A BOOK OF LISZTS

Variations on the Theme of Franz Liszt

JOHN SPURLING

Seagull
BOOKS

LONDON NEW YORK CALCUTTA

Seagull Books 2011

© John Spurling 2011

ISBN-13   978 1 9064 9 794 1

British Library Cataloguing-in-Publication Data
A catalogue record for this book is available
from the British Library

Typeset by Seagull Books, Calcutta, India
Printed and bound by Hyam Enterprises, Calcutta, India

for AMY

a kinder daughter than Cosima Liszt

Contents

Acknowledgements

Special thanks for help, advice and encouragement to Tariq Ali, Sunandini Banerjee, Rachel Calder, Richard Cohen, Audrey Ellison, Sohini Ghose, Daisy Gili, Kate Griffin, Penny Hoare, David Jennings, Naveen Kishore, Alison Menzies, Terry Mullins, Peter Nasmyth, Catriona Oliphant, Kathy Robbins, Alan Walker and, most of all, as always, Hilary Spurling.

Foreword

The chapters in this book are laid out mostly in the order I wrote them, but since they are all self-contained they can be read in any order. Chapter Four, 'Paganini in a Time of Cholera' for instance might be a better place to start than Chapter One, 'Incarnation'. To clear any confusion, there is a brief chronology of Liszt's life at the end.

I could not have written this book without reading and re-reading Alan Walker's masterly three-volume biography of Franz Liszt, and I recommend those who want to know and enjoy the real and full story of Liszt's extraordinary life to read it for themselves.

My excuses to the indignant shade of Franz Liszt himself appear in Chapter Seven, 'An Exchange of Letters'.

I 'discovered' Liszt's music six years ago and listened to almost nobody else's for the next four. I've made a selection from it at the end, in the hope that others may discover it too. Liszt has many passionate admirers, as is obvious from the great number of recordings of his music, the enthusiasm of the notes that accompany them and the roll-call of his distinguished performers. But he is still not generally given his due as one of the most stirring and innovative composers of the nineteenth century. I trust he will be in this year of the bicentenary of his birth.

John Spurling,
London, 2011.

This colossus, who rose so far above the merely astonishing . . . his life-course expresses itself, for me, in variation form. Here there is simply the original theme, always repeated, yet always unchanged; ornamented, embellished, now the virtuoso, now the diplomat, now the warrior, now the ecclesiastic, always the artist, always charming, always himself, at bottom unlike anyone else, and therefore presenting himself to the world only in variation form.

—*Richard Wagner*

I. Incarnation

Has God appeared on earth only once, in the person of Jesus Christ? The Society of Holy Plurality believes not. God, it maintains, has taken human form many times, in various guises. This secretive society meets privately in its members' houses and circulates papers and discussions in a magazine called *Avatars*.

There is much argument about whether God has ever been a woman, and even more about exactly who he has been. Indeed the Society welcomes argument and for this reason it has never split into sects. Truth, it believes, thrives on disagreement and God himself loves change and variety.

The list of God's avatars does not so far admit any twentieth-century Incarnation, although many members have argued energetically that there must have been at least one. Most members hold that it is too soon to tell and one or two fear that since the invention of moving pictures and sound recording there never will be another appearance. Would God, they ask, allow himself to be pinned down permanently in that way? Others riposte that he would be perfectly capable of evading, scrambling or erasing any evidence of his presence that displeased him.

However, there is no disagreement about whether God appears more than once in the same period of time. It is assumed that he does not. Of course he *could*, but it is unlikely, if only because he might meet himself (or herself). Thus in the constant arguments about who he has been, dates become crucial. Michelangelo died on 15 February 1564, while Shakespeare was born on or around 23 April of the same year, so it is possible for both to appear on the list. In fact they do not.

Raphael is preferred to Michelangelo, partly because his work is considered more sublime and less aggressive, partly because it seems unlikely that God cared to walk the earth again almost as soon as he had left it. No one doubts that God took the form of Shakespeare.

There is broad agreement about the criteria for recognizing one of God's avatars. Although the Society is at odds with the Christian Church over its belief in the uniqueness of Jesus Christ, it neither denies that he was God nor quarrels with the portrayal of Jesus in the Gospels. A Christ-like character is what the Society tends to look for in every appearance of God and this is surprising in view of the Society's belief in plurality. Some of the more provocative members have argued that if God really loves change and variety he would surely never have exhibited the same characteristics twice. These people question whether his purpose in reappearing is always to show the right way to live and suggest that he may simply enjoy moving *incognito* among his creatures, as certain absolute rulers have in the past, and that he has not necessarily always taken the form of a good person. He might have been Ivan the Terrible, Robespierre or Rasputin. Some with Manichaean leanings believe that these and others of their type were Satanic not divine avatars. Satan, they claim, also likes to walk the earth from time to time in human form. The consensus, however, is that God can be recognized only in a person who is good, wise, clever, sensitive, charismatic, primarily spiritual, prophetic, unselfish and essentially humble, though he might, like Jesus, sometimes show impatience and flashes of anger. He would certainly always stand out from the crowd and probably flout the conventions of the day, but perhaps not to the point ever again of willing his own execution.

The following is a paper published in *Avatars* under the name of S. Ramirez, arguing that God's last appearance on earth was in the nineteenth century:

'Franz Liszt was born in the autumn of the year of the Great Comet, 1811. His mother, Anna, was told by gypsies and firmly believed that the child she was carrying would be a great man and so it proved. He himself always believed that he was "chosen". Both parents were of peasant stock, though the father, Adam, had risen to be manager of a large sheep-station, responsible to his employer Prince Esterházy for thirty thousand animals. There must have been plenty of shepherds available to salute the child's birth under the shooting star.

'Both Adam and his father, Georg, were musically talented, but Franz's gifts were of an altogether different order. At the age of six he watched closely as his father played a concerto on the piano and coming in later from playing in the garden sang the theme; at the age of nine, after lessons with his father, he gave his first public concert in the nearest town, playing that same concerto and his own improvisations on popular tunes, with such success that his father immediately arranged a further concert in the city of Pressburg, after which a group of noblemen started a fund for his education in Vienna. His teachers there were Czerny, for piano, and Salieri, Mozart's alleged murderer, for composition. Czerny took the eleven-year-old Franz to play to a reluctant Beethoven, who disliked infant prodigies. But when Franz finished his triumphant recital with the first movement of one of the Master's own concertos, Beethoven held him with both hands, kissed him on the forehead and said: "Go! You are one of the fortunate ones! For you will give joy and happiness to many other people. There is nothing better or finer."

'The prophecy was amply fulfilled. Of his first public concert in Vienna, the same year, the *Allgemeine Zeitung*'s critic wrote, " . . . a young virtuoso has fallen from the clouds . . . There is a god amongst us." Liszt took the musical world by storm and his dazzling technique was matched with overwhelming spiritual and emotional intensity. His career as a virtuoso coincided with the full development of the seven-octave pianoforte, then in demand everywhere as a way of bringing music into the home and an instrument capable of standing in for any other instrument and indeed for a whole orchestra. In addition to his outstanding gifts as a pianist, Liszt was certainly the greatest transcriber for the piano of music written for other instruments by other composers, including the full orchestra and the human voice. He made piano solo versions of Schubert's songs, passages from operas by Mozart, Verdi, Wagner and others and all nine of Beethoven's symphonies.

'By the age of thirty Liszt had become an international superstar. People fought to possess his handkerchief and gloves, his broken piano strings and even his cigar stubs, one of which a court lady wore in a locket round her neck, to the consternation of anyone who came near her and caught its musty smell. A Russian critic who heard Liszt play in St Petersburg wrote: "I was completely undone by the sense of the supernatural, the mysterious, the incredible. As soon as I got home, I tore off my coat, flung myself on the sofa and wept the bitterest, sweetest tears." "Words cannot describe him," wrote the piano-teacher Oscar Beringer, " . . . I have seen whole rows of his audience, men and women alike, affected to tears, when he chose to be pathetic; in stormy passages he was able by his art to work them up to the highest pitch of excitement; through the medium of his instrument he played upon every human emotion." Wagner said of his playing of Beethoven's Sonatas Opus 106 and Opus 111 that "his was not a re-production—it was a re-creation."

'At the age of thirty-six Liszt abandoned his career as a virtuoso to concentrate on composing, conducting and teaching. After that he only played in private or occasionally in public to raise money for charities—orphans, floods, the rebuilding of Cologne Cathedral. His soft heart for good causes was equalled by his generosity towards young musicians—he never took any payment from his relays of pupils from all over Europe and America. He arranged and conducted performances of the works of Berlioz and Wagner when no one else would. He sheltered Wagner when he was a fugitive from political persecution, sending him money and encouraging him in every way he could. In his early years as a concert performer he agreed for a very large fee to take part in an arduous tour of England, Ireland and Scotland, but when the tour turned out to be a financial disaster for the impresario who had organized it, Liszt cancelled his contract and took nothing. His motto throughout his life was *génie oblige*.

'The adulation he received made him many enemies. With some it was simply envy, but with others it was a refusal to allow him more than one talent. Such people did not object to Liszt being the greatest pianist alive, but they could not see him also as a great composer. His detractors included erstwhile friends such as Robert and Clara Schumann and the great violinist Joseph Joachim; also the influential Viennese critic Eduard Hanslick and the much younger composer Johannes Brahms. As a very young man Brahms had visited Liszt at his home, been thrilled to hear him play one of Brahms's own pieces and then fallen asleep while Liszt played a work of his own.

'Liszt revered Beethoven and when the proposed Beethoven monument and centenary celebrations in his native town of Bonn were nearly aborted for lack of funds and the sloth and mismanagement of the memorial committee, it was Liszt who came to the rescue. But although his music owed much to Beethoven and the Romantic movement in general, it was also innovatory and experimental in ways which were not fully appreciated until long afterwards, by composers of the twentieth century such as Strauss, Debussy, Ravel, Rachmaninov and Schoenberg. Bartok called Liszt the true father of modern music, while Busoni went so far as to say that Bach and Liszt were the two poles, the two centres of gravity of all music. But when Liszt and his supporters annoyed the traditionalists by claiming that theirs was "the music of the future," Liszt, with his usual generosity, urged his pupils to leave his own compositions out of their concerts rather than incur the displeasure of managements and audiences.

'His father, Adam, was deeply religious and, as a very young man, before he settled for running the sheep-station at Raiding, entered a Franciscan monastery, but was dismissed after two years for "his inconstant and changeable nature". Liszt too, as a young man, already recognized as a prodigy after giving many public concerts, felt a powerful religious vocation and nearly abandoned his musical career. His father managed to dissuade him: "You belong to art, not the church". Nevertheless, as he approached old age Liszt took minor orders in the Catholic Church, never moving on to the later stage of becoming a full priest, but always wearing the clerical dress and being known, often with mockery, as l'Abbé Liszt. In his early twenties, while living in Paris, he met and was deeply influenced by the controversial Catholic priest l'Abbé Felicité de Lamennais, a social reformer who eventually broke with the Church. Lamennais believed that God was made manifest in art and that the artist was a kind of priest, the bearer of the beautiful. Liszt, in his first published article, written when he was twenty-three, envisaged a new kind of music which would unite "the Theatre and the Church". He remained a fervent Catholic all his life and once said to his friend, the then atheist Richard Wagner, "Everything is transitory except the Word of God, which is eternal— and the Word of God reveals itself in the creations of Genius."

'Many of Liszt's compositions were overtly religious—oratorios and masses as well as piano pieces—but all his best works are essentially daemonic, clashes between order and chaos, the peaceful and the violent, the spiritual and the emotional, the love of life and the fear of death. His only two symphonies were called The Faust and Dante, while his Two Legends for piano were based on the stories of St Francis of Assisi who preached to the birds and St Francis of Paola who walked on the waves and tamed a storm. When Liszt transcribed Paganini's violin studies for piano, he was not just honouring the other most famous soloist of his time, he was meeting an implicit challenge. For in all the stories the violin is the devil's instrument and Paganini, the impossibly brilliant violinist, was widely believed to be in league with the devil, his music and playing literally fiendish as well as fiendishly difficult. Certainly his grisly death of syphilis and the subsequent grotesqueries of his burial went far beyond the legendary descents to hell of Don Juan or Faust. So to translate this supposedly fiendish music for the fiend's instrument into music for the piano, the instrument of order, balance and omnipotence over all other instruments, was surely to meet and quell the demonic with the daemonic, to assert the power of life over death and the comprehensiveness of God over the narrowness of Satan.

'From infancy and throughout his life, Liszt was afflicted by chills, fever, violent shuddering and fainting fits. On one occasion, just before he was three years old, he appeared to have died and his distraught parents actually ordered a coffin from the local carpenter. In his twenty-fourth year, he fainted in the middle of giving a concert in the assembly hall of the Hôtel de Ville in Paris. One member of the audience who was seated at the side of the platform, his chair placed on the same board as the piano, said, " . . . as the closing strains began, I saw Liszt's countenance assume that agony of expression, mingled with radiant smiles of joy, which I never saw in any other human face, except in the paintings of our Saviour by some of the early masters; his hands rushed over the keys, the floor on which I sat shook like a wire, and the whole audience were wrapped in sound, when the hand and frame of the artist gave way; he fainted in the arms of the friend who was turning over for him, and we bore him out in a strong fit of hysterics. The effect of this scene was really dreadful. The whole room sat breathless with fear, till Hiller came forward and announced that Liszt was already restored to consciousness, and was comparatively well again."

'Liszt never married. The Countess Marie d'Agoult and the Princess Carolyne von Sayn-Wittgenstein were his only long-term partners, but many other women were in love with him and he had brief love affairs with several. Does his sexual history rule out his claim to be an avatar of God? On the contrary. Who made us lustful? And was it only for the purpose of procreation, as Christians insist? Or so that a few saints or master-craftsmen might sublimate their sexual desires into religious ecstasy or art? Liszt fulfilled both these purposes and yet had love to spare.

'I submit that God appeared in Liszt's form in the nineteenth century not only to enhance the power and popularity of music-making and to give a spiritual direction to its future, when it was in danger of descending into sentimental and commercial entertainment, but also to demonstrate his absolute approval of human sexuality, which most religions have mistakenly tried to suppress.'

II. *The Interpretation of Railways*

In the 1980s, Ulrich Krings . . . stressed the role of architectural and art history for the interpretation of railway stations.

—footnote in *The City and the Railway in Europe* (edited by Roth and Polino, Ashgate 2003).

This is a time of almost universal ignorance. Our darkness is lighted with flashes of random knowledge, gained mostly from the media and the internet; and here and there, by bursts of extraordinary knowledge and intellectual exploration on the part of a very small minority. It has always been so, except that the flashes of random knowledge, called 'hearsay' or 'proverbial wisdom' or 'received ideas', used to come from the small local communities in which we all once lived and now, with the arrival of better communications, come from all over the planet.

My own ignorance is fairly comprehensive, except that every so often I become immersed in some particular subject—guerrilla warfare, the British Empire, Saddam Hussein, fourteenth-century China—and perhaps for a year or two, know more about it than almost anyone except the specialists I have learnt it from. Of course, the picture I form of my subject is itself only a part of the whole and, once formed, it excludes all the rest of the knowledge I have acquired on that subject, so that my expertise, such as it is, lasts only until I have selected from it and made use of it. My knowledge, which grows deeper and broader as I pursue a subject, grows shallower and narrower again when I shape it into a story; then, fixed in a certain pattern, the story is, as it were, ejected from myself to stand on its own and much of the selected knowledge that has gone into it begins to leave my memory, while the greater part, the part that has not been used, is already mostly forgotten.

It is the process of going from ignorance and uncertainty to knowledge and meaning that fascinates me. I might compare it to a long journey, a journey by train rather than air, chosen seemingly at random, towards a destination whose name I know, but little more. Why am I making this particular journey rather than some other? It's mysterious. I suspect that the reason is neither the journey nor the destination in themselves, but a combination which transcends both— the journey towards that destination and the significance of that experience. And isn't this also true of music, a symphony, say, or a sonata or better still—since it has a distinct literary or visual element—a symphonic poem? And isn't the mystery partly explained by that romantic definition offered by Franz Liszt, the inventor of the symphonic poem: 'Music is a series of tones that long for and embrace each other'?

Franz Liszt was constantly making journeys and for the first half of his life he had to make them by coach and horse. He travelled from Hungary to Austria, through southern Germany to France, through England, Ireland and Scotland, to Switzerland and Spain and Italy, to Bohemia and Saxony, to Prussia, Poland and Russia, to Ukraine and Constantinople. He jolted and rattled all over Europe's bad roads to satisfy the curiosity and wring the hearts of music-lovers with his miraculous piano playing and then, at the age of thirty-six , just as the first railways were being built, he abandoned his public career as a pianist. His incessant travelling—as composer, conductor and organizer of music festivals—continued until the end of his life, but now by train.

Did he ever share a carriage or even the same compartment with a man twenty-two years older but bearing almost the same name, Friedrich List, former Professor of Economics at Tübingen? This List had been imprisoned in Württemburg, where he was a member of the legislature, for advocating an all-German Customs Union and beyond it a federation of all the various states into which Germany was then divided. Today, without risking a prison sentence for it, he would surely be an ardent supporter of a Federal Europe. Deported to America, he returned in 1832 as the American Consul at Leipzig and prophesied that river- and sea-traffic would soon give way to land-traffic by rail. 'It is a Hercules in the cradle,' he wrote, 'which will free the nations from the plague of war, national hatred and unemployment, ignorance and laziness. It will fertilize the fields, galvanize manufactures and mines, and make it possible for the lowest to educate himself by visiting foreign countries, to find employment in far-flung places and to improve his health in distant spas.'

The first German Customs Union was formed in 1834 and the first German railway—between Nüremberg and Fürth—opened in 1835. Professor, now Consul, List did not have long to savour the accuracy of his ideas, but when he committed suicide in 1846 most European countries already had railways. The first short section of the line on which Friedrich List and Franz Liszt would have been most likely to meet—between Dresden and Leipzig—opened in 1837, against bitter opposition from the peasants, List's 'lowest', for whom he foresaw such advantages.

A journey, then, from ignorance to knowledge might take the form of joining Friedrich List and Franz Liszt in that railway compartment in, let us say, 1846, the year of List's death and the year before Liszt's retirement from virtuoso performance. Where would one start? In the railway station, of course, on the outskirts of Leipzig. It was only later that stations found themselves in the middle of cities. The stations began by taking the place of the old city walls, defining the point where city and countryside met, but soon the expanding cities—whose populations grew monstrously as the railways allowed List's 'lowest' to travel in search of better lives— swallowed them. The architects of the stations used a variety of traditional styles to dignify their new buildings and, in the contemptuous eyes of early twentieth-century architects—those 'modernists' preoccupied with the idea of progress towards a machinist Utopia—pandered to the conservative tastes of the international bourgeoisie with reminiscences of Roman baths and basilicas, mediaeval castles, Renaissance palaces and baroque cathedrals. But our less puritanical postmodernist view, if I understand it correctly, is that it was only natural and tactful of those nineteenth-century architects to recycle all kinds of favourite old styles for the purpose of humanizing buildings with a completely new and alarming function. Franz Liszt also recycled the music of the past so as to appeal to the conservative taste of his international audiences, but he moved easily between past and future, for he became what one might call a 'proto-modernist'.

Friedrich List would have had no difficulty in recognizing the thirty-five-year-old man sitting opposite him. That handsome pale face, long straight nose, shoulder-length hair, the narrow hands with their long powerful fingers, that combination of relaxed good manners and latent energy, those glittering pale eyes, at once penetrating and mystical, that air of almost royalty—of being constantly looked at and fawned on—could only add up to the most famous musical performer in the Western world (now that Paganini was dead). But they may already have known each other, since Liszt had certainly met List's daughter, Elise, some years earlier in Paris and gone to some trouble to launch her career as a singer. In recommending Elise to the Princess Belgiojoso, Liszt even made out that Elise was his cousin and spelt her name 'Liszt'.

Franz and Friedrich's conversation could have been in French or German, depending on whether Friedrich had reasonable French. Franz's German was no more than adequate at this point in his career. He had been born in Hungary, then part of the Austrian Empire, but, although his first name is sometimes given as Ferenc, he did not speak Hungarian and, having moved to Paris when he was still a child and been based there ever since, had exchanged his childhood German— an Austro-Hungarian peasant's German, since he had had no more than a village education except in music—for a sophisticated adult's French. If they did converse in Liszt's inadequate German or List's possibly inadequate French—or maybe in English, which List would have spoken with an American accent and Liszt very sketchily from what he had picked up during his concert tours of Britain—they might have ranged over any number of topics. They were both men of the world, both famous, self-confident, articulate and highly intelligent. But for our purposes, joining them as we do in the role of inquirers and interpreters, we are only interested in their specialities and where their specialities meet: railways and music.

FRANZ. What an extraordinary experience this is! When I was in Russia I travelled over the frozen steppe on a sleigh pulled by dogs—it seemed wonderfully smooth and fast compared to one's usual mode of travel behind horses over roads, though disturbingly close to the ground. But this is like being pulled in a high carriage across a continuous sheet of ice by thirty horses.

FRIEDRICH. It is remarkable, but nothing to what will come. We shall soon be able to travel at three times the speed of a horse and over infinite distances, with only brief pauses to take on more water, coal, goods or passengers. Believe me, our world is changing now for ever. All narrow horizons are lifted. Those who come after us will almost be a different race of men.

FRANZ. A better race?

FRIEDRICH. I fervently hope so. Better fed, better educated, better employed, healthier, more open-minded, more ambitious for further necessary change, more egalitarian, more peaceable, more socially responsible . . .

JS. May I ask you—either of you—if you think travelling by train alters the nature of the journey?

FRANZ (*smoothing his long hair and lighting a cigar*). It's certainly more comfortable.

JS. I mean, as an idea?

FRIEDRICH. Provided the fares are set sufficiently low for the third-class carriages, of course it will. People will be able to contemplate a journey to the nearest city—or even to a further off city, or even a foreign city—to buy something they can't get in the village or to see a better doctor or to visit relatives, in a way they never could before.

JS. I mean, as a metaphysical idea. Does it alter the nature of the journey as such?

A pause in which the two distinguished Lis(z)ts briefly exchange puzzled glances.

I mean, what effect does the new railway have on your interpretation of journeys?

Another pause, in which Franz looks down at his hands and Friedrich looks out of the window.

FRANZ (*looking up from his hands*). If you would be so kind, Sir, as to give us your own interpretation of journeys made *before* the invention of the railway, perhaps I or my distinguished fellow-passenger might be able to interpret your question and attempt an answer.

JS. Correct me if I'm wrong, since I never knew any journeys before the invention of the railway, but I would suppose that they were great distractions. I mean that, although they were slowly and very uncomfortably taking you to your destination, they must, over so many hours, days, or even weeks—if you were going to Moscow, for instance, or Constantinople, or from Leipzig to Rome—have almost blotted out any sense of your final destination. They would have been full of quite irrelevant incidents—a lame or runaway horse, a wheel off the coach, a snowstorm or a flood, nights spent in inns, highwaymen, mud, rain and bitter wind, the closeness of the other passengers, the smell of their clothes or themselves, their irritating personal habits. Not only would the journey itself have been a jerky, disintegrated succession of such events, constantly disturbing the smooth progression of your movement from A to B, but you yourself would surely have lost much of your sense of your own identity. You would have begun to feel more like a piece of luggage, identified only by the address to which, after many batterings, it was ultimately consigned.

FRANZ. I cannot say I ever felt like a piece of luggage. People were often waiting to set eyes on me or even speak to me at the major stopping-places. They might have been waiting all day, knowing that I was due to give a concert in Magdeburg or Berlin in a few days' time. They would quickly have reminded me of my identity in case I had forgotten it. Latterly, in any case, I had my own specially built coach, a sort of hotel room on wheels, following the example of Lord Byron, who was himself imitating Napoleon.

FRIEDRICH. Long distance coach travel was not quite as dislocating as you imagine, Sir, if only because we were used to it. Neither we nor our ancestors had any idea of any easier alternative.

JS. I suppose it's the significance of the railway line itself that I'm trying to get at. The sense of a continuum, of an unbroken stream from A to B.

FRIEDRICH. Ah, you are thinking of the line as a kind of river laid over the land.

JS. Exactly. And a swifter river. And just like a river, you sweep past cities and towns, hardly touching them or even being aware of them except as names on a station platform. A and B, the starting-point and terminus of your journey dominate your thought, or as a matter of fact, perhaps only the terminus does. A is already behind you.

FRANZ. I don't think I'm sitting here concentrating on Dresden, you know, although that's where I am going. All sorts of thoughts may fill my head—my work, my friends or enemies, the scenery, the weather, the flight of birds, something I've said which I regret—just as at any other time.

JS. Of course. Your thoughts are quite free and may be as jerky as you like, but your journey, your unbroken movement through time and space is inexorable—unless you suddenly decide to get out at a station on the way.

FRANZ. But, my dear Sir, that applies to my life too.

JS. Yes! And does it also apply to the composition of a piece of music?

FRANZ. Indeed, that is a kind of journey, but why particularly a railway journey?

FRIEDRICH. Because it's smooth and unbroken—is that your meaning?

FRANZ. Composing a piece of music is no such thing. Fits and starts all the way.

JS. But not when it's finished and performed.

FRANZ. Of course not, unless very ineptly performed.

JS. Then it's the performance that resembles a railway journey.

FRANZ. Not at all. A piece of music changes rhythm and dynamic, pitch and speed all the time. It would be deadly dull if it simply repeated the same succession of notes without such changes.

FRIEDRICH. Clickety-click, clickety-click, clickety-click . . .

FRANZ. With the odd whistle and puff and squeak of brakes. Something could be made of it, I suppose. But a ride on a horse would be more promising material. Mazeppa, for instance, who was tied to a horse, which galloped across the Ukrainian steppe until it died of exhaustion. You must know the poem by Lord Byron?

JS. I know your own symphonic poem, *Mazeppa*.

FRANZ. Then you have the advantage of me. I have written no such thing. Only a transcendental study for piano with that title.

JS. Forgive me! What year is this?

FRANZ. 1846.

JS. I'm so sorry, I've mistaken my dates. Your twelve symphonic poems are a few years ahead, composed during your period as the Grand Duke's special kapellmeister at Weimar.

FRANZ. You know that?

JS. As well as I know that we shall soon reach Dresden. No, better. As surely as I know that we have already left Leipzig.

And there we have it. Our journeys by rail—barring accidents—are, as it were, already completed as soon as we are rolling, and in that they resemble the sense the composer has of the completed composition while he is still composing it, also the performance we hear while it is still unfolding—especially if it is a work we know well and may have heard already several times, so that it is both familiar and repeatedly fresh. And, reverting to my original inquiry, railway journeys also resemble our sense of the passage from ignorance to knowledge as already completed while it is still going on. They give us a glimpse of hindsight from the future while we're still in the present.

III. Constantinople

You're sitting in the foyer of a small theatre in Paris with your journalist friend Janin. It's the second interval and groups of people are standing about, seated or brushing past, eyeing you surreptitiously. You're used to that.

A tall young woman appears, treading lightly, holding a bouquet of white camellias, twitching her skirt to avoid it brushing the dirty parquet, showing her ankle in a pale pink silk stocking. You're instantly fascinated by her small oval face, framed in black hair. And as you stare, she looks at you and comes towards you.

'Who is she?' you ask Janin.

'Don't you know? It's Marie Duplessis, "*la dame aux camélias*". If she wants you, she'll have you.'

She smiles and sits down beside you.

'Monsieur Liszt, I heard you play the other night at the Théâtre-Italien and you set me dreaming.'

Her eyes are very dark. She talks and you talk, volubly, showing off. In her ears are pearls which shake gently when she laughs. Her smile is irresistible. If she wants you she can have you.

The three knocks sound and the foyer empties. You and she remain behind. She is shivering.

'You're cold, Mademoiselle.'

She goes and stands beside the hearth, where the logs are blazing fiercely, puts her foot on a fire-dog. You join her and the talk continues. Then as suddenly as she came she leaves. Through the window you watch her ride away, wrapped in fur, in her open carriage. Janin is still sitting where we left him, not pleased to have been entirely ignored.

She does want you. Next day she sends you an invitation through a mutual acquaintance, the fashionable Dr Koreff, who is treating her for a persistent illness. The day after that you visit her luxurious flat on the Boulevard de la Madeleine. A footman takes your hat and coat in the hall. There are hanging baskets of fresh flowers, and creepers rooted in wooden pots climb the golden trellis round the walls. The man opens a door on the right and ushers you into the dining room.

White camellias everywhere in Chinese vases, Spanish leather on the walls, cabinets filled with silver ornaments, a statuette of two classical lovers embracing. Green curtains over windows and doors, matching green velvet on the twelve chairs set round a carved oak table. Two places laid under a chandelier with six candles.

She enters from the room beyond, with her smile and her dark eyes.

* * *

His deepset eyes are sea-green, his nose long and straight, his lips full, his mouth large and mobile and the hard curve of his jaw, with the soft mound of his chin at its prow, is tilted upwards. His thick, fair hair, brushed away from the high sloping forehead, hides his ears and curls over his collar. This is the most beautiful man who ever sat down at your table.

'You failed to tell me, Mademoiselle, what you were dreaming of when you heard me play.'

'I dreamed of you sitting at my table.'

'Did you imagine I could refuse your invitation?'

'I couldn't quite believe you were real.'

'And now?'

You watch his long, long fingers playing with a piece of bread.

'I'm not sure,' you say. 'It's still more like a dream.'

'As you are to me.'

'But here you find me, a real woman, living in a real flat on the Boulevard de la Madeleine.'

'Yes, I came from my own familiar flat and entered yours from a real street, as Odysseus landed from his own familiar ship on Circe's magic island. But now that I've eaten and drunk at your table, I've put myself in your power. Circe has cast her spell on this everyday Odysseus and soon I shall be turned into a beast.'

'You?'

The idea is laughable. You do laugh and he gives you his broad, generous smile. No one could be less of a beast—or less everyday—than this captivating genius.

'But you, Monsieur Liszt, were the first to cast a spell on me with your music. You are Orpheus, not Odysseus. Where did you get such magic?'

'Practice. Much tedious practice. I couldn't play so well when I was a boy of nine and gave my first public performance in my native Hungary. Czerny in Vienna hammered me into better shape and I have done nothing but sit at the keyboard ever since.'

'If it was only practice, many others could do the same.'

'Others do.'

'No, not a bit the same.'

'No doubt something was given me.'

'By whom?'

'By my father, my grandfather—both good musicians.'

'But not magicians. Who gave you such power over our emotions?'

'Who?' His bewitching smile again. 'Not my mother, certainly. Who else could it have been?'

He puts down his knife and fork and holds up his hands, palms towards you, as if to show the answer, or rather no answer, written there.

'The devil, do you mean?' he says. 'They accused poor Paganini of getting his magic from the devil.'

No, not the devil, you think, when he sits down at the piano in the drawing-room after dinner and begins to play rapturously by heart and to your heart that piece—Weber's *Invitation to the Waltz*—which you yourself often play uncertainly from the score with stumbling fingers. But if not the devil, and if no man . . . and no man, surely, not even Paganini, ever made a mere instrument sound like this, as if it played itself for its own pleasure.

'Why does music have such power over us?'

'It is a kind of love,' he says, beginning another piece, a soft dreaming piece you have not heard before. 'But more ephemeral. The effect of music lasts only a minute or two after it ceases to sound . . .'

You don't care to interrupt his playing to disagree—the effect of his music at the Théâtre-Italien kept you awake all night and as for love, you have no experience of the sort he means. Unless the old Count's, who keeps you in this flat and pays for your carriage and horses and servants and much else besides because you remind him of his dead daughter . . .

* * *

You watch her beautiful face under the effect of the music. You would like to say that music comes from God, reflects God, nourishes the soul and returns to him like incense, expressing our deepest feelings about this world, his creation. But does one invoke the name of God in the presence of a courtesan? Not because God has abandoned her—that you cannot believe—but because it might be a lapse of taste, a suggestion of moral judgment. 'God' on the lips of men and women is too often a word of reproach. Perhaps even to mention love was equally tasteless. So you keep your mouth shut and play another piece.

But what you did not like to put in words your fingers cannot help finding on the keyboard and she is too sensitive, too emotionally intelligent not to understand. So when you pause and ask if she is tired of listening she replies:

'You play for me as if you were playing for some great lady. I wish I deserved such playing.'

'When I play well—and I *am* playing well tonight—it's because my audience brings it out of me. And you *are* a great lady.'

'No, not at all. I'm the ape of a great lady. I dress like one, I ride in a carriage and wear pearls or diamonds, I go to the theatre and draw all eyes to my box. I entertain rich noblemen here in the manner and surroundings they expect. But you know as well as I do that it's all play-acting. In reality, I'm a peasant from Normandy who by some chance was given the gift of beauty and used it—for this. The illusion of love and luxury. I tell you this because, unlike those noblemen whose greatness is only in the names and wealth they have inherited, you are really a great man and it would be stupid of me to pretend to be your equal.'

* * *

He doesn't reply at once, but flexes his hands as if to play again, then lays them in his lap and stares at his feet on the pedals. You have broken the spell. What made you speak like that? Great musician though he is, he is also a man like any other and came for the illusion.

'I am honoured,' he says at last, 'to be treated as a person to whom you can speak in this way, but what made you do so is not what you think. It is because we *are* equals, both creatures from the fields, from outside this sophisticated society whose manners we ape, both play-actors, both clever enough to know it and sometimes to hate ourselves for it. But why should we? What were we to do with these gifts from God or the devil—your beauty, my music—if not use them in the world as we find it and for the pleasure of others as much as ourselves?'

'For pleasure only?'

'And perhaps for the good of others.'

'But is what I do—the use to which I put my beauty—for anybody's *good*?'

'Dear Mademoiselle, we are not Puritans, are we? Puritans never approve of play-actors. They cannot see what "good" we do and they even accuse us of doing harm—moral harm. But we play-actors not only entertain people, carry them away for a while from their hard or dull or unhappy lives, we also lead them, if we are skilful enough, into the deeper parts of their feelings, re-introduce them to their souls, which the ordinary business of their lives makes them forget or even despise.'

'You're speaking of your profession, not of mine. What has my profession to do with souls?'

'As much as any other. Is making love for money really so different from doing anything else for money? Didn't Christ say to the Magdalen, "Much shall be forgiven thee because thou hast loved much"?'

'I have often thought of that saying,' you reply. 'It cannot mean, can it, that she will be forgiven for making love professionally because she has so often made love professionally? It must mean that she can be forgiven for making love professionally because she has often really loved people. And I don't think I have. I am quite cold, you know, quite calculating, quite attached to jewels and expensive clothes and all the good things my beauty has brought me. But love, no, I never considered love was what I was paid for, only its semblance, and I never felt real love in myself for anyone . . .'

* * *

What a strange woman this is! She lives—and lives sumptuously—by acting the coquette, but she has nothing of the coquette inside her, no vanity at all, no illusions. She goes to the theatre to be seen and perhaps she reads books and plays her piano as she dresses and furnishes her flat, so as to appear the kind of woman her clients wish her to be. But is that how she listened to your music? Not at all. She responded by stepping out of the role she performs so brilliantly, out of her clothes and jewels, one might almost say, with alacrity, with a kind of relief, not as if the music put a spell on her, but as if it released her from one.

'. . . until I saw you, Monsieur Liszt, and heard you play in that concert. And now I do understand how detached I have been. Perhaps when my clients speak of love they sometimes mean it. What do you think? Have I a soul, after all? I thought I had long ago sold it to the devil.'

And having found it, she offers it to you. You came here from a mixture of desire, curiosity and, yes, of course, vanity. It raises your stock, doesn't it, to be singled out by the celebrated Marie Duplessis? How are you to respond? Her offer puts everything on a different footing. It is souls now more than bodies. Come now! Don't be a fool! It was the bodies that brought the souls together. Let your body respond, then, and your soul look after itself! But if she feels real love for you and you don't for her—or not yet—then, if your body responds as it would like to, the roles are reversed and you are the prostitute.

* * *

At last he turns and looks at you. His pale eyes seem to give out light from within.

'Do you never look at yourself, Marie? Your soul is in the beauty of your face, self-evident, just as the Magdalen's must have been in hers.'

He talks kindly, smoothly, but it's only talk. He's right that his music is a kind of love, but his words are not. Are we both no more than we have been given, he his music, I my face?

'Shall I lose my soul, then, if I live to be old and lose my beauty?'

'I didn't mean that your beauty *is* your soul, but that the one expresses the other, as I try to express my soul through music. But as for growing old, what has that to do with us? It seems to me that old people's souls are often as wizened as their faces.'

'Well, I shan't live to be old. I am ill, you know. Though Dr Koreff, who carried my invitation to you, pretends he can cure me.'

'You don't believe him?'

'Is anybody cured of consumption?'

'They say that warm, dry places help, if the disease is caught in time.'

'Yes, people have told me that. But my living is here in Paris. I have nothing really, you know, of my own. All this luxury belongs to my protector, Comte de Stackelberg, and as for the jewels men have given me, they wouldn't begin to pay my debts. What a sad subject! It makes me ill just to think of it. Won't you play something else?'

And he does, a simple, gentle piece.

'What is that called?'

'I'm not quite sure yet. "Countryside" do you think?'

'Yes, and how I would like that! To be there, in that countryside you conjure up with your magic, far away from all this! Please take me there again!'

He plays the same piece, but differently, more passionately. You close your eyes and hear a little stream rippling through buttercup meadows, and feel the warm sun rising over a row of poplars, and then the vision dies away, and of course, you know that it was only a dream, only a painter's sketch of the countryside city-people like to imagine.

The real countryside of your childhood was not at all like that, but harsh and messy, raw and violent, a cold, wet, overclouded place where miserable people, like your parents, beat their children and their animals indiscriminately, without love or pity.

* * *

She opens her eyes and looks at you for a moment with a strange expression, as if she had been somewhere else and is not sure where she is now or who you are. Then she smiles with a sweet recognition that overwhelms you. You go and sit beside her on the divan and take her hand. She nestles against you, you put your arm round her and she lays her head against your chest. It's as if you had known one another long before.

'That was what I dreamed of when I first heard you play,' she says, 'of going far, far away from all this. I also dreamed of inviting you here, but that was more realistic.'

'Perhaps if one dream has come true, the other may. I have much the same dream as you, to leave all this. No longer to be the circus-monkey that I am, forever astonishing the public with my tricks, which they'll forget as soon as my back is turned. To find some remote place where I can compose in peace and perhaps not be altogether forgotten.'

'You could easily do that.'

'Not so easily. I have three children. Perhaps when I've earned enough to put aside for them, I can stop performing. Yes, that's what I mean to do, but meanwhile I have a punishing programme ahead of me. My travelling circus must now go east—to Prague, to Pest, to Transylvania, to Kiev and Constantinople.'

'Constantinople!'

'At the invitation of the Sultan.'

'Constantinople! The East! How I wish I could go with you!'

'How I wish you could! But you would not be able to stand the journey. I go by road most of the way—Heaven knows what the roads will be like in Transylvania and Ukraine—and finally take ship across the Black Sea . . .'

'For Constantinople! But I could take ship from Marseille and meet you there.'

'Of course. Why not? And now you mention Marseille, my friend Erard who makes the instruments I play, is sending one by sea to Constantinople. You could come with it.'

'I could, I could. I will.'

And so suddenly this bizarre bond is formed. You do not go to bed with her, but you and she become virginal lovers, whose plans for the future are all centred on the voyage to Constantinople. Constantinople is to mark the end of your servitude as a virtuoso and the end of hers as a *demi-mondaine*. And then, when the honeymoon is over?

But that is never in question, the future does not reach beyond Constantinople. Why should it? Isn't that sufficient future to make us happy now? And we are extraordinarily happy, as full of joy and hope and love, we tell each other, as either has ever been. Dr Koreff is astonished at the improvement in Mariette's health, which is partly due, no doubt, to her ceasing to take his prescriptions.

You often attend her to the theatre when you are not giving a concert and she comes to hear you when you are. And whenever she is free of her own professional obligations you go to her flat and play music to her through the night or read your favourite books to her or look at illustrations of the Orient and talk of what you will see together in Constantinople. And she repeats like a refrain:

'Take me with you, Franz, lead me wherever you like! I shan't live long and I don't mind. This life is too much for me, I don't value it. I can't bear it any more. I shan't get in your way. I'll sleep all day, and in the evening you can let me go to the theatre, and at night you can do with me what you will.'

But how can Constantinople be more than a dream? The laws and customs of Muslim countries are even more rigorous against women's freedom than those of Christian countries. How can such a person as Marie appear on my arm in the palaces or even the streets of Constantinople? It's a fairy-tale city that fills our thoughts.

Meanwhile your secretary Belloni makes plans and fixes dates for your concerts in Hungary, Transylvania and Ukraine. He informs the

Ottoman Ambassador that you hope to be at the service of his master the Sultan in the summer of next year, he makes inquiries about sailings across the Black Sea and he settles with Erard, the transport of a brand-new pianoforte by sea from Marseille to Constantinople. But the addition of a beautiful woman to this precious cargo is never discussed and after a while, as the time of your departure draws near, the fairy-tale city falls out of your conversation with Mariette.

When you come to take your farewell, Marie's health has deteriorated again. She clings to you feverishly as if she has quite forgotten you were leaving.

'Where are you going, Franz?'

'To Prague, Mariette.'

'Must you go so far?'

'I have concerts to give and a banquet to attend in honour of Hector Berlioz.'

'And when will you be back?'

'As soon as I can.'

'A few days?'

'Longer than that. I have other engagements beyond Prague.'

'A week or two?'

'I will write to you from Prague. Will you write to me?'

'Of course I will. And if you are going to be longer than a week or two I will come and join you.'

'If only you would.'

'Take me with you, Franz, take me wherever you like! I shan't get in your way. I'll sleep all day and go to the theatre in the evening, and at night you can do what you like with me.'

'Dearest Mariette, I shall come and see you as soon as I return and then I promise you I shall give up these circuses for ever.'

'And I shall give up this life I hate.'

Life itself, or the kind of life she leads? The ambiguity is surely deliberate, for they are really, you now understand, one and the same. You fail to write to her from Prague, where you drink too much at the banquet and Berlioz has to help you to your hotel. Nor does she write to you. But while you are kicking your heels in Galatz—quarantined on account of some local epidemic before crossing the Black Sea—you write to Dr Koreff to ask how she is. Do you somehow imagine that she is waiting for the word to take ship from Marseille to join you? No, you are salving your conscience for not having been able to tell her that her journey with you to the East could never happen.

A few days later you receive Dr Koreff's reply. Mariette died four months ago, aged twenty-three. With that letter in your pocket and aching sadness in your heart, you take ship for Constantinople.

IV. Paganini in a Time of Cholera

Franzi's life was ruined. His father had brought him to Paris nine years earlier as a child prodigy, astonishing audiences in Austria, Germany, France and England with his virtuosity on the keyboard. Then, as they returned together from a third season in London, his father, who had been his first teacher and managed his career from the start, died suddenly of typhoid in Boulogne. The sixteen-year-old boy saw his father buried and then returned to Paris, where his mother, left behind in Austria during those exhausting concert tours and while Franzi was continuing his studies with two distinguished music teachers in Paris, came immediately to join him. But what could she, an Austrian peasant who had been a chambermaid in Vienna before marrying his musical father and bearing this extraordinary child, do for his career? She was bemused by his genius and in fact wholly dependent on him, financially as well as emotionally, without any idea of how to direct his energies or organize his professional appearances. He was admitted to the highest circles of society, playing for the guests in grand ladies' salons and teaching their daughters. His mother never even met such people.

Tall, thin and pale, with translucent eyes and long golden hair, he looked as well as played like an angel. It was inevitable that he would be adored by his employers and his pupils and that sooner or later he himself would fall in love. Caroline was seventeen, the daughter of King Charles X's Minister of Commerce, the Comte de Saint-Cricq. The Comtesse chaperoned her daughter's lessons with the angelic boy and could see that if she were not present they would soon be in each other's arms. The Comtesse was half in love with the boy herself and as she sat there in a corner of the salon, ravished by the mighty octaves and rippling arpeggios he was demonstrating to her daughter, she even allowed herself to dream that they could be married. She said nothing of this to the Comte however, since, as soon as Franzi and Caroline took their hands off the keys, she knew that it was only a dream. Franzi's gifts were celestial, but his social status on earth was hardly better than a servant's.

And then the Comtesse fell ill and died. Caroline and Franzi grieved for her and their mutual grief further broke down the barriers between them. The Comte, continually occupied with government business, saw no reason to discontinue his daughter's piano lessons, which were now to be chaperoned by Caroline's maid or the house-keeper, both of whom delighted in the happiness radiating from their young mistress and her even younger teacher and did not always think it necessary to be actually in the same room as long as they could hear the piano being played. Neither Franzi nor Caroline had ever been in love before and they were spellbound by each other, though too inex-perienced to do more than hold each other's hands and exchange kisses whenever they were alone. Franzi, of course, could only visit Caroline's house two or three times a week—they did not dare ask her father for more time together and besides Franzi had his usual demanding schedule of salons and other lessons to attend. But at least by arranging his lessons with Caroline as often as possible in the evening after he had finished all his other engagements, he could extend them well beyond the prescribed hour, and this was what brought about their catastrophe.

One evening when the Comte was away from Paris for the night, their lesson, and the intense discussions of literature and religion, as well as music that went with it, occupied them so exclusively that it was midnight before they noticed the chimes of the clock. Caroline hur-ried Franzi to the door. It was locked and she had to wake the porter. Grumbling and resentful, he let the boy out, but it never occurred to Franzi to give the man something for his trouble and the next day the porter complained to his master. The Comte, alarmed and angry, summoned his daughter and demanded an explanation. The poor girl, innocent as she was, guilty as she felt, could only say that she loved Franzi and wanted to marry him and that she thought her mother had approved of their love. The Comte's anger turned to fury. Marry a piano teacher! Marry a foreigner! Marry a servant! Her mother could not have dreamed of such a thing. Caroline was never to see the wretch again. Her father would arrange a marriage for her, a suitable match with someone of her own class and meanwhile she would be confined to the house and the presumptuous boy forbidden to enter it.

Caroline's misery made her seriously ill and she resolved to enter a convent rather than marry anyone but Franzi. The Comte, however, had his way. Caroline was married to the son of another government minister and taken far away to an estate looking on to the Pyrenees, where she bore a daughter and, neglected by her husband, lived not very happily for the rest of her life.

Franzi himself also sought relief in religion, but not in any spirit of resignation. For him the appeal to God's authority over the Comte's took the form of a grim, self-destructive mania, during which he haunted St Vincent-de-Paul, the church nearest the flat in the rue de Montholon where he and his mother lived, and spent his days kneeling on the cold flagstones in a side-chapel, praying to become a martyr rather than a musician. He refused or ignored invitations to appear at salons, he forgot or was late for lessons and gave no care to improving his pupils' skills. He appeared at two concerts which had been prearranged, but played with such cold and empty virtuosity that even his admirers thought he had lost his powers and would soon be forgotten like so many other promising prodigies. His mother could do nothing with him, though with the help of his confessor, the Abbé Bardin, she did succeed in discouraging him from immediately entering a seminary and becoming a priest.

But this only had the effect of diverting his attention from the consolations of the next world to those of this. He could not stop giving lessons—he and his mother lived off them—but instead of coming home to a quiet supper and the desolation of his own thoughts, he went into bars, attached himself to bad company, drank for oblivion and reeled home late at night. Often his mother cooked meals which he was not there to eat and next morning she would find him still dressed, asleep on the stairs in a fume of alcohol. His life was ruined. He knew it. He regularly told her so, when he spoke to her at all, and he seemed to revel in it, as though he was taking revenge not on himself but on all those admirers who wanted him as an angel but not as a man.

He was rescued briefly by the Revolution. The elderly King Charles X attempted to put history into reverse, to bring back the *ancien régime* that had ended with his brother Louis XVI's execution thirty-eight years before. After Napoleon's defeat the victorious allies—Britain, Russia, Austria and Prussia—had restored the Bourbons to their throne, but the French had no great love for them and when Charles and his reactionary ministers dismissed the elected assembly, curbed the freedom of the press and restricted the number of those who could vote, the Parisians resorted to their favourite form of democracy—barricades in the streets, torn-up cobblestones and hand-to hand battles with the forces of authority. Franzi heard the gunfire and the chants of 'Lafayette, Lafayette' in support of the old revolutionary general who was leading the insurrection, and rushed out to join in. No doubt he was still seeking martyrdom, but now at least his target was no longer himself but an unpopular government, one of whose leading members had spurned and crushed the love of his life. He was only too happy to bruise and bloody the delicate fingers that gave such pleasure to his social superiors by gouging out cobblestones for his stronger and more skilful comrades to hurl at the government's soldiers.

The fighting went on for three days, with much bloodshed, and ended with the surrender of the royal troops, the flight of the king to England, and the return to his mother's arms of an exhilarated Franzi. The French enlisted Charles X's cousin, Louis Philippe, as their constitutional monarch, and entered a new period of rule by the rich middle-class, but Franzi sat down eagerly to compose a *Revolutionary Symphony*. It did not get very far and as the excitement of 'The Three Glorious Days' receded and people became disillusioned with their 'Citizen King', Franzi too lost his new sense of hope and purpose. He was back on the treadmill of lessons and salon lollipops, praying, brooding, drinking, heading for ruin all over again, but now less blatantly, so that even his mother believed that 'the gunfire had cured him'.

He found a new friend at this time, the Belgian organist at his church, a man of such pure moral principles that although he was the leader of the orchestra at the Paris Opéra, he would only play his violin with his back to the stage, so as not to catch sight of the lascivious movements of the dancers. He always wore a sky-blue tailcoat because that was the traditional colour of the Virgin's robe and he adored the composer Franz Schubert, who had recently died and whose works were hardly known beyond his own family and friends in Vienna. Schubert's music seemed to Chrétien Urhan to be the only work by a modern composer which was pure and innocent, uncontaminated by worldly ambition, showmanship or aggressiveness. To Franzi it was less the innocence of Schubert's music that appealed than its romantic content, the yearning melancholy of lost love, lost hope and the pathos of Nature's indifference to the fate of its individual creatures. Setting aside his *Revolutionary Symphony* he began to transcribe Schubert's songs for piano alone and introduced those he liked best to his salon recitals.

But his life was still a ruin. Love was forbidden—he could never love another after Caroline. Music was his daily bread, but he could see no glorious future in it as he grew older among so many other highly skilled competitors. As for religion, Urhan's pure fervour made him aware of how juvenile and inconstant his own faith was by comparison, and he particularly envied Urhan's ability to express his religious feelings directly in music, on the church organ in public or in private in his own compositions for the viola d'amore. The music Franzi played—was required to play—was mostly trivial stuff, mere entertainment. Sometimes Franzi felt that he had lost his way through his own faults of laziness and vanity, sometimes that he was being made to pay now—by fate or perhaps God himself—for the dazzling success of his childhood.

One day in summer he attended a concert given by the Italian violinist, Niccolò Paganini. It was a strange and unsettling time. Cholera had broken out in Paris and was spreading swiftly. Those who could afford to were fleeing the city. The streets were jammed with carriages hurrying towards the country and carts trundling corpses to the cemetery. Those who remained in the city were preoccupied with the imminence or actuality of death—their loved ones', their friends' or neighbours', their own. And in the midst of this, making no alteration to his plans, appeared the most famous virtuoso of the age. But of course he was not afraid of cholera, people said, since it was well known that he was in league with the devil, if not himself the devil incarnate. The unprecedented brilliance of his playing was inconceivable without some kind of demonic assistance, no one ever saw or heard him practise his instrument and even at orchestral rehearsals he never played his cadenzas, but kept them strictly for performance in front of an audience. Paganini himself did not try too hard to correct this element of his unsavoury reputation. It helped to pack out his concerts and he was, after all, a showman. But he did vehemently and publicly deny the worst story in circulation—that he had murdered his mistress and used her intestine to make the fourth string of his violin and had then spent twenty years in prison perfecting his technique.

Franzi read this denial in the *Revue Musicale* and reluctantly believed it, but liked the myth better. One of his favourite books was Goethe's *Faust* and the moment Paganini stepped out on to the stage, an emaciated wire-like figure all in black, with lank black hair and bristling side-whiskers, a beetling brow and a long tragic face already wrecked by syphilis and bad dentistry, Franzi was sure that if this was not Mephistopheles himself it was someone who wanted to be mistaken for him. But when the man began to play, the hairs rose on Franzi's neck and goose-pimples ran down his arms and legs. Was this instrument even a violin? Who had ever heard a violin emit such sounds, such swoops and leaps and trills, so high as to be almost out of earshot, so deep as to evoke mountain abysses or booming sea-caves, so fast that the heart raced to keep up, so lingeringly slow that your head swam with vertigo and you almost toppled forward out of your seat? And then, under the intolerable pressure of the bow and the impossibly articulated fingers of the left hand scurrying along it, a string snapped. The audience gasped, a small sardonic smile appeared on the maestro's diabolical face and he played on with three strings, even more brilliantly than before. Another string snapped and it made not the slightest difference—this magician could make two strings do what no other human being could have done with four.

Franzi heard someone in the interval say that Paganini's strings snapped so often that it must be one of his tricks—no doubt he deliberately weakened the strings in advance, so as to excite his audience still further Another person added that he had been known to get down to one, but that somehow that last one always held out. But Franzi thought they were wrong, for Paganini was not just a circus-trickster, though he had certainly mastered every trick in the book and invented a good many of his own. He was also a true artist, both as performer and composer—many of the pieces he played were his own.

His incomparable technique was not an end in itself but was in the service of his music, music which came from his own emotions and which went straight to the emotions of those of his audience, those at least, such as Franzi himself, who were not worldly-wise cynics but still in love with life. And this was the overriding impression Franzi carried away from the whole extraordinary experience, that this man who looked like death and played without fear in the middle of a city haunted by death, was celebrating life, was a giver of life.

Franzi left the concert reeling, as if he were drunk, overwhelmed with a kind of revelation. If Paganini had made a pact with the devil in order to play like that, then perhaps the devil was not what people thought. Perhaps he was on the side of life, not death. And this idea gave rise to another, which Franzi would have preferred to ignore, but found he could not. His deeply religious friend Chrétien Urhan was a fine musician, but could not hold a candle to Paganini either as composer or performer. Urhan's eccentric asceticism and studied innocence in the service of his sternly pure God, now seemed to Franzi a kind of desire for death, or at least an exclusion of the life most humans were naturally inclined to live.

So if Urhan was inspired by God and Paganini by Satan, Franzi was perhaps being tempted by the latter at the very source of his faith, his belief in music and poetry as the highest expressions of human spirituality. If it was so, he had already succumbed, since he knew now as he came triumphantly home to the flat in the rue de Montholon, that his way ahead was clear, that his life had a new meaning. His own room would be his prison. There he would study and practise, practise and study until he could do on the piano what Paganini could do on the violin, not only technically but emotionally. Yes, and play on regardless when the strings snapped. He would emerge from the chrysalis of his deadly years as a frustrated lover, would-be Christian martyr and ruined prodigy to be the greatest pianist the world had ever known, and to take with both hands what the world had to give in the way of life, love and applause.

V. *My First Countess*

Repetition, recollection, reversion. Isolated in snowbound Ukraine with my first Princess, I am repeating, recalling, reverting to the winter I spent with my first Countess in her husband's château in Savoy.

I'm no Don Juan. On the contrary. He captivated and took possession of his innumerable victims, scalped their maidenheads and moved on immediately in search of others. Whereas for me it's the other way round: the women captivate and take possession of me. I need their attention, their surrounding femininity, their desire to be in love, their desire to make a lover of me. The sexual act itself matters less than the direction they give to my life. True, it's only for a time, short or long, but no less intense and all-embracing for that. And when we move apart again, having used up our need for one another, I am briefly rudderless until the next one sees my plight and closes in. I live, in other words, not in my own dominating identity, like the Don, but in the diffusion of theirs around me, their scent, their flavour, their warmth, their will. Leporello's list of his master's conquests, according to Mozart and Da Ponte, is all numbers and nationalities—six hundred and forty in Italy, one hundred in France, ninety-one in Turkey, one thousand and three in Spain—but any list of my mistresses—the *mot juste*—would be much shorter and consist of individual names.

Adèle, then, I am thinking of you, fifteen winters back, when I was nineteen and you were thirty-five, when I'd lost my first great love and dallied with others, but not been to bed with any of them. That was a shame, which I preferred to conceal, since the sexual act for Frenchmen, among whom I'd lived half my life, is a quite mundane thing, an appetite to be satisfied just like eating and drinking, whether expensively and intensely with married women or cheaply and casually with prostitutes. Love—real love—is something different, marriage something different again. Adèle was married to the much older Count L., but like most French upper-class marriages it was a financial and familial arrangement, a legal contract without love or much respect on either side even at the beginning and certainly none by the time Adèle set her heart on me.

She was a pretty woman, fair and blue-eyed, with a retroussé nose, of medium height, growing a little plump, lively, restless, emphatic. She *loved* my music, she *loved* my shy manner as I *sidled towards* the piano and then my *magical transformation*, as she put it, into the *Supreme Master* as I began to play. She could not have enough of *real music*, she said, and whatever would she do without it during the cold winter weeks with her husband in their château in Savoy? So what if I were to be their guest? The Count had no ear for music, but he would have plenty to do there, mostly outside the house, inspecting and regulating the estate, hunting, shooting, riding, and he would be glad to know that his countess would not be as bored and sulky as usual, but happily occupied in improving her piano-playing and perhaps her singing.

Well, as I said, I'm always pleased to be directed by a firm feminine hand, especially accompanied by a pretty face—my father pointed this out to me just before he died and warned me to beware. But why beware of such a kind and intriguing invitation from such a superior person? A Countess, no less, inviting me as a guest, not a servant, and with such a mischievous look that I could not entirely attribute her purpose to the mere desire for company in a remote place, still less for piano lessons. I accepted at once and soon after Christmas travelled with the Count and Countess in their monogrammed carriage to the Château de Marlioz, a few miles from the famous spa town of Aix-les-Bains.

The château was a tall, elegant, compact building with a steeply-sloped roof and thin pencil-like towers, set in the middle of a large park in the English style. Sheep grazed the broad green pastures, which sloped down to the main road and overlooked the dark blue Lac du Bourget, with the Mont du Chat beyond, while directly above the pine-woods at the back of the house rose the snow-clad Bauges Mountains and the peak of Le Grand Revard. It was a lovely place, an

Arcadia, as different from the long, low mansion in the flat Ukrainian steppe which I inhabit now, as Savoy is from Russia or the pretty, flighty, very French Countess Adèle from my beloved, learned, profoundly serious Princess Carolyne. But I am a very different person myself now from that uncertain, awkward nineteen-year-old, whose shyness, pallor and extreme youth must have convinced the elderly Count that he was not extending his hospitality to any sort of rival. As I climbed into the carriage, he said:

'So you are the prodigy my wife is always chattering about! She will have told you I have no ear for music and my sister who lives at the château is quite deaf, so you will have a poor sort of audience. But you look as if a dose of clean mountain air and a course of our disgusting mineral waters would do you good and I daresay the Countess will profit from your tuition.'

He was a man of few words and that was the only time he ever addressed me directly.

During the first week of my visit the sun shone and the days were relatively warm. The Count was out most of the time with his bailiff, visiting his tenants, checking walls and fences, blocked drains, leaking roofs and all the myriad disorders that plague a landowner. Adèle meanwhile, a little flushed, but uncharacteristically subdued, walked me round the more accessible parts of the estate and induced me to try the warm, health-giving but revoltingly sulphurous water that sprang here and there out of the ground into stone basins or fountains. She also made some attempt to improve her piano-playing with my help and in the evenings I myself played some of the shorter, simpler pieces from my repertoire for my audience of three, two of whom quickly dozed off.

The weather gradually grew colder and the sky clouded over. The Count, who talked more to his sister than to his wife, received a letter from France which seemed to annoy him and announced that he would have to return to Paris for a few days. Adèle hardly even pretended that this would inconvenience her and early the next morning the Count's carriage was at the door and he and his valet entered it and drove away as a few snowflakes drifted down on a cold wind from the mountains. Adèle and I set out to walk up to a viewpoint beyond the woods at the back of the house, but the snow was thickening, the sky had become very dark and we turned back. She suddenly took my arm as we quickened our pace down a long open slope towards the château.

'I *love* snow, don't you, Franz? Perhaps we shall be snowed in. I do hope so. What luck that the Count left today! He is not a person to be snowed in with, I can tell you. Quite the opposite to you, Franz. You are the very person to be indoors with. We have provisions to last for weeks, and wood to last the whole winter and we can snap our fingers at the rest of the world. What *fun!*'

Indeed, she was right. The snow continued to fall for several days, then melted a little, before the temperature suddenly dropped and everything froze. The roads were impassable. Adèle and I and the Count's old sister, with half a dozen servants, were suddenly as isolated as if we had been on a desert island. It made no difference to Mlle L. who had lived alone in the château for years and seldom went out in any case, but to me it was at first a worry. Since the age of nine, I had only lived in cities and been constantly busy with teachers, pupils, friends, admirers. In myself I was a solitary boy, whose only close relationship since my father's untimely death was with my mother, but because of my fame and my need to earn a living for my mother and myself, I was seldom alone for long, except in my own small room when sleeping or practising.

'Play for me, Franz!' Adèle demanded, as we left Mlle L. embroidering cushion covers and went into the morning-room where the piano stood. 'Play me the most exciting thing you know!'

I chose part of the *Symphonie Fantastique*, that brand-new work by my brand-new friend Hector Berlioz, which had been performed for the first time only a month earlier and which I was sure was the greatest orchestral composition since the death of Beethoven. This symphony opened a new era in music with its literary content and recurring motif, the *idée fixe*. Berlioz was inspired by his then unrequited passion for the Irish actress, Harriet Smithson—later she agreed to marry him and I was a witness at their wedding—but the music depicts the horrible dream of a lover in which he kills his beloved and is guillotined for her murder. I'd already begun to make my own piano transcription of the symphony and flattered myself that I had caught something of its wild romantic colouring.

Adèle sat on a sofa at right-angles to the piano and whenever I glanced up sideways from the complexities of the fingering, I could see that she was hardly able to keep her seat. Her naturally prominent eyes were bulging. Soon she could sit there no longer, but came and stood directly behind the piano-stool and as I started the 'March to the Scaffold' she put her hands on my shoulders. I heard her gasp as I came to the moment when the guillotine falls and, as I rolled the severed head lingeringly into the basket, her hands were on my chest and I could feel her breasts and belly pressing against my back.

'Franz, Franz,' she said, 'You are a *miracle*. You are a *Hungarian* miracle. I'm sure no Frenchman or German, no one in the world, ever played with such *fire*.'

But just as I was edging round to kiss her, for I was sure that was what she wanted, she broke away and went to the window.

'Look at that snow!' she said, 'thicker and thicker. What *fun*!'

I got up from my stool and went and stood beside her, then put my hand on her arm.

'No, Franz,' she said, pulling her arm away. 'Not now. We have all the time in the world. Let us enjoy ourselves to the *utmost*! Fire and snow! Snow and fire!'

So we put on our boots and coats and went out in the snow, which had begun to fall again, and walked twice round the house, leaving footprints which were already being obliterated as we returned indoors. And now, in the lobby where the boots and the coats were kept, having slipped out of her own boots while I was still struggling to remove mine, she suddenly knelt down on the stone floor and pulled off my boots for me. Then she ran her wet muddy hands down her cheeks.

'See! I am not a countess now, only a slut. Isn't that easier for you, Franz?'

I knelt down in front of her, put my arms round her and kissed her cold, red *retroussé* nose. We were still wearing our coats. She undid mine and threw it on the floor. I did the same for hers and then put my hands on her breasts. Immediately she jumped to her feet.

'Do you dare, little Franz, do you dare? Oh, disgraceful!'

And she ran out of the lobby, only to run back a moment later, as I was still asking myself what next.

'I am going to my room, do you hear? I am taking *refuge* in my own room. Don't you *dare* follow me there, you brute!'

What to do? Was this still the game of fire and snow, or was she serious now? I hadn't the experience to judge, but she had aroused me enough to make me choose the bolder alternative and I went through to the hall and the fine double staircase that curved up both sides to the first floor. She was standing at the top looking over the rail.

'Disgraceful boy! How slow you are!'

But as I began to run up the right-hand staircase, she ran down the left-hand. I stopped half-way up, she stopped half-way down. I started down again, she started up. I stood in the hall and looked up. She stood by the rail at the top again and looked down.

'How will you ever catch me, Franz?'

I ran up the left-hand stair, she started down the right-hand, then seemed to trip and sat on the third stair from the top, nursing her ankle.

'Now you have hurt me, you nasty creature!'

I ran across and sat beside her.

'I'm sorry, very sorry if you're really hurt.'

'Of course I'm hurt. Chased like a poor startled hart in my own house. My husband's house.'

'I'm truly sorry.'

'Now you must carry me to my room.'

Which I did and laid her on the bed.

'What do you think, dear Franz? Is there a bruise or a swelling?'

'None that I can see.'

'Sit down and look more closely.'

I sat down on the bed beside her foot and bent over and kissed the ankle. She put her hand on my head and ruffled my long hair.

'You are an angel, Franz, and I'm sure my ankle will soon be better. But now you must go. A servant may see us and draw unfortunate conclusions.'

This was ridiculous. There had been no sign of the servants—it was not the time of day when they were busy about the house—and if they had been anywhere but in their part of the building they would surely have heard us at our game of fire and snow in the hall and up and down the stairs.

'We must postpone our joy, our *passionate blaze* until tonight.'

'Must we, Adèle? You have stoked me very hot already.'

'I can see, sweet boy, I can see the *flame* rising.' A smile on her lips, her eyes on my crotch. 'Remember, we have all the time in the world. This snow was sent by a kind providence. We should make the best use of it. We are here now for the winter and there is no one to disturb us.'

Almost the very words spoken by my beloved Princess here in Ukraine, when the snow began to fall in earnest, but with what a different tone and meaning! For our lovemaking now is more intellectual and soulful than sensual. Our fire is less in the loins than in the head, where all our individual ideas and understanding of the world and art and literature and religion are thrown together and mingle and fuel a great blaze of mutual energy.

I suppose that what I really want from a woman is both: the sensuality and sexual enticement of Adèle with the intellectual and spiritual fervour of Carolyne. But is that combination really possible? It seemed possible, certainly, with Marie, my *second* Countess, and perhaps was so for a time, but then everything went wrong, deplorably wrong, and I'm inclined to think now that the reason was Marie's inability to combine the two qualities satisfactorily to herself. Or was it my fault, unable to reconcile her demand for my exclusive attention and my need to practise my art, which also demanded my exclusive attention? And, unlike my beloved Carolyne, my once beloved Marie had no real belief in the love of God. No more of this here! The story of my second Countess is a far, far more complicated one than that of my first.

Fire and snow! We dined politely with the Count's sister, then adjourned to the morning-room for music, when I accompanied Adèle in some local Savoyard songs—her voice was small and untrained, but charming enough for these simple airs—and then played a few of my Schubert transcriptions. After that Mlle L. retired to bed and Adèle and I looked at one another silently, boldly, hungrily. But as I moved towards her, she turned away and went to a bookcase, where she found a volume of poems by Lamartine.

'"The Lake," she said. 'You know Lamartine's beautiful poem about our lake?'

'No, I don't.'

She sat down on the sofa, patted the place next to her and then, holding the book so that I could also see the text, read the poem aloud to me.

> *'Aimons donc, aimons donc! De l'heure fugitive,*
> *Hâtons-nous, jouissons!*
> *L'homme n'a point de port, le temps n'a point de rive:*
> *Il coule, et nous passons!'*
> *. . . O lac! rochers muets! grottes! forêt obscure!*
> *Vous que le temps épargne ou qu'il peut rajeunir,*
> *Gardez de cette nuit, gardez, belle nature,*
> *Au moins le souvenir!*

> 'Let us love, then, let us love! The fleeting hour
> Let's hurry to enjoy!
> Humankind has no harbour and time has no shore:
> It flows on, we pass by!
> . . . O lake! and silent rocks, caves, pines on the dark height,
> You whom time can make young again, you time sets free,
> Keep, keep, I beg you, lovely nature, from that night
> At least the memory!'

It was indeed a beautiful poem—I came to know and love Lamartine himself later—but on this occasion I was struck more by the way its sentiment seemed to contradict Adèle's repeated refrain that we had all the time in the world.

I have also wondered since—though at the time I was too young and too amazed by my new status as the lover of a countess, a married woman from the highest society, to pose the question even to myself—whether this was a regular performance? Did the Countess habitually choose some innocent youth to play sexual games with in the absence of her husband? I think not. I think she was improvising and herself as uncertain as I was, of how to behave if one found oneself released from the normal restraints of the social code. She could not, after all, have predicted that we would be snowed in just as the Count left for Paris.

'And now,' she said, 'now it's *bedtime*. I shall go to my room and you must go to yours. I daresay you will find it hard to sleep, but do not even *think* of stealing into my room like a thief. But if you do, *without* thinking, you must close the door behind you, because I warn you that I may easily scream and we do not want to disturb Mlle L. , who is not *stone* deaf.'

With that ambiguous encouragement, after I had undressed and was in my night-shirt, I stole along the corridor to her room like a thief and found the door ajar. Adèle was sitting up in bed reading a novel by the light of several candles and wearing a diaphanous nightdress with a low-frilled neckline. As she turned towards me with a charming smile, the nightdress revealed most of her splendid breasts. I closed the door and moved eagerly towards her.

'What bright green greedy eyes you have, Franz!' she said. 'They *frighten* me. Come here and sit down with your back to me!'

When I did so, she immediately drew a silk scarf from under her pillow and tied it round my head so as to blindfold me.

'Now,' she said, 'You will not be able to *paralyse* me with your basilisk stare and we shall be on more equal terms.'

I heard the bed creak as she got out of it on the far side and then suddenly felt her hand touch my raised *bâton*.

'Wicked boy!' she said. 'Do you mean to *rape* me without remorse?'

'Yes,' I said, 'But not if you don't want me to.'

'Oho! Then you will have to find me!' and she moved away. 'Come on, then! I am just here by the window.'

I took a few steps in the direction of her voice and stubbed my toe on a leg of the bed. She laughed as I stooped to rub it and coming nearer, gave me a little slap on the buttock. But my stooping had slightly loosened the blindfold and with one eye I could see her standing in front of the fireplace, warming her bottom. She had removed her nightdress and was completely naked. Then she danced away to the other side of the bed. Seriously aroused now, I quickly felt my way round the bed and blocked her into the space between the bed and a window.

'Now I have you!' I said.

'No, you don't!'

She darted along the wall towards a second window. I caught hold of her by one naked arm, but she pulled herself free and ran towards the door.

'You're *cheating*,' she said. 'You can see everything.'

'I certainly can and I love it.'

'I shall run out into the corridor and scream for help.'

'Scream away!' I said.

'My sister-in-law will come to my rescue,' she said.

'Let her! I'm ready for all comers.'

I advanced on her again, my arms stretched out so as to prevent her escaping towards the windows, but this time she didn't even try to slip away, but waited until I had pinned her against the door. Then she gripped my head in both hands and kissed me lavishly on the mouth, when I grasped her soft buttocks and lifted her off the floor. And in that awkward position, her bottom against the door, my face, still half blinded by the silk scarf, in her breasts, her hands lifting my night-shirt and guiding my *bâton* inside her, I made real love for the first time in my life.

When I was in love with my second Countess, I had to pretend that this earlier affair with Adèle was brief and unsatisfactory. Indeed it was brief, lasting only the month or so when the roads around us were impassable. But unsatisfactory? On the contrary. During that month we made love many times a day—with due attention to the regular comings and goings of Mlle L. and the servants. The latter at least must have known what was going on, but took care to behave as if they did not.

By the time the snow began to thaw and the Count was expected back from Paris, I had almost had enough of this exhausting game. The Countess, however, found all kinds of ways to vary and prolong its excitement.

'You are a virtuoso,' I told her, lying in her arms after we had made love on the floor beside the piano. She had been playing a simple piece by Mozart and, at every mistake, took off part of her clothing. It did not take long for her to be seated on the stool completely naked and the lesson ended abruptly without the piece being finished.

'No one ever said a nicer thing to me. Do you really think so?'

'I think that what we do is *real music*. The other kind is just an idealization. And this kind, of which you are the virtuoso, makes me understand the other kind better. The notes, if they are composed and played with true feeling, long for each other, just as we do, and fall into each other's arms—and that's how all the best music is made.'

Sometimes we pretended to be children, talking baby-talk, examining each other's parts—laughing at our pretence when we came to her generous breasts or the golden bush of hair below her belly. Once we were two naked Greek statues facing each other from either side of the room and trying not to be the first to move. I rushed to seize her when I saw her breasts stir, but she declared that she had won because she'd seen my *tower* go up first. Sometimes she was the great lady and I was the humble servant, sometimes I played the Count and she the chamber-maid, and on one occasion she gave me a riding-crop and demanded that I *ride* her *hell-for-leather* to the *finishing-post*. I could not do it as seriously as she seemed to want, but I heard the gossip years later that another lover had been more accommodating and had hurt her seriously.

In spite of what I told my second Countess, I cannot be too grateful to my first for her teaching and above all her sensitivity. A coarser woman would have treated me as a mere instrument, hauled me into bed and satisfied herself without too much thought of how this new experience would turn out for me. Adèle introduced me to one of life's greatest pleasures with the science, invention and enthusiasm of a true artist and the consequence is that I can never think of it as morally bad, but on the contrary as the body's best and most natural activity, its music, its God-given purpose: 'male and female created he them'.

We parted badly, however, because I was afraid to meet the Count when he returned. Adèle insisted he would never notice a thing, but I was certain I would be unable to conceal how we had spent the month of his absence. I made the excuse of urgently leaving for Geneva to stay with a pupil, which indeed I had arranged, and promised vaguely, deceitfully, to return in a week or two. She sent many letters after me, full of reproaches and wild laments over her unhappiness and my cruelty. I answered them as best I could and then ceased answering at all when I fell in love with my second Countess and there was nothing more to be said. My conduct was wicked and ungrateful and I'm afraid characteristic of my selfish and uncouth character at the time, but I was not yet twenty when Adèle and I loved each other and I believe I have improved myself a little since.

The snow that keeps me indoors with my Princess, has brought this episode back to me as if it were yesterday and I must admit that, happy as I am now, loving and beloved, I have moments when I could wish to be back in that snowbound Château de Marlioz with the naked adorable Adèle. Of course she must be fifty now and I have become so famous that I could make love to most of the women in Europe if I cared to, but . . . that was the first time and it was very good. The water has flowed down the lake as if we had never been there, but I do not share Lamartine's sadness. What we were given, we took with all our hearts, knowing it was as brief and superficial as the snow, delighting in it all the more for that reason. I shall not show this to my Princess. She is a very different person from my first Countess.

VI. *The Abbé's Messenger*

You can be an infidel, a deist, an atheist: no one will be the least alarmed, or even annoyed. But be careful not to offend the opinions of the theologians or the interests of the hierarchy. For that they will not forgive you.

—Abbé Felicité de Lamennais

I feel the need to write something about the last two and a half weeks, if only because I have been profoundly disturbed. We met in Paris last year through a mutual friend and immediately felt drawn to one another. This young virtuoso from Hungary is a beautiful boy, spiritually, I mean, as well as physically, all soul and ardour. His enthusiasms are the same as mine: religion, the life of the spirit, liberty, equality, truth and love. The difference is in our experience of the world—I have almost thirty years' more—and in the way we have channelled our enthusiasms: he through music, I through the priesthood. Yet if he had not been born with his genius for music he would surely have been a priest and I would not be a priest if I had been born with a genius for anything.

It was only when I realized that I had no special gifts, but was simply an intelligent and sensitive person who wanted not to waste life but to find the truth and try to live according to it, that at the late age of thirty-four, I followed my elder brother into the priesthood. I think Liszt envies me and I certainly envy him, for what is my priesthood now but a running sore? Indeed, since the Holy Father's latest encyclical condemning my little book, *Paroles d'un croyant*, I am a priest only in name and though I have not been formally excommunicated, there is no question of my ever again performing any of the duties of a priest. Except, of course, to bear lonely witness that God is God, Creator of the Universe, that Jesus Christ came to show us the truth and save us all and that the Church which professes to speak with his authority, and to which I still belong, has lost its way—*his* way.

Should I then, have stayed outside the Church and concentrated on writing the truth as I saw it? No, it seemed to me important to do so *as* a priest, to demonstrate 'what a priest is', as I said when I was tried and fined for my earlier book, attacking the way our religion in France is linked to our politics and therefore our rulers. If there is not at least one priest who tries to live as the founder of the Church lived and taught, then what is the Church for? Am I then saying that I am the last best hope of the Church? No, I believe there are many good priests going about their proper work in Christ's name, but perhaps not choosing or needing to confront the hierarchy with its mistakes as I have done. And they are much wiser than I am, since all my efforts and the opprobium and outlawry they have brought me, appear to have been perfectly useless.

Liszt envies me because from an early age he has understood that the basic reality in this life is our relationship with its Creator and therefore our primary purpose should be to concentrate on that relationship, to love him, to love his creation and, if possible, convey that understanding to our fellow men. The only profession specifically dedicated to that task is the priesthood, but of course from an even earlier age he had been dedicated to the profession of a musical virtuoso, so that he feels in a sense that he has been sidelined, that his musical genius has prevented him following the only true way.

The second or third day he was here, after his lunch, which he took alone, since I do not eat at midday, we went out for a walk together and he raised this question. Should he abandon his musical career and become a priest or at least a monk?

'I don't think God wants that of you,' I said.

'Will you ask him?'

'I don't speak directly to God,' I said, taken aback by the naiveté of the question.

'If *you* don't, M. l'Abbé, who does?'

'I mean that He does not speak directly to me. I'm not a saint, only a humble priest.'

'How did you know that he wanted *you* to be a priest?'

'I didn't *know*. I thought it the best thing I could do.'

'And you don't think it the best thing for me?'

'I think God has given you—gave you from the start—a very clear message about what he wants you to do.'

'Then why do I feel so uncertain and so inadequate?'

'We all do, if we are honest with ourselves.'

'Christ never said anything about being a musician. He wanted us to live for other people, especially for the poor. Do I do that? No, I play mostly for the bourgeoisie.'

'You talk in political terms,' I said, 'but music is above all a spiritual thing. The Church has always made use of it as such. What are hymns, oratorios, musical settings of the Mass but means of awakening the spiritual part of us, stimulating our emotions and directing them upwards? With a heart and mind and talent like yours you can do as much as or more than any priest to serve God and that was surely God's purpose in giving you the gifts you were born with.'

He seemed satisfied with that and began to talk about how he fervently wishes to unite music with the Church, to abolish the distinction between secular and sacred music, to make all music a vehicle for the spirit.

Liszt is indeed very young. He is also very spoilt by the life he has led. He has had nothing but adulation since he was a small child and remains, in a way, that same small child, accustomed to adulation, hungering, crying for attention if for a moment it is withdrawn. He does not quite understand this, because of course he has no means of knowing what it is like to be an ordinary person. Naturally, he has experienced frustrations and disappointments and severe discipline— he could not play as he does without it. The sudden death of his father (who was also his musical director), must have had a traumatic effect on him, but he never speaks of it. I think he is lonely (he has innumerable acquaintances, but seems to have no close friends and never to have had any), and he is often a prey to melancholy and depression. But always beyond and above these more or less normal human afflictions, he is at the same time the incomparable, the unique Franz Liszt. Not that he is arrogant or domineering. Oh no, on the contrary,

extraordinarily humble, deferential, even to someone as socially marginal as me, whom he chooses to consider wise and divinely inspired—
God knows, I wish I were. Grafted on to his child-like consciousness of
being always the centre of attention is an adult's sensitivity to others
and an adult's learned manners. A prince, that is what he is, with a
prince's grace and condescension and complete ignorance of what it
is like not to be a prince.

He came here to escape as much from himself as the world—probably more so, because, isolated and set on a pinnacle as he is by his
genius (and one must say also his physical charm), his world is himself.
I put him in the room next to mine on the first floor, but he spent
much of his time, of course, in the salon on the ground floor, practising on our poor piano there and also beginning to compose a piece of
his own, strange sounds to my ears after Mozart and Meyerbeer,
Haydn and Hummel. But though I love music, I am hardly an expert.
The very peculiar Hector Berlioz is Liszt's current musical idol. This
piece of Liszt's is inspired by and named after a collection of
Lamartine's poems, *Harmonies poétiques et religieuses*. Lamartine's pref-
ace, which Liszt intends to quote from at the head of his score and
which he read to me one morning over coffee, with his habitual nervous mixture of pride and deference, speaks of 'souls raised by solitude
and contemplation towards ideas of the infinite, towards religion; their
thoughts turned to rapture and prayer, their whole existence a silent
hymn of praise to God and hope for the future'.

'Isn't this exactly what you want music to be, M. l'Abbé?' he said.
'I have composed nothing like this before and already, after only a
week here at La Chênaie with you, I feel altogether renewed. Enough
of virtuosity and playing merely to entertain! I've found my métier. I
shall be first and foremost a composer.'

Yes, I was like that at his age, unable to separate the pursuit of a
spiritual life from my obsession with myself. And I know from my own
experience how dangerous that thoughtless contempt is—'playing
merely to entertain'—that easy dismissal of the rest of the world, the
majority of mankind, as unenlightened, unredeemed. He will learn
painfully, as I have, that sublimities—which I do indeed believe to be
the true realities—are hard to keep hold of amid the dark, smoky
seeming realities of this world. Hardest of all because of the constant
shadow cast by oneself. And besides he will be quite unable to resist

the demand for his virtuosity, since he is, I have to admit, much as I like and admire him, in some ways a weak character.

He came here expecting austerity and solitude and found it. Our other incumbents, young Boré and Kertanguy, who are about Liszt's age, and the two 'teenaged boys, are immersed in their studies and mainly silent at dinner-time, the only point in the day when we all regularly meet together. They were all the more silent, of course, in the presence of such a famous and glamorous person as Liszt. And for the first week our monastic regime appealed to him—he was pleased with the simple food, the constricted premises, the long hours alone when he read or did his exercises on the piano. His eyes were bright, his talk full of joy and hope, he was flatteringly attentive to every word I uttered—and I'm afraid that with such an eager listener I scarcely ever stopped talking. But by the next week, he was no longer so ready to be left to his own devices, he was smoking more and evidently missing both company and alcohol. He seemed even to have tired of reading.

I thought at first that he was merely bored, that he had made a mistake about himself and did not really relish solitude at all, but there was more to it than this, as I discovered a day or two before he left, when we were playing *écarté* together and the postboy arrived. Liszt fell upon the letters and extracted one for himself with almost frightening transports of delight. His emotions are very near the surface and, again like a child's, quite unconstrained. I did not see him angry during the time he was here, though once irritated by a crass question from one of the children about the length of his golden hair, but I suspect that he must have a fierce temper if baulked or severely contradicted.

His letter, as he could not help telling me in his great excitement, was from the Countess d'Agoult, with whom he has been conducting an on-and-off affair—I do not speculate whether platonic or otherwise—for a year or two. He told me that she is a devout Catholic—she cannot be altogether devout if she, a married woman with two daughters, is prepared to have this sort of relationship with a boy considerably younger than herself—and does not much approve of my writings, but that he is always arguing my case with her and hopes eventually to persuade her that I am 'the one bright light shining in the Church's dim penumbra'. He wanted her, he said, to come to La Chênaie herself so as to see with her own eyes and hear with her own ears what a haven of true Christian faith and reason it is, in a world gone insane with the struggle for power and material gain. How much she would enjoy, he added, paddling with him in our little lake and joining our daily walks through the countryside in the evening, though I would have to moderate my pace which was almost too rapid even for his long stride!

He meant, I'm sure, to show me that she was not a snobbish aristocrat, but a genuinely simple person and that she and I might share a love of nature, even if our opinions did not quite coincide. But the very suggestion made me shudder. What naiveté to imagine that he could introduce his lady-love to our strictly masculine society or that my ideas of liberty include free sexual relationships! The whole business clouded our last days together, for what had begun by seeming a real meeting of minds—however distanced by our relative ages—a kind of discipleship on his part, and on mine the privilege of influencing a chosen vessel of God's purpose, a truly gifted artist, now looked more like a whim, a jaunt, a sulphur bath for the soul, a mere episode in his busy social schedule.

I am being too negative. He *is* religious, he is not a *flâneur*, he means most of what he says and although he is certainly more at home in a society salon than a monastic cell, he also appreciates, though not for long at a time, solitude, contemplation, the idea of sainthood, and the attempt to be good, not just for himself but for others. He is very much moved by the suffering, helplessness and hopelessness of the poor and takes their side unequivocally against the rich and powerful. His main problem, as I mentioned, is weakness of character, especially where women are concerned. Of course they flutter round him in swarms like moths to a candle and he in turn is quite stupefied by their attentions.

Well, coming late to the priesthood as I did, I have experienced that too—the charm of women and to a small degree their capacity for worship when they come across a man set apart by his gifts or even just his superior notion of himself and his ideas. But Liszt's attraction for women is on an altogether different scale from any that I may have had at his age and I fear that for all his high ideas and noble aspirations, women will always keep him partly tethered in that narrow yard of tittle-tattle, fashion, fripperies, interior decoration and trivial emulation from which so few of them seem able or even wishful to break free. No, let me defend myself, in case any woman should ever read this, and protest that men can be just as constricted by mundane concerns and conventional aspirations. No, I do not say that all women are like this, but only that in our society most are and that I have seldom met one that was not. It comes simply to this: it is easier for men to escape the superficialities of social life, and a few do, whereas any woman who did so would have to be a kind of freak—a George Sand, let us say—and her worst enemies in that case would certainly be other women, just as my worst enemies are other priests.

I am going astray. I had no intention of getting involved with the woman-question, not even as it affects Liszt. I wanted to explain to myself why Liszt's visit disturbed me so much and it is really nothing to do with his weakness of character, which in any case I might have foreseen and which I have probably over-emphasized. No, it is *my* weakness of character that has been revealed, *my* desire to be a surrogate father to this boy who lost his own at such a crucial point in his life. And why? Probably because my own father was no father to me, but entirely taken up with the failure of his business and indeed his whole life. So he handed me, already motherless, over to an uncle, who more or less left me to my own devices from an even earlier age than Liszt. My elder brother was the nearest I had to a father and he directed me, almost inexorably, into the monastic life he had embraced. Its discipline was not at all to my taste and it was only after much heart-searching and many escapades that I eventually settled for the seemingly less constricted vocation of priest.

I said that I envied Liszt for his genius, but I envy him even more for his faith. I believe, yes, I do believe in what I try to teach others to believe, that God is our Father and that Nature, his creation, is our mother. But the more I hammer out my argument with the Church, that Nature evolves and adapts, that this is the law of Nature and therefore God's law and ours, as part of Nature, so that the hierarchy's insistence on stasis and infallibility, its resistance to reason, its alliance with all the reactionary elements in our society is not only wrong but devilish, the more my doubts grow. What *is* my faith? Is it only faith in reason, in the betterment of society through justice and liberty and equality for all humanity? Do I believe in God because I have been told he is God or because I have first-hand evidence of his existence? I have never been in direct communication with God. I love what the Gospels tell us of Jesus Christ and his teachings. I love Nature, which

I believe to be some sort of reflection of God. I love reason, which must also come from God, since everything does. I love my fellow-men in general and a few in particular. But God himself? I pray to him constantly. He does not answer.

That assumption of Liszt's, that I could put a direct question to him and receive a direct answer, took the ground from under me, I realize now. I could never communicate with my own father, I cannot communicate now with our Father in Heaven. And because I cannot and never have, I have turned my frustration and dissatisfaction on the Church and become a politician myself instead of a priest. I want justice, liberty and equality for all humanity and promise it in the name of God, but the more I demand that the Church gives evidence for its dogmas and pronouncements, the more I am forced to go back to the one 'fact' for which my only evidence is the Bible: the existence of God and his love for us and the rest of his creation. What if God did not exist, if Liszt's genius were mere chance or heredity (both his father and grandfather were musically gifted, even if they only practised as amateurs), if my own life were based on a false assumption? That would not invalidate my claims for the rights of humanity, of course, but it would reduce their authority, reduce them to politics, which is what my enemies already say they are. No, the evidence for God the Father and for God's love is our existence in the universe and the self-sacrifice of his Son. And Liszt himself is evidence too, for his faith is in a way stronger than mine. I have made myself, after much hesitation and many stumblings, a servant of God. But Liszt knows he is—his doubt is only about how he should act on that knowledge.

I have never met anyone like him before, one of the elect. He looks like an angel and I begin to think he is an angel. His human failings, which I have dwelt on too much, are just that, human, the inevitable weaknesses of flesh and blood. But his spirit and his ability to project his spiritual powers in the form of music are sublime. I felt this otherworldly radiance from the moment he arrived, but because I am so helplessly human myself, so mired in the flesh, I mistook my feelings for something else, for carnal love. Yes, I reproved and constrained and punished myself for what I took to be my impurity in lusting after this angelic youth, and even imagined that I would have a hard time if he took to staying here regularly.

Now I suddenly realize that it was his all-too-human reaction to his Countess' letter that by stages has brought the truth home to me. The first stage was irritation at the intrusion of that world of women on our hermitage. The second stage was jealousy—he was clearly in carnal love with her and had only spiritual love for me. The third stage is my recognition now that *spiritual* love is precisely what he came to bring me. He was a messenger from God, though not, of course, realizing that consciously, any more than I did. He thought I communicated directly with God and I smiled—almost jeered—at his naiveté. But *he was* my communication with God. That is how God works and now at last I have the evidence I always lacked. It has been a long wait—half a century—and I was slow to see it even when it came under my own roof at La Chênaie. No wonder I feel so disturbed.

VII. An Exchange of Letters

Bayreuth,
Germany
20 August 2007

Dear Mr Spurling,

During my lifetime, people frequently spread false rumours about me, misinterpreted my motives and even wrote trashy and libellous novels about me (though they partly disguised my identity with other names and occupations).

When I was young, I hastened to correct their lies or misunderstandings by writing either to them personally or to the newspapers which had published them, but when I was older and had grown a thicker skin I ceased to bother, unless the lies were so gross and widely-circulated that they might distress my friends or family.

Your book (which does not even attempt to disguise my identity) can do no harm now to anyone I cared about and very little to me. My reputation has had its ups and downs, but in spite of some neglect in your country—which from my many triumphs there in my lifetime, I might have expected to honour me more than others—it is now, I believe, securely established, even if somewhat diminished still by my former protégé, friend and son-in-law, the incomparable genius and self-publicist Wagner. Yes, I can be generous to real greatness even from my grave in the shadow of his theatre.

But since you profess to admire both me and my work, indeed to be so absorbed by both that you have thought about little else for the past three or four years, I would like to ask you why you take the liberty of fictionalizing me in this way, freely inventing whenever the established facts of my life fail you. You put words in my mouth, discover thoughts in my head and ascribe actions to me which, if I were still alive I would robustly repudiate and for which, even if I could not be bothered to call you to account publicly in the newspapers or the courts, I would find it hard to forgive you. Do you really wish to offend the person you have taken so much trouble to study?

If you were doing this for money, I would understand. In my younger days when I was short of money and wanted more of it, I travelled and played, played and travelled and put up with infinite irritations, pains, sicknesses and tedium for the sake of earning money. When I was older I was short of money again, but since my children were grown up and I did not by then want much for myself beyond cigars and alcohol, I no longer cared to make myself a martyr to money. However, neither my reputation probably nor certainly yours is sufficient to earn you more than a sorry sum from this long labour, so what is the point of it?

The novels written about me in my lifetime by friends or lovers (George Sand, Balzac, Daniel Stern,* Olga Janina) were intended either to earn their authors money and further success (Sand, Balzac) or to take revenge for blighted love-affairs. But your love affair with my long-departed spirit and my still living music is not yet blighted. Perhaps it would be, if I had any say in the matter and could stop this book of yours in its tracks, but I do not think you would continue to write it if you were to become disillusioned, like those two vengeful women, with your erstwhile hero.

So what the devil do you think you are doing? What service to me or yourself do you imagine you are performing with this ersatz tissue of fact and fiction?

I am, Mr Spurling, yours very truly

F. Liszt

---

*Daniel Stern was the pen-name of the Countess Marie d'Agoult, mother of Liszt's three children.

Beulah,

Wales

21 August 2007

Dear Dr Liszt,

I have no wish at all to offend you. I am, as you say, a passionate admirer both of your life and your music. I might perhaps have written another straight biography of you, but since the publication of Alan Walker's three-volume life, which everyone who loves your music should read, there is no need for that and besides I am no biographer.

Still, I clearly have offended you and will continue to do so, since my book is scarcely begun and I shall continue to invent as the mood and the material lead me. You did after all write to your official biographer, Lina Ramann: 'My biography is more to be invented than written after the fact.' And I am only doing what you constantly did with your own compositions, taking a motif and very often—in your wonderful transcriptions, 'paraphrases' or 'reminiscences'—another composer's motif and running away with it.

No, I am not writing for money or revenge and I don't imagine that I'm writing on your behalf—whether to add to your already glorious reputation, to inspire fresh interest in it or to illuminate your life and music in some way that straight biography can't. I'm writing primarily for myself, to tease out and if possible clarify whatever it is that you have aroused in me—my one-sided love-affair—and to discover in the process some fresh approach to writing fiction which often in the last half century has seemed to be a dying art, but never actually is because it has no discernible boundaries. You, I know, felt just the same about your music.

So forgive me if you can, dear Master, when I say that although your life and music and reputation are my subjects, as, for instance, Byron's *Mazeppa* or Goethe's *Faust* were the subjects of works of yours, what I'm really trying to do is to make you into something else, as you made those literary works into pure music. Not that there is anything pure about my book—except that it's pure words—it is precisely, as you have pointed out, an ersatz tissue—or shall we say a Hungarian goulash?—of fact and fiction.

But if you could think of yourself less as the great Franz Liszt, who lived and played and travelled and loved and composed with such inexhaustible energy, and more as a motif or series of motifs which can be stated, transformed and improvised upon and might or might not in the process emerge as an independent work of art—whether successful or futile in the outcome I can hardly say, but that is the intention—then, I believe, you might forgive my presumption and perhaps even wish me success.

Your humble admirer,

John Spurling.

VIII. His Second Countess

> . . . *Nessun maggior dolore,*
> *Che ricordarsi del tempo felice*
> *Nella miseria* . . .
>
> (Nothing sadder than to remember the good time in the
> bad)
>
> —Dante, *Inferno* V, 121–3

1. LOVERS MEETING: PARAPHRASE OF MADAME D'AGOULT'S *MÉMOIRES*

If Dante saw truly, then the fate of Paolo and Francesca da Rimini—to
be whirled around for ever in the winds and darkness of 'the second
circle of hell'—will be ours too. *They* came to illicit kissing very quickly,
after reading together the story of Lancelot and Guinevere. Franz and
I took longer, though our heady, intimate conversations started from
the very moment we met, in the salon of the old Marquise Le Vayer in
Paris.

I was invited to an evening of choral singing. The piano accom-
paniment was to be played by the famous Hungarian prodigy, one of
whose pupils was the Marquise's niece. I say he was famous, but just
then, at the age of twenty-one, his fame was fading. Something had
upset him—people said it was a frustrated love affair and that he was
thinking of entering a monastery. He still continued to teach a few
pupils, but he never played in public any more and only very rarely in
private salons. If people spoke of him now it was more as an enigma
than as a prodigy.

I arrived late, but Franz was even more late. I had never set eyes
on him before and, having heard most of the fashionable virtuosi, had

no particular wish to hear another. The boy I saw come through the door was tall and excessively thin, with a pale face and huge sea-green eyes, which shone with sudden flashes like waves catching the sun. He looked unhappy, but also masterful, and the way he glided rather than stepped across the room, distracted, uneasy, made me think of a ghost whose hour for returning to the shadows was about to strike.

Yet as soon as he was introduced to me, he sat down beside me, politely, confidently, and began to talk as if he'd known me for years. I was attracted by the power and freedom of his spirit. He talked impetuously, vehemently, abruptly. His ideas, his judgements, cutting across all the banalities and received ideas I was used to, astonished me as much as his appearance. His flashing eyes, his gestures, his smile—sometimes sweet and gentle, sometimes caustic—seemed to demand either that I contradict him or wholeheartedly agree with him. I found it difficult to reply.

The piano was opened, the candles lit on either side of the reading desk. Franz left my side and in a daze, almost involuntarily, I followed him to the piano, where the small group of girls assembled by the Marquise was waiting to sing, and, taking a mezzo-soprano part from one of them, joined the chorus. It was a piece by Weber. When it was over and Franz got up from the piano, he caught sight of me among the singers who had been standing behind him. His expression lightened for a moment and then became sombre again and for the rest of the evening he made no further attempt to speak to me. When I went up to him among the others to say something polite about his playing, he inclined his head without speaking. It was late when I got home. I had difficulty sleeping and when I did sleep I had strange dreams.

The Marquise visited me next day with one of her relations. They had thought I looked unwell the night before and came to see how I was feeling. But without really listening to my reply, the Marquise burst out with exclamations about Franz's genius.

'And yesterday,' she said, 'he surpassed himself. His pupils say he has never played like that before. You inspired him. It was you he kept looking around for. When you applauded, his face lit up.'

Her relation interrupted her to talk about artists' eccentricities and how difficult it was to have them in one's house on an equal footing with the other guests from one's own milieu. The Marquise took no notice at all, but continued to praise Franz, his character—'as beautiful as his genius'—his soul—'as noble as his talent'—his evangelical goodness, always trying to help the poor though he was poor enough himself.

'You should invite him to call on you,' she said to me. 'He deserves the honour. You would make him proud and happy.'

Her relation made a dismissive gesture, as if to say this would be quite out of order. That gesture decided me. I asked the Marquise for Franz's address and sent him an invitation to one of my soirées. Writing the invitation, short as it was, cost me infinite time and pains. I had felt, when he talked to me, that he was very conscious of the difference in our social status and was afraid it might come between us. So I was anxious that he shouldn't find my invitation condescending. He didn't reply, but he came.

He was well received by my circle of friends and when I asked him, came again. There was nothing to stop us from meeting as often as we liked. My taste for music was well known, my reputation was secure after six years of marriage, and I had complete independence both from my husband and my family. We conversed greedily and enthusiastically about every sort of serious subject: God, religion, human destiny, politics, literature, art and, of course, music. We never talked trivialities, never said anything flirtatious, never descended to saying anything about ourselves, except that we had both often been unhappy. We were very young, very earnest, very profound, very naive, and were soon meeting every day, alone or in company. I had been well educated, he hardly at all, but his quick intelligence and keen curiosity had already broadened his mind far beyond mine. His passionate, extreme feelings about the world's injustice and materialism and the better world he hoped for, his revolutionary ideas for a reformed Church and a Republican State went against everything I had been taught and carried me into an altogether new way of thinking. I was not seduced so much by his music—the overwhelming sensuality of his playing which reduced most listeners to tears—as by what lay behind it: the ambitious energy, the spiritual aspiration of his mind. Providence, chance or God chose me to be an aristocrat, a member of a privileged minority, but he belonged to a still smaller minority. We use the word 'genius' too loosely. A real genius, a person gifted from birth with powers beyond the ordinary human compass, is very rare. I never had any doubt but that in Franz I had met one, and of course I was mesmerized.

Sometime later he wrote a piece for the piano, ostensibly in honour of the Virgin Mary.

'This is my Annunciation,' he said, 'and it is for you, Marie.'

'Then I suppose you are the angel Gabriel.'

'I suppose I must be.'

'You look just as I imagine him from the paintings.'

'But, of course, he was only the messenger.'

'Whereas you . . . ?'

'I am staying the night.'

The same thought struck us both and we looked at one another, almost challenging the other to say it aloud. Neither of us did—our belief in that Christian myth was still too well rooted. He was always more of a Catholic than I was, and has remained so. But since I have abandoned my religion I can say it now: 'Is that what happened? Did Gabriel stay the night?'

But there was no question of his staying the night in that first phase of our relationship. In fact, quite soon it lapsed for a while, when I went back to my place in the country and became immersed in all the usual humdrum—and now, to my newly expanded spirit, sickeningly tedious and narrow-minded—activities of aristocratic country life. The Château of Croissy, dating back to the time of Louis XIV and a short distance from Paris, was a large and elegant property which I had only just acquired. I could not take any pleasure in it now. Franz's letters were my only consolation, but like a wind blowing on embers they inflamed my irritation with everything around me—and especially the constraints and proprieties of the neighbours. My intervention in his life seemed to have renewed his confidence and ambition. He was giving public concerts again, with growing success, meeting new and interesting people—Hugo, Heine, Dumas, Berlioz, Chopin—and discovering new books to read and new ideas to share with me. But *his* intervention in *my* life had simply made it seem even more pointless and insufferable than before.

What of my husband, the Comte d'Agoult? He was a kind and decent man, fifteen years older than me, who had been a dashing cavalry colonel in the days of Napoleon I, but was now, like most military men in retirement, looking only for a quiet life without disturbance. He had married me in order to unite two old noble families and because I was beautiful and my family, unlike his, wealthy. I had married him because no one else more suitable presented himself, and because girls of my class either got married or went into convents. After the birth of our second daughter we had had enough of each other and agreed to live separately. He came to Croissy for a while that spring to remind the children that they had a father and when he had gone, I began to think that I might throw myself into a river, as my elder half-sister had done a few months earlier in Germany. I was desperate. I wrote to Franz and invited him to Croissy.

My two daughters were with me in the salon when he was announced. He stopped in the doorway. I could see at once that I had made a terrible mistake and that he was on the point of going straight back to Paris. What was the matter? The disparity in our social status was certainly part of it—the grandeur and luxury of the house—but much worse was the light he now saw me in, as a married woman with small children and somewhere, even if not in evidence, a husband. I was suddenly a person pinned down by reality, in a world which we had absolutely ignored in all our high-flying letters and conversations. Of course he lived in another real world, at least as constricted as mine, with his mother, but we had ignored that too. And, as I have said, he was a very religious person, and it had clearly not occurred to him until this moment that he was intruding on a marriage.

He did not leave, but many times over the next few days I almost wished that he would. We spoke only in broken sentences. We mostly avoided one another. All the power and energy of his longing for the infinite and the heights of human experience were now turned downwards and inwards and awry. I had seen him as almost an angel, now he seemed demonic. Even his voice changed. He could not speak of anyone or anything without sarcasm and bitterness, and I knew very well that it was me, poor me, the person who had brought him down to earth with such a crash, who was the real target of his venom. I urged him to play the piano, thinking that might restore his spirits, but no, not at all. He had lost none of his technical brilliance, on the contrary he exaggerated it, loud, soft, fast, slow, glissandi and octave leaps, glittering arpeggios, crossing hands, devilish trills, dissonant chords, mighty hammerings which broke several strings, all the time with a kind of leer or sneer on his face, as if to say, 'Is this what you wanted, Madame? The Paganini of the piano: every trick in the book and a lot more of my own invention? Your tame mountebank obliges.'

And then, after a day or two of hardly speaking, he began to talk glibly, with a sentimental smile, like an actor in a play, like Molière's Tartuffe, and that was worse.

'Such a palace you live in, Madame! The view over the park is heavenly! What lovely mirrors! Are they heirlooms or did you buy them specially for these walls? They are quite perfect. Everything is perfect: the wallpaper, the flower-arrangements, the chandeliers, the bibelots—is that the right word?—the pictures, and especially their frames. Such impeccable taste! The horses in your stable—would that I had ever been taught to ride like a proper gentleman! And to have your own cook . . . ! The food is beyond praise. What a paradise you have admitted me to, Madame! This poor musician is truly over-whelmed by his good fortune and thanks you from the bottom of his heart.'

At last I could stand no more. I meant to say something—'Please stop!'—instead my voice came out as a small cry, a sob. I burst into tears. He stared at me in silence and the sickly smile disappeared. His lips trembled. His whole body shook as if some battle was going on inside him. Suddenly he went down on the floor at my feet and clasped my knees.

'Forgive me, forgive me! What was I thinking of? How could I? I'm sorry, so sorry. Can you forgive me?'

I took hold of his hands—they were even hotter than mine—to pull him up, but instead he pulled me down. This was no longer for-giveness, but an explosion of love, a vow, a promise of love undivided, without limit, without end, on earth and in the skies for ever and ever.

Oh, Paolo and Francesca, our love was a match for yours, indeed I think it far surpassed yours in intensity, in breadth and depth, and—since no angry and vicious husband broke in and stabbed us to death—in duration too. If Dante saw truly, we shall join you there in the black whirlwind, with all those others, Antony and Cleopatra,

Heloise and Abelard, Tristan and Isolde. Our love was no less passionate, no less doomed than theirs, indeed the love of Franz and Marie deserves like theirs to be retold and remembered, and if it is not, it will only be because we did not die of it, but lived to see it die in us. At least, it died in Franz. Alas, it never died in me and that is my own Circle of Hell, here on earth.

2. THE *RATZENLOCH*: REMINISCENCE OF ANNA LISZT

I am Franzi's mother. He and I had a difficult time after my husband died. It was Adam who made Franzi a famous pianist. Adam always wanted to be a full-time musician himself. After he died, I came to live in Paris to look after Franzi, while he finished his studies and taught pupils. We were very hard up, but things became even more difficult after Franzi fell in love with one of his aristocratic pupils. She was in love with him too—of course most of them were—but when her father made her marry somebody of their own class, Franzi became quite wild with grief. He wanted to be a priest or a monk—my husband had the same idea at the same age, long before we were married, and was a novice for two years in a Franciscan monastery, but he didn't take to the life and I'm sure Franzi wouldn't have either.

Fortunately, our confessor Abbé Bardin and I got him off that idea and I decided the best thing was for him to get married, because what he always needed was a woman to look after him. When a boy reaches his age he needs things from a woman that his mother can't give him. I don't mean just the physical thing, though that's important enough, but a meeting of minds too—especially Franzi, who was a very bright boy bursting with ideals, and ambitions, and big ideas, most of which I could hardly understand. We had a very loving relationship, but he couldn't talk to me about all the books he was reading and the thoughts he was having about them. And I have to say that because of his talent, and his looks, and the pupils from the aristocracy he was teaching, he was always attracting women and was getting quite loose in his morals as a consequence, going off sometimes for jaunts with various young women—and some older ones too. There was a Hortense and an Adèle and others too, but he didn't tell me anything about them.

Madame Laborie, who lived almost next door, had a pretty daughter called Charlotte, about Franzi's age, and when they met, they definitely liked each other. With Madame Laborie's approval, I suggested to Franzi that he ask Charlotte to marry him. He wasn't all that enthusiastic, but I pointed out that if he really wanted to be a great musician, he couldn't afford to be constantly distracted by girls throwing themselves at him, he needed a home of his own and a wife he could rely on, and that Charlotte was a sweet and gentle person. He agreed. Oh, dear! It still makes me squirm to think of what happened next. One day he came home and announced that he was going off for a trip to Savoy.

'You went there last winter,' I said. 'Is this the same lady, the Countess you stayed with before?'

'No,' he said. 'I've finished with Adèle. This is a different person.'

'May I know her name?'

'It won't mean anything to you. Mademoiselle Barre.'

'Mademoiselle? That's not quite the thing, is it, when you're engaged to Charlotte?'

'Mother, I'm not exactly engaged to her and I've decided I can't marry her. She's a nice girl, I'm not a very nice person. I would make her unhappy.'

'You'll certainly make her unhappy if you break off your engagement.'

'I told you, it wasn't exactly an engagement.'

'Her mother and I certainly thought it was. And I believe Charlotte did too.'

'I'm sorry. I don't in the least want to make her unhappy. But better that than a whole life of unhappiness.'

And then he delivered one of his long excitable speeches. As I recall, it was something to do with the importance of living in the future as well as the present. He always had a whole rigmarole of explanation for any course of action he was taking and then two or three weeks, or sometimes only days later that would all be forgotten and he'd be off on some other track with another explanation. Oh, he was a handful! His father could have managed him, but I couldn't. I didn't really have the words. He spoke beautiful French by then, but my French was still very limited, and his explanations were mostly French.

So the upshot of this was that he wrote to Charlotte and returned all her letters, and I spoke to her mother and it was dreadful. He was ashamed, I was ashamed, Madame Laborie was understandably angry and poor Charlotte was devastated. Meanwhile Franzi went off to Savoy with his Mlle Barre and seemed to have enjoyed himself, but I never heard another word about her. Charlotte was very low for a long time—her mother and I remained friends, but Franzi and Charlotte were careful to avoid meeting. I'm glad to say that some years later she made an excellent marriage in the aristocracy, whereas Franzi never has got married at all and surely never will now.

His second Countess—well, she may have been his fifth or sixth, but his second to my knowledge—was called Marie d'Agoult. Her husband came from a very old family of the aristocracy, and so did she. Her father was the Viscount de Flavigny and her mother was the daughter of a rich German banker in Frankfurt. They had met when her father was in exile from France during the Revolution, and they came to live in France again after the defeat of Napoleon and the Restoration of the Bourbon kings. Madame d'Agoult was particularly close to her father, but he died when she was still a girl, and that may have been part of what drew Franzi and her together—they had both lost beloved fathers at a very vulnerable age. Madame d'Agoult was living apart from her husband when she met Franzi, but she had two young daughters, her mother was still alive and she also had a brother—who was now, of course, the Viscount de Flavigny—as well as the rest of her mother's German family, still living in Frankfurt. She must have been very seriously smitten by Franzi to contemplate giving up her whole family and her position in society in order to live with him.

But I don't think she did contemplate that at first. She was several years older than him, not at all frivolous or light-hearted, quite different from the ladies Franzi had been involved with up to then. They met in somebody's salon, and then started to see each other regularly and write long letters to each other. I thought in those early days that their interest in each other was mostly intellectual, not physical. But then the lady invited him to stay at her grand château outside Paris, and after that he told me that he was madly in love with her and she with him and they didn't know what to do about it. He didn't ask my advice because he knew perfectly well what I would say about being in love with a married woman. However, what he did do was rent a separate apartment, and when I protested at the expense and even cried a little at the thought of not sharing my life with him any more, he put his arms round me and became very tender and loving:

'Dear mother, you always take everything so hard! I'm not going to stop living here with you. The apartment is just for working in. I'm seriously composing now as well as practising for my concerts—and you will be freer to see your friends, especially Madame Laborie, without disturbing me. Or me disturbing you, for that matter, with *my* friends and all my coming and going. I may spend the night there sometimes, of course, but it's not very far away and we can still see each other every day. We'll go round and look at it tomorrow and you can tell me what I still need to furnish it.'

So we went round there and as soon as he opened the door he said:

'There you are, mother! That's my *ratzenloch*,' using the German word for rat-hole.

I was shocked:

'Whatever do you mean—*ratzenloch*? I see no rats, nor any signs of any. It's a nice apartment, clean and tidy. And you told me it cost two hundred francs. You should have more respect. Why do you call it a *ratzenloch*?'

But he only smiled in that enigmatic way he has and wouldn't explain.

Of course I soon understood what he really wanted the apartment for. It was so that he could meet her in private, because their relationship, which perhaps up to then had not gone beyond the bounds of decency, had now evidently reached a new stage. And why *ratzenloch*? I don't know for certain. He never did explain, but I suppose it was a kind of joke with her—though I never noticed that she had much sense of humour—that she, the proud countess with a fine apartment in the best quarter of Paris as well as her great château in the country, now had to come to her lover in this very humble place.

But I don't know that she came very often that year. In the summer she was in the country with her children and then Franzi went off to stay in the country with a strange rebel priest he admired, Abbé de Lamennais, and soon after he (Franzi) got back to Paris, a terrible thing happened to Madame d'Agoult. The elder of her two daughters, Louise, six years old, became very ill and died, just before Christmas.

As far as I know, Franzi and the Countess never met during that time and though he certainly wrote letters to her I don't think she replied. So I began to think that the whole thing was over. I believe Franzi did too. He had been quite busy recently, performing at private concerts and because, while he was out of the public gaze, he had been improving his technique, he made a big impression. I thought that what with this new success, and poor Madame d'Agoult's dreadful loss, he would put this latest affair—like all his previous ones with smitten ladies—behind him. We never discussed it, but a mother knows her son pretty well and, although I could see he was not happy, I thought he was slowly recovering.

I was quite wrong. He suddenly announced at the beginning of spring that he was going to leave France and never come back. And he must have written to Madame d'Agoult to say the same thing. At any rate, he went to see her 'for the last time' and when he returned, his mood had changed completely—his eyes were shining, he was full of energy and he was chatting away about anything and everything, whereas all through the winter he was almost silent. And whereas, he had hardly used his '*ratzenloch*'—horrible name—since the previous spring, now he was often there and I don't think he was alone.

3. THE SWALLOWS: REMINISCENCE OF THE ABBÉ LAMENNAIS

After he left La Chênaie that autumn, I did not hear from Liszt, except for a brief letter of thanks. The sad news of the death of Madame d'Agoult's daughter reached me from other sources and I wondered what effect it would have on Liszt's love for this woman. I do not myself believe that God inflicts these things on us either as punishments or warnings, but I would not have been surprised if she had seen it that way. She was, by all accounts, a superstitious person, and besides, such unforeseen and shocking events knock us all off balance. We are only too ready then to believe ourselves specially marked out for disaster, instead of merely unlucky. However, I did feel that her misfortune, in this case, might ultimately turn out to have good consequences—as misfortunes often do—in that it would surely put an end to a liaison with Liszt that was likely to be harmful to both.

I believe that for a time it did, and for more ordinary people might have acted as a call to order, a reassertion of reality. But they were neither of them ordinary people, and besides, the Romantic current of that age—at least among the leisured and educated classes—ran very much against the pressures of reality. The poems of Lord Byron, Goethe's youthful novel *Werther*, Senancour's gloomy *Obermann*, Chateaubriand's *René* were read and admired by all cultivated and thoughtful young people and induced them to see themselves in a somewhat theatrical light, as lonely, tormented figures in revolt against the world as they found it. As it turned out, Madame d'Agoult's loss did not repair her marriage nor separate the lovers. On the contrary, it brought them together again with even greater passion.

What drew my attention to them at this point, was a strange incident in the spring, at the Hôtel de Ville in Paris, where Liszt was taking part in a concert, his most important public appearance for some years. I made sure of being in the audience and was deeply impressed, as was everybody there. This was no run-of-the-mill virtuoso. His technical command of the instrument was astounding enough, but his command of our emotions even more so, not only through his playing but through the expressions on his face—a gamut between joy and suffering. And then, all of a sudden, in the final piece of the concert, as he was taking part in a duo for two instruments, that expressive face, pale at the best of times, was drained of colour, his hands fell from the keyboard and he dropped sideways into the arms of his page-turner. A moment's stunned silence in the hall was followed by cries of consternation. Some people rose to their feet, others whose view they blocked followed suit, and soon half the audience was standing, as Liszt was carried out by his colleagues on the platform. The page-turner—his friend Ferdinand Hiller, another piano virtuoso— soon returned to reassure us that Liszt was already conscious again and had merely been overcome by the heat. That was, of course, the end of the concert, but many of the audience were not reassured and were convinced he was dead.

Rumours of his death had swept Paris some years before and one newspaper had even printed an obituary. There was always something about Liszt which aroused public hysteria. Those of us with liberal opinions like to believe that all men are intrinsically equal. I'm afraid they are not and if anything in particular changed my own opinion on this subject, it was my acquaintance with Liszt. Some part of his phenomenal effect on the public might have been intentional, willed and shaped by him in the manner of a consummate actor, but the larger part, I'm sure, was far from intentional and was even sometimes distressing to him. Where did this effect come from? People said that Paganini's power came from the devil and they might have said the same of Liszt's. For myself, I don't believe in the devil as such, only that there are sometimes devilish tendencies in human beings. Not, I hasten to say, that I ever saw such tendencies in Liszt. His effect was a combination of his music and his own magnetic personality and for simple people—even sometimes for more sophisticated people—the powerful emotions aroused by music, especially as he played it, could not be separated from his physical presence. We all have a limited experience of the world and its infinite variety, and my experience has provided me with no one quite comparable to Liszt—I never saw or heard Paganini. I must therefore fall back on the only credible explanation a priest can offer: God made him like that and must have some purpose for him, which may or may not be revealed to those who, unlike me, will live to see Liszt's life as a whole.

The next day I called on him at his mother's house and found him quite recovered. At least he was recovered from whatever had been the immediate cause of his collapse—I was inclined to attribute it less to the heat in the hall than to the extreme tension of the occasion.

'It often happens like that,' I said to him, 'that one bears up through the really difficult part and then, just as one is coming through, beginning to relax, one gives way. As even our Lord seemed to in his last moments on the Cross, crying out, "My God, my God, why hast Thou forsaken me?"'

'I *was* nervous when I began,' he said. 'But I soon felt that the audience was on my side and then I felt perfectly confident. No, I had something else at the back of my mind . . .'

He seemed to be about to go on, but fell silent. I did not break the silence. I could see that he both wanted and did not want to speak about something that was troubling him. At such times it is often just as unhelpful to interrupt a silence as it is to break into a flow of words.

'You may remember,' he said at last, 'that I had a letter from somebody just before I left La Chênaie last year. It was from Madame d'Agoult. We were in love with each other, but then her child died. I wrote and wrote to her, but she never replied, so I stopped writing. I wanted to die too, or at least go somewhere where I could begin my life again as somebody else. That's what I finally decided to do, but before leaving I wrote and asked her if I could see her one last time, and then she did reply. I rushed to see her and we fell in love all over again. She was there in the audience last night, but I avoided looking at her until we were playing that piece by Mendelssohn. And when I did catch her eye, it was very strange, as if we had changed places and I was her and she me. And the next thing I knew I was lying on the floor off-stage, looking up into Hiller's face. That was odd too, because, you know, Hiller was born in the same year as me, 1811, the Year of the Great Comet, and people had told me that he had also been very much in love with Marie—Madame d'Agoult—before I met her. My first thought on coming to my senses was that Hiller must have knocked me down in a jealous rage. That was sheer delirium, Hiller and I are good friends.'

He laughed, and then seeing how intently and anxiously I was watching him and that I could barely manage a smile, went on:

'I know she is a married woman, I know you can't approve of this, Monsieur Féli, but there is really no alternative. We have become true lovers and we are going to have to leave France. She will write to her husband and ask him to forgive her, and to care for their remaining child and we shall live together in another country.'

Of course, I could not approve, but I tried to show sympathy and asked him if there was not some way in which they could remain friends, loving friends, without throwing their lives away in this catastrophic manner.

'This is a flight from reality,' I said. 'Whatever country you fly to, however much you are in love, you cannot, as swallows are supposed to, stay for ever in the air.'

'I understand that,' he said. 'But she does not, cannot.'

'Yet it's she who will lose most.'

'Perhaps that's why she has to do it. She is an all-or-nothing person.'

' Would you like to change her mind?'

'There is no question of that. I love her so much that nothing else matters to me except her happiness. Therefore I must do what she wants, whatever it costs us.'

'Have you told your mother this?'

'Not yet. No one but you, though I don't know why, since it can only hurt you to see how far I have fallen from the good life you exemplify.' (Or something to that effect. He could chatter and flatter in very good French with as much panache as any of the smart people he met in the salons.)

The more we talked the more gloomy he became, but in the end it all came down to the same irremediable fact, that he had abdicated his own volition in this affair and would go where the wind and Madame d'Agoult took him. It seemed to me less like love than misplaced loyalty.

I was very distressed by this interview. Why had he made me his sole confidant if not to ask for my help? Yet he had insisted that he was impervious to my advice and that there was no help to be given. Surely he had not expected me to be angry, to try to browbeat him into a better course of conduct, as perhaps his real father might have done? What good would that have done? Perhaps it would have made him feel better, bolder, stronger, more romantically rebellious. As it was, my combination of sad sympathy with suppressed disapproval drove him deeper into his depression without changing his mind.

I brooded on this as I walked towards the friend's apartment where I was staying, and on the way went into a church and prayed to God to help me to help him. I remained there a long time and gradually my thoughts turned from Liszt's problem to my own perennial worries, and those of other people, and then towards longer, clearer perspectives of acceptance: 'Thy kingdom come, Thy will be done!' Leaving the church I went and sat in a little park in the spring sunshine, rested my head against the back of the park-bench, contemplated the soft blue heavens and almost forgot to worry about anything, when I noticed a pair of swallows (the first I had seen that year), high up, diving, skimming, and soaring after insects. My thoughts went straight back to Liszt and his Countess. And immediately I understood what I had to do, what Liszt really wanted me to do, though he couldn't say so. *She* was the one who had taken the disastrous decision to break up her life and become a wandering musician's mistress. It was *her* I must dissuade, though I had never met her and though Liszt, obviously, could not introduce me to her, because by doing so he would be, as it were, endorsing my opinion. The thought of undertaking such a task filled me with apprehension. I could well imagine how this proud and wilful woman might receive me, a person whose outlook and way of life I knew she already had doubts about when Liszt came to stay with me.

But if I have learnt anything from my years as a priest and unworthy follower of Our Lord Jesus Christ, it is that one's own pride and fear of humiliation, are the first base instincts to be overcome. I had only the remainder of this day in Paris before returning to the country, and I had meant to spend it discussing with friends and colleagues what I should do, now that my writings had brought me into direct conflict with the Vatican. That must wait. I must discover Madame d'Agoult's address in Paris and, if she was still in town after attending her lover's concert, call on her. Otherwise, I must make my way to her château at Croissy, though I dreaded seeing her in that palatial context still more than in the fashionable Faubourg St-Germain.

Fortunately she was in Paris. The footman who opened her front door looked down on me with open contempt. He was a tall young man and I am a small old one. My battered shoes, my blue peasant stockings and ancient frock-coat were quickly registered and no doubt reported to his mistress. I do not recall even giving my name before the door was shut, while he went to find out if she would see me. A few minutes later I was admitted and ushered into her presence.

She was *en déshabillé*. Taller than me, with long golden hair, blue eyes, a high forehead, a strong, straight nose, a fine womanly figure and the smooth skin, elegance and poise of her class, she was a formidably beautiful person and, it seemed to me, at this first glance, likely to be as impervious to my plea as a marble statue.

'My name is Felicité de Lamennais,' I said, hardly managing more than a whisper, so horrified was I at the thought of what I had come to ask her, 'and I am well aware that it is a great impertinence to call on you like this without any introduction or invitation. I have no excuse, except that time presses, I have to go back to the country, and I have something very urgent to say . . .'

I had been talking to the floor. I looked up to see that she was observing me with an intense, penetrating stare. I dried up completely and could not think of what to say next.

'I know who you are,' she said, very gently, 'I guessed as soon as Léon described your appearance to me.'

'I'm afraid I am not dressed for calling on people in the Faubourg St-Germain,' I said.

'I am not dressed for callers either,' she said. 'You took me by surprise. I have read some of your writings, I know how much Franz admires you, I have heard nothing but praise for your courage and goodness, and I have the greatest respect for you, Monsieur l'Abbé. It is an honour to me to receive you and always will be, at any time, with or without an invitation.'

This was generous and encouraging, but her intelligence and sensitivity seemed to make my task even more impossible.

'I saw Liszt yesterday,' I said, 'and was glad to find that the incident at his concert was nothing serious. But in the course of our conversation he told me that you and he were . . .'

I found that I could not meet her gaze. Most of my subsequent speech, setting out the danger they ran by not taking thought for the future, pursuing their love outside the bounds of society, in a vacuum which could not be sustained, and so on and so forth, was delivered to the floor, the furniture or the windows. I spoke for some time, worked myself into quite an ardour and was scarcely interrupted, except by a few exclamations of dissent. But finally, coming to my peroration, I did succeed in confronting those sharp blue eyes:

'The social norm is inexorable,' I said, 'wherever you may go in the civilized world. People who might be eager to entertain him for his talent and fame will not be willing to entertain you. You will be isolated and shunned. However close you are to him, you can neither of you be happy in those circumstances. It may be possible one day for society to change but, as it is, it is ruthless towards those who break its rules. I beg you to think again before it is too late.'

She was still silent, but I could tell immediately what she was thinking, that I myself was a well-known rebel against all the rules of my Church, and that if I had the courage for that, so did she to rebel against the rules of Society.

'Madame,' I said, 'I am a single man, near the end of my life, with no close relatives left in the world. I dare to believe that my rebellion against the authorities of the Church is what God wants of me in order to turn the Church back to the path he meant for it. That is what gives me courage, not my own strength. You and Liszt, however, mean to break God's law as well as man's, and for nothing but your love for each other. If you will not consider yourself or him, at least think of your remaining child, deprived of her mother at this moment when she has already lost her sister, of your mother deprived of her child as well as her grandchild, of all the rest of your family. Your rebellion will harm them as much as yourself.'

Now I could see tears in her eyes and I pressed my advantage by going down on my knees.

'At least put off your decision!' I said. 'Let some weeks go by, even months, while you consider what I have said.'

'Please don't kneel to me!' she said, and when I would not get up, 'I can remember almost word for word something you wrote in a letter to Franz. "Love is not just a flavour to life, it is life itself. We should love one another on this poor earth, we should love one another until the end, so that we can love one another again in that real life beyond, where nothing ends." Surely love is at the very heart of your teaching?'

'Indeed it is. And I have no desire whatever to stop you loving one another. It is because I love Liszt and because, now that I have met you, Madame, I understand why he loves you, that I am making this ridiculous exhibition of myself at your feet. No, you must not stop loving one another. But you must do so without making yourselves exiles. Because once you have opened yourselves to all the malice and scandal which will come your way, even your love may be put at risk. I have said nothing of God's love. You will have that whatever you do, it is the basis and condition of our existence. But you will find it harder to love him if you are breaking his Commandments, and harder to reconcile your love for each other with that eternal Love. Will you promise me to defer your decision?'

She looked at me with an expression I couldn't read, almost mockingly, then shook her head. Her golden hair flowed round her shoulders and from my place on the floor seemed haloed by the light from the tall windows. There were dark patches under her eyes. No doubt she found it hard to sleep.

'I could give you that promise, Monsieur l'Abbé, in order to get you off your knees, but I would have to break my promise as soon as you left the house. It's already too late to change our decision. Did Franz not tell you? I have got another child inside me and it is his.'

About a month later they left Paris separately and joined one another in Switzerland.

4. *YEARS OF PILGRIMAGE*: REVISION OF FIRST YEAR—SWITZERLAND

What a fellow I am! Here I sit in my study revising—no, recomposing *Album d'un voyageur*, which itself grew out of Marie, *Poem in Six Melodies for Piano*, my wordless songs of love to the Countess d'Agoult, composed all those years ago in Geneva, when our first child was newly born and our love for each other seemed absolute and eternal. And now I am settled in Weimar with my Princess, and our love for each other is absolute and eternal.

Is my soul made of shifting sand? Am I a travelling *saltimbanque* in love as I used to be at the keyboard? Where does my loyalty lie? Of course it lies here with my Princess, exclusively with my beloved Carolyne, who has sold her estates in Russia and come here to live with me; and we are to be married as soon as she gets permission from the Czar and the Pope to divorce her husband. In an hour or two she and I will sit down to lunch together and look at each other with love in our eyes and hearts.

But meanwhile I'm seated in my Blue Room at the keyboard of my Boisselot. My eyes are on the published score of *Album d'un voyageur*, and my thoughts return to that lost world of Marie and Franz. Nostalgia? Not at all. What I mean to do is remake this score with all my augmented skill and experience, transcribing this transcription of that lost world into fresh music, better music, cleverer, more poignant, more complex music. Already, in their published form, when the love of Franz and Marie was guttering, reigniting itself, guttering again, those love-tones were mixed with tones of religious and revolutionary fervour. So it is not the past that I shall be invoking so much as the future, transforming that youthful, naive, intimate love-music into a celebration of love itself—the love of God and his Creation and the love between lovers.

Is there any conflict of loyalties there? Should I fear that the love of Marie and Franz-Then, Franz-23, may burst into flame again and singe the heart of Franz-Now, Franz-37? Surely not? Music and memory are abstractions. They burn in the mind, but are extinguished by the real world. The real world—and especially the real Marie—slowly extinguished the heat of that wild, romantic, tender, passionate, precipitous Swiss honeymoon, whose essence still lingers in this music. Correcting its clumsy passages, adjusting, clarifying, expanding its expressiveness, I shall no doubt rediscover the feelings that went into it, but the *persons*, no. They are long gone, their love evaporated, or, dare I say, transfigured into sounds.

La chapelle de Guillaume Tell (*The Chapel of William Tell*)

Who was this hero? Did he exist? Someone like him, or several like him must have, to lead a revolt against the Habsburg overlords which in time brought independence to the whole of Switzerland. Schiller's play lifted Tell from a local hero into a universal symbol of revolutionary courage and national pride. Rossini's opera, which I saw in Paris in 1829, gave him the additional glow of noble music. My own piano transcription of Rossini's overture was one of my most reliable crowd-pleasers in the days of my travelling circus. I played it in London at Willis' Rooms in St James' Street in 1840:

'The most complete orchestra by which we have ever heard it performed never produced a more powerful effect . . . even could description convey any idea of Liszt's performance, its possibility would appear incredible, except to those who have heard it' (*The Times*).

And during our tour of Ireland, I played it in the wilds of County Cork, in a hotel sitting-room in Clonmel, on a Tompkinson square piano, to a sleepy audience of twenty-five. (The Irish will never achieve independence if those people were anything to go by.) And then again at my first concert in Berlin in 1841, unleashing the full fury of

'Lisztomania' (Heine's catty phrase), and again in St Petersburg in 1842, in the Assembly Hall of the Nobility before an audience of three thousand.

'We had never in our lives heard anything like this. We had never been in the presence of such a brilliant, passionate, demonic temperament, at one moment rushing like a whirlwind, at another pouring forth cascades of tender beauty and grace. Liszt's playing was absolutely overwhelming . . .' (a Russian critic, Vladimir Stasov).

I must try not to dwell on my press cuttings and ephemeral triumphs as a performer, but concentrate, as the Princess constantly reminds me, on my real work as a composer . . .

All this was still in the future when Franz-23 and Marie visited Tell's chapel beside the deep fjord of Lake Uri. Here Tell was supposed to have jumped out of the evil Austrian Governor's boat during a storm. Franz was much moved by his thoughts of the mediaeval mountain hero as he helped Marie out of their own boat on to the landing-stage, beneath the crags and forests of the Canton of Schwyz, and approached this holy place, but it was in poor condition and there was little to see inside . . .

A solemn, slow processional, a little muted as if heard from afar, carries us up to and through the doors of the chapel. Distant echoing trumpet-calls from the left-hand rouse flutterings and stirrings of unrest and revolt from the right-hand, until, grander and bolder than before, the hero's processional returns. Inside, in the presence of God, the march of triumph grows more thoughtful, more spiritual and at last more tender, intimate, rapturous . . .

Franz and Marie stood hand in hand before the altar in that empty chapel, as if waiting for the priest or pastor or friar to pronounce them man and wife. But, unlike Romeo and Juliet, it could not be done, even in secret, without abjuring their Catholic faith, and they were both believers. Their love was not blessed by the Church, although to them it seemed blessed by God none the less, for otherwise how could they be so happy?

The trumpet-calls and the fervour of rebellion are heard again, fading into memory, and the hero's processional swells up and dies away on a long sustaining pedal . . .

The Chapel of William Tell . . . the 'marriage' of Franz and Marie
. . . defiance and liberty . . . and love, the wedding-march of love . . .

Au lac de Wallenstadt (*On the Lake of Wallenstadt*)

In Basel, Marie was staying with her mother at the Drei Könige Hotel.
Those Three Kings, I suppose, who followed the star to Bethlehem to
worship the Christ-child in the manger: could the pregnant Marie
have chosen a more symbolic address? Franz arrived two days later,
took a room at the Hôtel de la Cigogne (The Stork Hotel—another
strangely significant choice) and going out at once to the poste
restante, found a brief note:

'When you read this, I *shall have told her*, at present I have still not
dared say anything. This is the last hard test, but my love is my *faith*
and I thirst to be martyred.'

That was a reference, of course, to Lord Byron's *Childe Harold*, a
book I had taught her to regard as one of the lodestars of our life
together, and our defiant break with conventional society:

> O Love! no habitant of earth thou art—
> An unseen seraph, we believe in thee,
> A faith whose martyrs are the broken heart . . .

'I am here, since you've summoned me,' Franz replied, adding in
awkward English, with the idea no doubt of sounding more like Byron,
'I shall not go out till I see you. My room is at the Hôtel de la Cigogne
number twenty at the first *étage*—go at the right side.' And she came.

From Basel—after her mother had been told, suffered a brief nervous crisis, and left Switzerland in dismay—the lovers travelled east-
wards to Lake Constance, visiting the Rhine Falls en route, then southwards to Wesen, where they stayed and took a boat-trip on the lake . . .

Gentle, rippling, lilting notes—a *perpetuum mobile* of love and happiness with only small variations in the tempo for the splashes of
wavelets, and the flashes of sunlight from their crests . . .

Marie loved this melody, it was the cradle-song of their love, and
I shall alter it very little, for it still brings back to me that enchanted
day on the pale green lake, their senses lulled by the rhythm of the
oars and the slow unfolding of the precipitous shore-line, but waiting
to leap up again, as they did that night—so many wakeful nights in

hotel rooms—slaking their lust for each other's naked bodies, rocking themselves in each other's arms, as if they lay not on a hard bed but soft lapping waves.

Pastorale

A little jogging tune, tipping its hat to the Great Master's Opus 28, the *Pastoral Sonata* . . .

Two in a rustic carriage trotting through the fertile uplands south of Zurich . . . creamy cows, wrinkled nut-brown peasants with faces like the bottle-stoppers they sell in the towns . . . the air so fresh and pure that the lovers wondered how anyone breathed without choking in the cities below, but whenever they reached a village it was scented with manure from the neatly-stacked conical middens outside every house-proud chalet . . .

It was lovely, but tedious, too—those long circuitous journeys, to see yet more pretty views recommended by well-meaning Swiss. I enjoy Nature, health-giving Nature, but in small doses, and descriptions, either in words or music, can be as tedious as excursions, so I'll keep this one short.

Au bord d'une source (*Beside a Spring*)

The lovers saw many springs, of course, when they walked beside lakes or up into mountains, and I forget which this was. Not the source of the Rhone, which emerges from a glacier (though they did see that), but something more humble, a thread of water oozing out of a bed of moss, half-hidden by grass, overhung with some creeping plant . . .

In spite of my prejudice against purely descriptive music, I have to say that this is a very fine example, bubbling and sparkling in the upper register, then deepening a little as the stream burrows between turf banks and down its rocky bed. Technically, however, it could be better handled and I shall improve it, give it more sparkle, more laughter, more of the serpentine . . .

Why do artists so often like to pose their nude models beside springs? Is it Eve in the Garden of Eden they are thinking of, or the virgin huntress Diana bathing secretly in the forest? Or something more explicitly sexual? A sly reference to the hidden opening, the source of pleasure and the source of life. Franz would have liked his

Marie to pose naked beside a spring. but he never asked her. It was not warm enough in early June at that altitude and although they were nearly always alone, there is not much cover on a mountainside if anyone should pass by or look up from below. Did he *com*pose her in imagination beside this glistening Alpine trickle?

'I catch a glimpse of her golden hair as she stoops to drink, a breast, a flank, a belly hardly yet swollen, and, in those last spaced-out, wide-eyed notes, she turns towards me . . .'

Orage (Storm)

How long have I been tinkering with this work now, returning to it ever and again between other compositions and all my other tasks here in Weimar and elsewhere, as conductor, concert-organizer, teacher, courtier? Franz-37 has become Franz-42, but I still cannot quite tear myself away from improving Franz-23's love-song . . .

Thunder and lightning over the mountains, the hands in turn running up and down the keyboard, then both hands working up a surging, angry melody, with rumblings in the bass, rapid strokes of lightning. The melody returns, the lightning strokes are further off, everything slows down into the deepest notes. Is the storm finished? Not quite. The lightning strokes reappear, the thunder booms and suddenly it's all over.

They had their own storms too, Franz and Marie. How could they not, such a pair of nervous temperaments? When one such person alone is infuriated by something, he takes it out on the furniture or a piece of china or the next friend he meets, but when two people are all day and all night in each other's eyes and arms, their irritations sometimes coincide and funnel up into huge black clouds of resentment which collide with thunder and lightning.

There were plenty of irritations in that Swiss Arcadia. The travelling was slow and uncomfortable, the hotels mostly clean, but rugged and constricted, with low ceilings and small rooms, the food hearty but unsophisticated, the people usually friendly, but not the least deferential and sometimes surly. Franz was used to such places, but Marie had never in her life, not even in her convent school, experienced such rude conditions. She was accustomed to the space that goes with luxury—large, airy rooms, high ceilings and, above all, space between persons—and to having several servants always on hand, whereas here there was only her equally disorientated French *femme de chambre*. Since Marie and Franz were travelling under false names, as a married couple, she had suddenly ceased to be a noble countess and become a mere woman. At first this gave her a romantic frisson, but soon enough it grated on her. Even the constant close presence of her lover in poky rooms, delightful in some moods, became aggravating in others. Her maid, accommodated in even rougher quarters and surrounded by weather-beaten yokels who often made passes at her in their incomprehensible dialect, was perpetually ill-tempered.

The wonder is that Franz and Marie did not quarrel more often. The worst storm, I remember, was in a very basic inn at Hospenthal. The day before, they had passed the 'Devil's Bridge', a great granite arch over a still older and ruined bridge below, spanning the deep gorge of the river Reuss. Marie, for all her intelligence, was a superstitious person. She crossed herself and clung to her lover's arm as their carriage passed over the bridge. Franz, for all *his* intelligence, could be an insensitive person. He laughed at her fear, ordered the driver to stop the carriage in the middle of the bridge, jumped out and seated himself nonchalantly, Byronically, on the parapet, leaning over to peer down into the abyss.

'Please! Please!' she called out, almost screamed. 'Please let us go on, Franz!'

There was a wind getting up and rushing quite strongly through that narrow corridor between the high mountains that were now all around them.

'Please, Franz, please! We shall be blown away!'

Indeed, the carriage was rocking a little.

'Come here and look down!' said Franz, pretending not to hear her cries, and strolled towards the carriage holding out his hand. 'Come!' he said. 'You'll be sorry to miss such an awesome sight. I will keep you safe. If the devil ever built that old bridge below he has not kept it in repair and is presumably no longer using it.'

But she would not come and at last, in a bad humour because she had not given way to him or trusted him, he climbed back into the carriage and they drove on.

Their mutual discontent continued over a poor supper at the inn in Hospenthal and after supper, Franz announced that he meant to rise very early and walk up to the St Gotthard Pass.

'Am I to go with you?' she asked.

'As you wish. It will be a steep road and perhaps too long and hard for you.'

'Then I will stay here and read a book,' she said.

So, banked down, their quarrel smouldered all night. They scarcely spoke, they did not make love. They slept fitfully. There were fleas in the bedding.

Soon after dawn, Franz got up and dressed. Only when he went downstairs to see if anyone was up to make him coffee did he notice that it was snowing. Snow in June! He could scarcely believe it. Clearly he had to abandon any hope of seeing the St Gotthard, stay indoors like her and read a book.

Even for people who love reading books, as they both did, a whole day of it in a small stuffy inn with bad light, bad smells and hard chairs is difficult to endure and, since they had only smothered, not extinguished their quarrel, they were still barely speaking to each other. I've forgotten exactly what small incident unleashed the fury of these two caged tigers. It might have been her rudeness to the innkeeper's wife, a pretty young woman with apple cheeks, with whom Franz was conversing animatedly, in spite of their equally but quite differently outlandish German (hers Swiss, his Austrian), when the tense, pale and puffy-faced Marie came down from upstairs. Or it was some passage from a book—*Childe Harold* probably, since that was one of the guidebooks to Switzerland they had brought with them—which he read out to her with the half-intention of wounding. Perhaps this:

Not much he kens, I ween, of woman's breast,
Who thinks that wanton thing is won by sighs:
What careth she for hearts when once possess'd?
Do proper homage to thine idol's eyes;
But not too humbly, or she will despise
Thee and thy suit, though told in moving tropes;
Disguise ev'n tenderness, if thou art wise;
Brisk Confidence still best with woman copes;

Pique her and soothe in turn, soon Passion crowns thy hopes.'

'I am growing quite tired of Byron,' she said. 'That predictable alternation of romanticism and cynicism. And I don't think you should see yourself as Lord Byron—you have neither his experience of the world nor his class.'

'What does that mean?'

'What do you think it means?'

'It seems to mean that you're saying I'm an ignorant peasant with ideas above my station.'

'You evidently prefer the company of ignorant peasants . . .'

'Prefer it to what?'

And after these flashes of lightning, the storm burst properly. She screamed out:

'To their betters! To those who have thrown everything away— name, rank, family, reputation—for what? For whom? A pseudo-Byron who makes eyes at every barmaid and poses as a fearless traveller . . .'

And he shouted back, in a transport of rage:

'*Poses?*'

'That's what I said. All that monkey-business on the bridge! And what about your great walk up the St. Gotthard which would be too hard for the women-folk?'

'Have you looked out of the window this morning?'

'A little snow, is there?'

'No one—not even a local guide—would go up there in this blizzard.'

All this, of course, was in French, so that at least the innkeeper and his wife could not understand the words. They were not in the same room, but certainly could hear everything through the open doors, as perhaps much of the village could even through closed windows and falling snow. The maid, who was in her room upstairs and could surely hear and understand every word, was probably enjoying herself for the first time.

Oh dear! what comical creatures we are when our pride is hurt! The indoor storm continued for some time, but the exchanges grew repetitive and the insults even more so. They were mostly hers, since civilized men are as averse to offering women direct insults as they are to striking them—much as they are sometimes tempted. Women, relying on their inferior strength, are easily capable of both.

'I wish I had never come to this benighted country,' she said. 'I wish I had fallen off the devil's bridge and never allowed myself to be shut up in a hovel with a person who is all pretences. Blizzard! What a ridiculously overblown word for a few flakes of snow! But everything about you is overblown. You are a Lord Byron parvenu! I shall walk to the St. Gotthard myself and show you what sort of man you are!'

She called to her maid to bring her walking-boots and cape and, having put them on, wrestled with the heavy front door and went out. Franz followed a few moments later and saw her staggering up a white slope in the wrong direction against a bitter wind thick with snow. She was already as white as the ground beneath her and the air around her. Franz, in slippers, without his cape, ran after her, sliding and slipping, caught her by the shoulders and turning her to face him, kissed her icy red nose and cheeks, then brought her back inside.

The snow continued all day, Franz soon had a heavy cold—I have always been a martyr to chest infections—but their quarrel was over.

This *orage* will be an entirely new composition, and I shall try to make it, what it never was before, a storm within a storm.

Vallée d'Obermann

Few people read Senancour's *Obermann* these days, but it was all the rage then and Franz and Marie had taken a copy with them. Its eponymous hero is a gloomy nihilist who has withdrawn from all society, finding his only solace in nature, especially the Alps, and whose small store of energy is devoted to fending off the unpleasant effects of being alive in a vain world, while scarcely hoping for a better one. What did this have to say to a couple who, after their brief quarrel, were as blissfully happy in each other's company as it was possible for mortals to be?

They left the inn at Hospenthal as soon as the snow storm passed; climbed the Furka in better weather to look down on the Glacier du Rhone; visited the confluence of the Saaser Visp and Mattervisp, and saw it as a symbol of their own confluence; travelled on to Martigny, where the fledgling Rhone begins to widen and turns suddenly northwards; made an excursion from there to the Grand St Bernard Pass; and arrived early in July at the little spa town of Bex, on the edge of the long, broad Rhone valley leading into Lac Leman. Here they found a comfortable hotel where they stayed for the next fortnight, exploring the lower slopes of the Vaudois Alps and recovering, in a relatively civilized place, from the discomforts of so much travelling.

Obermann, which they read aloud to each other, contains many fine descriptions of Alpine scenery in this particular region. But it was principally perhaps a kind of memento mori, reminding them of the unhappiness and insecurity they had both experienced before they found each other, the literary equivalent of sitting in comfort and security in front of a good fire while thinking of the poor souls caught in a storm outside; perhaps also a prophylactic, warding off any further storms inside.

This piece, cast in E minor and intended to juxtapose Franz and Marie's happiness with the discontent of the novel's hero, is altogether too uniform and monotonous . . . I would like less of Obermann and more of Franz and Marie . . . lonely unhappiness, after all, is common enough, but mutual happiness to that degree is rare . . .

And now, a year later, amongst all my distractions, they have found it . . .

The melody begins very gently in the lower register, long-limbed, rising and falling . . . repeated by the higher notes, with murmurs from the bass . . . slow, separate utterances, almost dying away . . . and the dialogue of bass and treble is repeated, slowed again by the left hand, with deep feeling . . . two or three sighs, grunts, until the right hand, surer, purer, sings an aria and is joined again—an almost operatic duet—by the left hand . . . question and answer . . . climax of passionate feeling between high notes and low . . . dying away to pauses and questions again . . . 'Do you love me?' 'I love you.' 'Do you really love me?' 'I love you really.' . . . and so to smooth flowing unison in the middle of the keyboard, with the left hand murmuring the tune, while the right hand makes lingering liquid sounds like the spring flowing down the mountainside . . . or lips meeting . . . and now the duet grows quicker and stronger, the two hands, the two voices alternating, then flowing together like the confluence of two rivers, to an ecstatic climax . . . rapidly peeling bells . . . slowing to a solemn march and a brief triumphant close . . .

This *Vallée d' Obermann*, recomposed by Franz-43, is what Franz-23 would have composed then if he had known how to, his monument against time, his long-ago love-song to Marie.

It has been possible, of course, only through the *unfailing* love of my Princess, who sits here in the same room writing her interminable letters to the authorities of Church and State, so that we can be truly man and wife.

Eclogue

A myth, a fairy tale it seems now, that honeymoon in Switzerland, and I have inserted this brief shepherd's song to salute, as it were, innocence from experience . . .

Hand-in-hand our happy couple walks on springy turf, on a hillside . . . crystal air . . . limitless vistas of green slopes and blue peaks capped with snow . . . they run, jump, skip like children . . .

Le Mal du pays (Homesickness)

A sad little piece—I have hardly altered it. Was it her homesickness or mine? I have forgotten. Most probably hers, since I was already well accustomed to being a stranger in other people's countries. Her moods came and went, seemingly independent of circumstances, and I would enter our room to find her in tears . . . did I fully appreciate then what she had given up to live with me in another country? . . . I believe this lament suggests that I did, that I shared her tears of exile . . . Of course, Franz comforted her, reminded her that she was not alone, nor ever would be . . .

Did I say that? Yes, again and again. But it was not I that broke with her, when the time did come. No, but the time came, and when it did, she *was* alone . . . and is still.

Les cloches de Genève (The Bells of Geneva)

From Bex they went to Villeneuve at the eastern end of Lac Leman, from there by boat the length of the lake to Geneva. It was still July and they had five months to find a home and settle down before the baby was due . . .

Such relief, such joy! . . . This music was composed after she was born . . . What could better celebrate Blandine-Rachel, the most beautiful child I ever saw, than the bells of Geneva?

I was pleased enough with the piece then, but now it seems inadequate. I shall remake it completely to be the fitting culmination of the first and sweetest of my years of pilgrimage, and follow those gentle bells with a fresh melody, expressing my never-ending love for that beautiful girl, now eighteen years old—first fruit of the lost love of Franz and Marie . . .

5. LOVERS SEPARATING: NOTEBOOK OF BARONE EMILIO MULAZZANI

She is a lovely woman, but very, very sad. I try to cheer her with expeditions around my beautiful city of water and stone and great art, but all she thinks about is her absent loved-one. He is not strictly her husband—she has left her genuine husband and their child in France—but this lover and she have been living together for some three years and have already had two children together, so in all but name they are a married couple. He is a Hungarian musician of outstanding talent but low birth. She is a noblewoman, at least on her French father's side—her mother's people, I think, are German bankers—and was married to an equally well-born Frenchman, though much older. She burnt her boats, as far as Parisian society was concerned, by eloping with this musician, first to Switzerland, then to Italy.

What am I to do? The Hungarian went haring off to Vienna to give charity concerts on behalf of his compatriots, whose principal city has been inundated by the Danube, with much loss of life and destruction of property. He left her behind here in Venice, partly because she did not feel strong enough to travel so far, but chiefly because her situation as his mistress makes it impossible for her to be received by the people of high society, who attend these concerts and welcome him almost as an equal. She cannot even allow herself to be seen at his public concerts without humiliation. I gladly undertook to look after her while he was away—they know hardly anyone in Venice, and his departure was sudden—as the floods were. His decision to go to the aid of his unfortunate countrymen was laudable, of course, and even she could hardly argue against it, but he has remained in Vienna far beyond the week he predicted, and she believes that his enjoyment of a way of life he had virtually abandoned for her sake has blotted out, at least temporarily, his feelings for her.

He writes to her regularly, but his letters—filled with the details of his triumphant success in that Imperial city where he last appeared as an eleven-year-old prodigy—are not calculated to calm her increasing panic at his absence. The more he boasts of the distinguished peo-ple—noblemen and especially noblewomen, including the Empress herself according to his latest letter—who salute his talent, and vie with each other to entertain and honour him, the more her spirits decline.

It might be better if she had at least one of their children here to divert her attention, but women of our class are not accustomed to caring for babies, and besides, she and her lover have been constantly travelling, so the little girls are being looked after by others—the elder is with foster-parents in Switzerland, the younger with a nursemaid in, I think, Como. Consequently she has nothing to do but brood over her lover, and his absence and to make a pretence of enjoying the sights of Venice. I'm afraid she hates my beautiful city—she disliked it even before the musician left for Vienna, and now she sees it as her prison—though she tries to veil her feelings from me, since she knows they would wound me and I am at present her sole friend.

Should I make love to her? I mean in earnest, for naturally my manner is to seem to court her—it is what she expects and what those who see us so constantly together, friends and relations of mine, as well as maîtres d'hôtel, waiters, servants, gondoliers, assume. But I fancy that to go beyond the outward forms of a *cavaliere servente* would not just shock her, it might even tip her over into real dementia. She is on the verge of it already, I have to say, and it alarms me. She is a very intelligent person, very sharp, very articulate, as well as beautiful, but there is a fiery core of volcanic disquiet inside her which I am frequently afraid will erupt in ungovernable fury. There is no question with her, I'm sure, of a brief pleasurable affair while her lover is away. It would have to be a serious relationship and although I do not fear the Hungarian, I do fear to become his permanent successor. Nor am I at all sure she would have me as anything but a courtier. She is a believer, an idealist, a romantic. She almost worships the Hungarian, who is indeed, for all his low birth, a superior man—I have heard him play, and heard him talk and can quite truthfully endorse her admiration for him, albeit without idolatry—but even if she enjoyed my caresses, there is nothing to admire in me beyond my distinguished ancestry, my youth, my sense of duty towards both of them and my small skill as a guide to Venetian art and architecture.

Yesterday in the Doges' Palace we came to Tintoretto's fresco of Bacchus and Ariadne and when, after a long silence in which she seemed to be puzzling out the meaning of the painting, I began to explain it, she said:

'Oh, I know the story of Ariadne, thank you, Barone—how she fell in love with the Greek hero Theseus and helped him kill the Cretan Minotaur, and then escaped the King her father's anger by sailing away with Theseus, only to be deserted by him on the island of Naxos. It is a story that speaks strongly to me now, as you may imagine.'

There were tears in her eyes.

'But it's not too sad a story in the end,' I said with a smile, 'since she is rescued by a God, no less, the generous, pleasure-loving God of wine and dancing and carnival.'

'What are you saying?' she demanded, without the trace of a smile, 'that I should take to drink and let my hair down and become a lost creature?'

'You would be incapable of that, Madame,' I said.

'I am glad you understand me so well. If I had been her, I would rather have died than give myself to Bacchus.'

'It would have been Theseus or no one, I'm sure. But what if he never returned?'

'You think he will never return?'

'I was only thinking of the story of Bacchus and Ariadne,' I said, pointing at the fresco and going a little red, since I had not at all intended to be misunderstood in that way.

'But what do you think about Franz?'

'He will certainly return. He is a man of honour and you have told me yourself that his letters are full of his love for you.'

'Not so full. They are mostly about his love for himself and how the whole of Vienna shares it.'

'He is a wonderful musician,' I said, 'and he can't help but be pleased that the musical capital of the world has recognized it.'

'And now those musical people will never let him alone. They will claw him away from me. It began to happen in Geneva, so we pulled up our roots there and fled to Italy, where luckily most people prefer opera and do not flock to hear pianists. But now these greedy people in Vienna have snapped him up and our quiet, private life together is ruined.'

'But surely, Madame, the reason you love him so much is that he *is* a great man? Will you deprive him of his métier and keep the world in ignorance of his powers?'

'His true genius does not lie in the way he plays. That is just technical facility and shallow celebrity. His true genius lies in the compositions he will give the world. Making clever versions of other men's tunes so as to please the crowds, and strumming the piano for them only distracts him from that, taking the time and energy he should be giving to his serious work.'

'Well, I'm quite sure that unlike Theseus he will soon be back.'

* * *

This morning being fine and bright I called at her hotel to take her on a trip to the Lido. She kept me waiting at least three quarters of an hour and when she emerged I could see that she had been crying. She was also shaking so much that Tonio and I had some difficulty in helping her safely into my gondola. I asked her if she would prefer to abandon the trip and return to her room to rest.

'Thank you, no! The best thing for me would be to fall overboard and rest on the bottom of the lagoon. Meanwhile, take me wherever you like, Barone, it's all one to me.'

I had been intending to point out the many beautiful views around us as we passed out of the Grand Canal, but she was sunk in her own sorrow. I soon discovered, however, that it was less sorrow than anger that afflicted her.

'Is he still delayed in Vienna, Madame?'

'Now he is talking of going to Pest to see the devastation for himself.'

'What can he do there? Play sonatas to the people driven out of their homes? Or does he mean to turn bricklayer and carpenter and help to house them again?'

'He talks of nothing but money and fame. The money he has raised—the largest private contribution to the relief fund, he says—and how he is never alone, with crowds of admirers always trying to gain admittance to his room or at least touch the hem of his garment. That was his first letter, but his second . . .'

'Two letters at once? You can hardly say he has forgotten you.'

'The second letter was addressed in his handwriting but sealed with a lady's coat-of-arms. It is clear enough how he spends his time between concerts.'

'And did he say anything about his return?'

'I have no idea. I tore the letter up as soon as I saw that seal. How dare he make love to other women after all he has promised me, after I have given him my life, my reputation, my absolute faith in his destiny?'

I was afraid that in her restless fury she would indeed fall into the lagoon and even take us with her, but Tonio watched her convulsive movements carefully, countered them with neat footwork and expert oarsmanship and kept the gondola steady.

We reached the Lido safely, but I can hardly say what we did there. Walked about, drank coffee, had a meal—of which she ate nothing. Her 'betrayal' was all she could think or speak about. She was more subdued by the time we returned to the city, but only because her anger had turned into a feverish fit of shivering. I had almost to carry her from the boat into the hotel, where she went straight to her room and I hope will sleep off her anger and indisposition.

* * *

As a music-lover myself, and one of those who consider Liszt's playing quite out of the ordinary run of virtuosity, I was shocked by the way she dismissed it. 'Strumming the piano' or 'doing his tricks,' as she called it on another occasion. She plays the piano herself, I know, but does music really mean very much to her? Or art, for that matter or beautiful things in general? She is an avid reader of books, a cultured person, but these things seem less important to her for their own sake than for their social value. Reflecting on today's wretched expedition to the Lido, as well as her attitude to the many rare things I have shown her, I ask myself what it is that she worships Liszt for. And I come to a strange conclusion. It is what everybody worships him for. In spite of the way she accuses him of seeking celebrity and soaking up adulation, she herself admires him as much for his fame as his talent. What she does not like is having to share that fame and talent with others. Her love for him is all about possession, exclusive possession, and therefore his celebrity too belongs to her. It has become *her* celebrity. So paradoxically, although his celebrity has been, and has to be earned in the common market-place, it is now to be locked up in her keeping and denied to the market-place. She is so fanatically jealous of the whole world that she would rather his fame was altogether extinguished than that she should not have it all to herself.

Isn't this some kind of madness? I wonder if Liszt himself had begun to suspect it before he left for Vienna. They were certainly not on good terms with each other when I first met them together and his evident delight in my city elicited the opposite response from her. 'Carthage!' she said. 'Nothing but materialism and vulgar display!' She was speaking to him, not to me, but he was ashamed that I had overheard. Yes, she was jealous even of Venice when he said he had fallen in love with it at first sight.

There was an embarrassing scene between them when I obtained permission through my contacts to see Giorgione's masterpiece *The Family of the Painter* in the private collection of Girolamo Manfrin. It is an enigmatic painting of a naked woman suckling a child on one side of a ravine, while a young man holding a long pole stares across at her from the other side. Behind them is a bridge across the river and the outskirts of a town, and in the sky above the town, are billowing storm-clouds cleft by a bow-shaped streak of lightning. The colouring, as in all this master's works, is rich and soft, and the lighting, of course, because of the imminent tempest, eerie and dramatic. Liszt looked at it with great concentration for some ten or fifteen minutes. She soon tired of it and walked about the room glancing at other things.

'What on earth can it mean?' he said at last. 'Both he and she look quite unprepared for the storm coming up behind them, yet they must surely hear the thunder from those massive clouds?'

'I don't think you should look for a literal meaning,' she said. 'It is an allegory.'

'Of what?'

'There have been as many interpretations as interpreters,' I said. 'No two of them can agree. It belonged originally to Giorgione's patron Gabriele Vendramin and perhaps illustrates some obscure Greek myth which appealed to them both.'

'It might be an allegory of male and female,' she said. 'She nurtures the child, which is no doubt his, while he stands aloof the other side of a gulf.'

'And the storm?' he asked.

'I daresay he will go off and find shelter. She and the child will be left to bear the brunt of it.'

'I don't think that can be right,' he said. 'He is looking at her, but she is looking out at the viewer, not at him. If it's an allegory at all, then perhaps it's an allegory of childbirth, of the way that alters the relationship of man and woman, distancing the man and perhaps bringing tempers and tempests in its wake.'

'Are you blaming me for bearing your children? Are you suggesting that I put them before you? How utterly unjust you are! Have I distanced you for the children's sake? On the contrary, I have distanced *them* and given all my care to *you*.'

'Let us not quarrel over a beautiful painting, Marie! Especially not in front of this kind young man who has given us the privilege of   seeing it. Personally I don't think it's an allegory at all, but simply a pastoral scene with a storm brewing. And if, as the title suggests, the painter has put himself and his wife and child in the foreground, he may only have meant to hint to his patron that a higher fee would not go amiss, since he now has to feed and clothe his family and give them shelter from the storm. And *we* can understand that only too well, can't we?'

'We have lived mostly on *my* money so far.'

'Exactly so. But that cannot go on.'

'You want to start giving public concerts again, do you?'

'Why not?'

'Why not! You know very well that you promised to keep away from all that trivial nonsense and devote yourself to serious music, and for that and your future as a great composer, I gave up everything and stepped into the void. No, Franz, I can see that you are nosing about for every opportunity to break our bargain and go back to your circus life. But if you do, I warn you, it will be the end of our life together . . . yes, the end of our happiness . . .'

And she began to cry. I stood there quite amazed at what Giorgione's innocent painting had provoked, but Liszt hurried to take her in his arms, and wipe away her tears and for the rest of the day, when I escorted them in my gondola down the Grand Canal and identified the various palazzos and their present owners, she seemed to enjoy herself more and thanked me warmly when we parted.

* * *

When I called at her hotel this morning to see if she had recovered, her maid came down to the foyer to meet me and told me she was much worse.

'Will she see me?'

'She cannot see anybody.'

'Well, I will return later in the day,' I said.

But the maid became very distressed and urged me not to go away. She had meant that her mistress was unable to see anybody because she was delirious.

'Has a doctor been called?'

'Not yet. I was waiting to speak to you.'

'Then I will get my own doctor to see her.'

I wrote a rapid note to Dr Ligonno and told the hotel receptionist to have it delivered immediately, then followed the maid to the Countess' room. Her delirium seemed to have passed for the moment and she was sleeping peacefully, her face almost more beautiful in repose than I had ever seen it. I wiped the sweat from her forehead without waking her.

When the doctor arrived soon afterwards and examined her, she was almost herself, though very weak, and hardly able to get out of bed. He prescribed some medicine and told me privately that he found nothing physically wrong with her—even her temperature was only just above normal.

'Nerves,' he said. 'Highly-strung nerves which have been twisted up beyond bearing by some mental anguish. She was naturally unwilling to speak frankly to a complete stranger, but perhaps you know of some cause for this anguish, Barone?'

'I certainly do,' I said. 'Her husband . . .' I used the word so as not to have to enter into further explanations. 'Her husband has been away in another country longer than he or she expected and she is desperate for his return.'

'Then you had better write to him and tell him to hasten back,' he said. 'That is the only medicine which will do her any good.'

I went home and did so, addressing my letter, since I had none of his to refer to, to Herr Franz Liszt, Klaviervirtuoso, Vienna, hoping that his celebrity would see it safely delivered. Then I returned to the hotel and spent the day at her bedside, reading to her when she was awake, contemplating her face or stealing out for a bite to eat and a cigar, when she was asleep.

* * *

The next day she was a little stronger and the next day stronger still, walking about her room and taking a little to eat and drink. We spoke of Liszt almost exclusively and tried to work out when he might get my letter, how long his journey would take and when he might arrive.

* * *

Today his reply came. Its contents took my breath away. He thanked me profusely for my 'loving care of the person who matters most to me in the world', but said that he was engaged for several more concerts and could not leave Vienna immediately. He asked me to urge her instead to come to him, borrowing money if necessary for the journey, since there was no time to send her any.

I now began to see the man very much as she sees him, engrossed with himself and his career, unworthy of the great love she bears him and the sacrifices she has made for him. She has certainly, as she told me, been his Beatrice, but had Dante's Beatrice lived and returned his love to this measure, would the great Dante have treated her like this? I'm afraid it is possible. Artists are obsessive people and do not live by the same rules as others—indeed they live in a world largely of their own creation, a construct of their own fantasy with rules and morals to suit themselves. Any woman who chooses or is inexorably drawn to enter that unreal world and share its creator's dreams, risks also being left behind in a reality which is all the more squalid and unbearable for the dreams which have proved illusory. Most people know better than to try to walk on water, but many unfortunately believe they can walk on clouds.

Yesterday, in her renewed hope of seeing Liszt again soon, the Countess had forgotten all her animosity towards him and spoke only of the bliss they had enjoyed together. She described the 'simple paradise' they had shared in Switzerland and at Bellagio on the shore of Lake Como, where he had completed, working in the same room as her, the first of the great works to which he aspired and which would carry his name down the centuries. Her part, she said, was only to inspire him and to protect his genius from all the snares and interruptions of the careless world, outside the walls of their paradise. She herself, she said, was nothing very much, as Beatrice was nothing very much in herself, but linked to him she became something quite beyond herself.

And now it was my task to tell her that this Dante was managing quite well without his Beatrice, that he was still walking on the clouds while she had fallen into a pit of despair. I contemplated tearing up the letter and pretending there was no reply yet, but I have never learnt to lie convincingly and I was afraid to do anything to complicate and worsen the situation. So with the greatest reluctance I went to the hotel, clutching Liszt's letter as if it was a dose of poison.

She was out of bed, looking quite ravishing in her nightgown as she stood by the window observing the activity below on the quays.

'Marie . . .' I said. It was the first time I had called her that and she looked round with a sweet smile. 'He has replied to my letter . . .'

On my way to the hotel I had decided to give her the gist of the letter without showing it to her. I thought that I might possibly make the contents sound softer than they were. But I was not quick enough. Her smile became an expression of great joy, ecstasy . . .

'He's coming, oh, he's coming, then!' and she rushed across to me and snatched the letter from my hand.

I could only watch in dismay as she read the letter, slowly turned white, took two steps towards a chair and fell down in a faint.

Her maid revived her with smelling-salts and we got her into bed.

* * *

I have written again to Liszt to tell him the effect of his letter on her and to say that at present she cannot even walk from her bed to her chair, let alone make the journey from Venice to Vienna, and that if he does not come to her in the very near future, I seriously doubt whether he need come at all, since his beautiful Countess will have left her hotel and gone to San Michele, the island of the dead. I really believe she may die. Her delirium has been raging for two or three days. 'Franz! Franz!', she cries out as she tosses and turns and fights with demons. The doctor looks grave and does what he can, but that is little, for he still insists that this illness comes from the mind more than the body.

'And that region we still know too little about,' he says. 'We can only pin our hopes on her husband.'

* * *

She is much better, thank God. I prayed for her ardently in every church I passed—though I'm not usually a very religious person—and my prayers seem to have been answered. Her beauty is only enhanced by her pallor and deeply shadowed eyes. I told her so partly to encourage her, partly because it was true, and she asked me if I was in love with her.

'Of course I am,' I said, and although I spoke with my usual light tone and she understood it as mere gallantry, I begin to think that I really am.

She always puts herself down when she speaks of Liszt and his genius, and I took this at first at face value and then blamed her possessiveness. Now I can see more clearly what Liszt sees in her and to understand why, when their relationship went more smoothly, it was something more than an ordinary love-affair. She is, I believe, as unusual a woman as he is a man. Her intelligence is such that one does not normally see far into her mind—she is too sharp and wary to allow it. But I have seen her now, been with her through many hours, when she was neither sharp nor wary, but gentle and vulnerable, and made me aware of the strength and subtlety of her mind, and above all of its capacity for love. Not for me, I hasten to say, except as she warms to all those who respect and are kind to her, but always for him, for Liszt, the first man who gained her real love, as he will surely be the last.   For whatever becomes of their great love for each other, however many other women he may fall for in his Byronic style—she was quite open to me about his tendency to be seduced by a pretty face—she will never stop loving him. She recognizes that he is not quite the god she first thought him, that indeed he is vain and sometimes short-tempered and too much addicted to cigars, coffee, wine, applause, and the flattery of grandees. She puts that last down to his humble birth. He can never quite believe, she says, that he, the son of an employee of the Esterházys, is at least as much courted in a smart salon as Prince Esterházy himself. But these are trivialities. She loves him for what, she says, is expressed in his music: his god-given power to touch the heart and give wings to the soul, his capacity for love. It comes full circle, then. His capacity for love meets hers and hers his and they set each other ablaze. But let his be withdrawn or seem to be withdrawn and hers begins to burn inwards, with the dreadful result I have witnessed.

But if he should not return? She is sure he will, she has written to him herself, she knows him better than I do, but yesterday when there was still no reply to either of our letters, she too began to lose confidence. I saw her spirits droop, her mouth tremble, her eyes grow dim.

'Marie,' I said, 'whatever happens, don't despair! I am nothing beside your Franz, but if my life, my soul, my love can be of any use to you, take them! Parents, friends, possessions, fortune, career—I abandon them all, kick them away, if I can make you happy.'

'Dearest boy,' she said. 'I know.'

And she kissed the top of my head. I had gone on my knees beside her chair as I made this declaration. I had made a fool of myself, but at least she was smiling again.

* * *

He has replied that he will be with us within a week. To see her face as she looked up from reading this letter was to see what no artist, even the greatest, has ever captured in paint or stone. Art is just that, mere imitation of the terrors or joys which we experience but cannot hold on to or even properly describe. I was not jealous to see such love for him flame up in her face, but on the contrary felt fortunate to be there to witness it.

* * *

It was a lovely May day and I accompanied her for a brief walk in the sunshine in St Mark's Square. The crowds made it a little difficult for her, but she leant on my arm and took small steps.

'I'm sorry for what I said about your city,' she said. 'You've taught me to love it.'

'Water, stone, air and sun,' I said. 'It needs all four elements to show at its best, but especially the last.'

'I too,' she said, 'but my sun is still lacking.'

At that moment somebody plucked my sleeve. It was a messenger from the hotel.

'The Signor has arrived,' he said. 'He has just now gone into the hotel.'

'Marie,' I said, 'Hold on to me and be calm!'

'What?' she said, 'what is the matter?'

'He is here. At the hotel this instant.'

She looked at me for a moment with no expression, her face quite closed, as if she were still expecting bad news. The next moment she was gone, had let go of my arm and was running, yes, running towards the hotel, passing through the crowds, parting couples, threading groups, as if they were merely shadows. I followed more slowly but when I entered the foyer I found them still in each other's arms.

6. LOVERS PARTING: PARAPHRASE OF LISZT'S AND MARIE D'AGOULT'S CORRESPONDENCE

The Mazeppa Cantata, *for soprano, tenor, bass and chorus, with piano or small orchestra.*

> *There was a gentleman of Poland called Mazeppa. In his youth he had an affair with the wife of another Polish gentleman, which was discovered. The husband had him tied naked to the back of a wild horse, which was then released. The horse had been brought from Ukraine and returned there, carrying Mazeppa, half-dead of exhaustion and hunger. Some peasants rescued him, he remained with them a long time and distinguished himself in many battles with the Tartars. His superior knowledge and intelligence gave him a high reputation among the Cossacks, and as this increased from day to day, the Czar was obliged to make him Prince of Ukraine.*

—Voltaire, *History of Charles XII*, quoted at the head of Lord Byron's poem *Mazeppa*

* * *

NARRATOR (*bass*). After his absence in Vienna, Franz returns to Marie in Venice. Together they tour Italy: Genoa, Milano, Lugano, Como; Bologna and Ravenna; Florence, Pisa, Siena, Rome. In Rome she gives birth to their third child, Daniel. From Rome they return to Florence; from there to Lucca, to San Rossore between the pines and the sea, to Pisa again, and back to Florence. And there they agree, for the time being, to go their separate ways.

MARIE (*soprano*). I love you so much and for *yourself,*
    I believe you still love *me.*
    But your heart is only mine in part.
    My love dries up and withers you.
    Five years you've freely loved me,
    And loved me *greatly.*
    Five years may be enough.

I know you feel shackled,
Confined and stifled,
I know you need to be free.
Let me go, let me leave you!
But when you need me, call me!
Call me and I will come!

NARRATOR. Marie, returning to Paris, goes westward, gathering their
two daughters. She leaves their baby boy with his nurse in
Palestrina, and takes ship from Genoa for Marseille.

MARIE. How can I leave this dear land, Italy,
Without a last goodbye?
How can I see those lovely years
Fall from my life without regret?
Oh, my dear Franz, I say with all my soul:
It is you who filled it with feeling,
Profound, imperishable.
Bless you a thousand times!

NARRATOR. And Franz goes eastward to Venice.

FRANZ (*tenor*). Here, Marie, I say my last goodbye.
Only in my heart and thoughts shall I find you again.
Sea and sky, St Mark's and the gondolas—
Everything here speaks to me of you
Echoing your dearest name.
Here I lost you and left you,
Here I found you again.
Here you were dying,
Here you came back to life!
Oh Venice, in your lagoons
What sweet enchantment lingers!

NARRATOR. He sails to Trieste.

CHORUS (*with the rhythm of a galloping horse*).
Two concerts in Trieste,
Six concerts in Vienna,
And a concert in Pressburg.

FRANZ. You can't imagine the scale of my success.
Day by day I grow more popular

In this propitious place!
Fifty people wait at my door
Just to see me come out.
Even my doctor's a celebrity now,
Making the rounds of his patients
Just to give news of my fever.

MARIE. My God, your fever! On my knees I beg you
Give up *coffee,* tobacco, wine! Do this *for me!*
Franz, how I love you! But in God's name
Sacrifice your vile regime!

FRANZ. I am sad and weighed down, my dear and dear,
My life is so empty, so stripped of joy,
All true and profound and intimate joy.
As for the women, yes, I must tell you,
It's not just one woman, but all of them,
Yes, universal infatuation.
But, believe me, I pay no attention.
Not one woman here attracts me at all
Physically speaking—no, not the slightest—
And as you well know that's always my weakest
Point, at least when I'm bored or distracted.

MARIE. You're *smoking again!* My God, will you not
Do this for me, sacrifice your cigar?
You've given up praying to God, you say,
But you will not give up your cigar!
I love you, I love you with all my soul,
Every day you're away I suffer more.
When, when, oh when will you return to me?

CHORUS. Nine concerts in Pest
And two in Pressburg,
Two concerts in Brno
And six in Prague.
Three in Dresden,
Three more in Leipzig.

FRANZ. How thoroughly I loathe my piano!
I never wished to play except for you,
And why these crowds should come and hear me

And pay me handsomely, I do not know.
Nor do I know what you can mean by asking
My permission to become unfaithful!
What? With whom? In general? You don't say.
No matter. I just want you to be free,
Completely free. Until the day, Marie,
When you can say that such and such a man
Has stronger feelings for you than I have,
Has understood more deeply who and what
You are—until that day you cannot be
Unfaithful. Nothing can change between us.

MARIE. Unjust and blind, imperious, unruly,
Mad, cruel passion! What a thing it is!
My head burns merely to remember it.
Oh, then I did not walk upon the earth!
Your every word, your every glance revealed
Some new expanse of Heaven or hole in Hell.
Potocki has declared his love for me
And, yes, I do confess, my heart leapt up.
Why? Why because my secret thought was this:
'I must be lovable if others love me,
And if so, dearest *Franz* can still love me,
And therefore I can make *him* happy still.'

FRANZ. I shall not live again until I see you.
Among these upturned faces, clapping hands,
These shouting voices and these teeming crowds,
I do not live, I am a man of stone,
And always utterly alone, alone.

MARIE. Even after this long separation,
After so many griefs piled up between us,
I swear no man was ever loved like you!
I try to see that moment when we meet,
To feel the first touch of your puissant hand!

FRANZ. A mighty thunderstorm broke over me!
Two thousand people called me back to play.
And this was Prague, Court of Appeal, they say,
For all musicians coming from Vienna.

Now my success, they say, surpasses
Paganini's, and there *is* no standard,
No precedent, no measure beyond his.

MARIE. I want you neither for your *power* nor *pride*,
I want *sublimity* no more today
Than then, five years back in the *ratzenloch*.
Be *good* to me! Allow for my weakness!
For six months now I have been ailing, ill,
But do you ever ask about my health?
Anxiety is what I'll die of soon:
Your coffee and cigars, the thought of you
In someone else's arms—I should go mad!
I'd give my place in Paradise to gain
Six cloudless months on this poor earth with you.
You think too much, dear Franz, of being *great*,
You feel too strong to think of others' weakness,
For you, no doubt, *everything is simple*.
Forgive me that I'm crying with misery
And losing hope of ever finding peace,
Since you can never now stoop down to me.
I am like other people, don't you see?
They share my faults, my fears, my jealousy
And my weak will, emotion's helpless slave.
But you, no, you are not the same as others.
Whatever I dare dream of, you will laugh at,
What I dare wish for doesn't count with you.
Proudly you soar, sensible of greatness,
Unable even to notice here below
The little cries and hurts of feebler hearts.

NARRATOR. He returns to her for a month in Paris, then leaves for
London, where she joins him.

CHORUS. Two concerts in Paris,
And four in London.

MARIE. Don't keep my box for Monday,
I shall not come into town.
At present I can do nothing—
Perhaps I never shall—
But be alone, alone.

FRANZ. This is what you have to say!
 Six years of devotion
 Bring you to this conclusion.
 Yesterday we travelled
 From Ascot to Richmond,
 No single word you uttered
 Not wounding or insulting.
 But why bring up these sorrows,
 Why count our hearts' complaints?
 Let's suffer and be silent!
 Love is not just, no never,
 Love is not dutiful,
 Love is not even *pleasure*.
 Love is a mystery
 Containing everything.
 It's there for all to see
 When it appears on earth,
 In lovers' perfect trust.
 Let's not bandy words, then,
 Nor bargain nor measure!
 If love still lives in *our* hearts,
 Then everything is said.
 But if our love has fled,
 There is no more to say.

NARRATOR. They leave London for Brussels and Brussels for the Rhineland.

CHORUS. Concerts in Brussels, in Bonn, in Ems,
 In Baden-Baden, in Frankfurt and Köln.

NARRATOR. They part in Rotterdam, she for Paris, he for England.

FRANZ. My life as a *saltimbanque* begins today.

CHORUS. Concerts in Chichester, Portsmouth, Ryde and Newport,
 In Southampton, Winchester, Salisbury, Blandford,
 In Weymouth, Lyme Regis and Sidmouth,
 Exmouth and Teignmouth,
 In Plymouth and Exeter.
 Concerts in Taunton,
 In Bridgwater and Bath.

FRANZ. Maybe there's too much passion, energy,
   Too much fire inside us, to settle down
   Like bourgeois people in the possible.
   Let's not complain nor make ourselves so sad
   With accusations! Let's not accuse fate!
   Let's just live as we can! Rest your arm on mine,
   Let me sleep gently up against your heart,
   Whose beating shall be my hidden tempo,
   My mystery, my rhythm of beauty,
   My symphony of everlasting love.

MARIE. Oh yes, exactly so, I feel the same!
   What divides us is nothing but a dream,
   A nasty nightmare, deceiving phantoms.
   All those bitter and lacerating words
   Are spat into our mouths by evil spirits.
   They drop from outside, settle on our lips,
   They have no proper roots within our hearts.
   So love and hope spring up again in me.

CHORUS. Concerts in Clifton and Cheltenham,
   In Leamington, Coventry, Northampton, Harborough,
   In Leicester and Derby, Nottingham, Mansfield and Newark,
   In Lincoln, Horncastle, Boston, Grantham,
   In Stamford and Peterborough, Huntingdon, Cambridge,
   In Bury St Edmunds, in Norwich and Ipswich,
   Colchester, Chelmsford and Brighton.

NARRATOR. Franz returns to France, spends two weeks with Marie at
Fontainebleau, then leaves for Hamburg.

FRANZ. Surely this was the first time that we parted
   Without discord and anguish. Was it chance?
   No, I think now we're surer of each other.

MARIE. What kind power has changed us or revealed us?
   None, I think. It's you alone have changed us,
   Changed everything by the power of your love.
   It's you I must thank for *crushing the snake*,
   For lifting me once again on your wings
   To that ideal world for which I'm longing.

CHORUS. Three concerts in Hamburg.

NARRATOR. Franz and Marie spend a week together in a small hotel
in Dunkirk, a *ratzenloch* revisited. She returns to Paris and he to
England.

CHORUS. In Oxford and Leamington, two concerts,
    In Birmingham, Wolverhampton, two concerts,
    In Newcastle, Chester and Liverpool, three concerts.
    In Preston, Rochdale, Manchester, three concerts,
    In Huddersfield, Doncaster, Sheffield, three concerts,
    In Wakefield and Leeds, two concerts,
    In Hull and York and Manchester again, three concerts.
    In Dublin three concerts.

FRANZ. Such sadness, such tedium
    Has gripped me these twelve days!
    I think of Geneva,
    I think of Lake Como,
    Where our two girls were born.
    Please tell me their birthdays—
    I cannot recall them.
    Every morning I wake up
    To see three young, bare trees,
    Shaken, beaten by wind.
    This image haunts my mind.
    I too am shaken bare,
    And beaten dry. Where's the green,
    The sap and scent we dream?

MARIE. You are so dreadfully sad!
    I would be too, but know
    You'll soon be here and then
    All this will drift away.
    Come back! We shall be happy.

CHORUS. Concerts in Cork and Clonmel,
    In Dublin again, in Limerick and Belfast,
    In Glasgow and Edinburgh,
    In Newcastle, Sunderland, Durham,
    In Richmond, Darlington, Halifax,
    And in London.
    Concerts in Brussels, Liège and Anvers
    And three concerts in Paris.

NARRATOR. In his first Paris concert since returning from Britain, Franz plays *Mazeppa*, his transcendental study for piano, and has a triumphant success.

MARIE. You were so deathly pale when we parted
    And I was sick at heart. Today your star
    Shines over me again and confidence returns,
    We shall meet again—this time for ever.
    I failed to tell you then what *good* you did me,
    Your time in Paris. You were so fully,
    So greatly, nobly *mine!* Yes, you gave me
    Your gift again, it seemed, for the second time,
    The gift of your whole soul, your life, your love!

CHORUS. In London, one concert.

NARRATOR. Franz rents a private island in the Rhine, the island of Nonnenwerth.

FRANZ. And if you'll come to Nonnenwerth, my star
    Will light my way again. A *candle* now
    Is all the light I have. What vanity,
    What obligation makes me go on
    Playing this sad, interminable game,
    Demanding every ounce of energy?
    Pity me, Marie, bear with me, help me!

CHORUS. A concert in Hamburg and in Copenhagen, ten.

NARRATOR. She joins him on the island of Nonnenwerth, while he makes excursions to play in nearby cities.

CHORUS. Concerts in Bonn, in Ems, in Köln, in Koblenz,
    In Frankfurt and Wiesbaden.

MARIE. *Madness* invades my brain.
    I cannot stand it, can't live
    With these disturbances.
    I'm leaving now for Paris.
    Better *friend* than *lover.*
    I don't reproach you, no,
    But staying I shall suffer
    And make you suffer too.
    And so goodbye, dear Franz—
    No *break* but an *adjournment.*

CHORUS. In Mayence, Baden-Baden, Frankfurt, concerts,
  In Köln, in Aix-la-Chapelle, in Liège,
  In Köln again, in Elberfeld and Düsseldorf,
  In Düsseldorf again and Elberfeld again,
  In Crefeld, Münster, Osnabrück,
  In Bielefeld, Detmold, Kassel and Göttingen,
  In Weimar, in Jena, in Dresden, in Leipzig,
  In Altenburg and Halle.
  And seventeen concerts in Berlin.

FRANZ. My success is huge in Berlin, vanity
  Well satisfied—but what exhaustion!
  My friends say I've grown thin—fever most nights.
  I long to end this mania—mine and theirs.
  Oh, something quite unheard of, by the way,
  The King of Prussia came to three whole concerts.

MARIE. I beg you, Franz, *take better care of yourself*!
  Think of your children, lovely creatures now!
  Think that there's in my heart a place so deep
  Even you don't know it. In there you live
  A life unseen, as if you were a god.

FRANZ. I'm nervous, ill, worn-out, on my back
  Four days now, and delirious two hours—
  Devouring need to rest or sleep or die.
  Eight concerts in a row, four matinées
  For the Princess—and dinners and soirées,
  Balls and smoking-rooms, conversation,
  Correcting proofs, instrumentation . . .
  You must know how I miss *you*, only *you*.

NARRATOR. Before setting out for Russia, he spends two days at
Müncheburg with the beautiful young Berlin actress Charlotte von
Hagn.

CHORUS. Concerts in Elbing and Königsberg,
  In Lithuania, Riga and Estonia.

FRANZ. You know, you say, that I've opened my heart
  To *an affection much more serious*
  Than before. How do you know? Who told you?
  Can you believe there's room in my poor life

For any other *serious affection?*
I've freely staked my life once and for all
And have no power, nor appetite, nor will
To stake my life again. Nothing has changed.

MARIE. The spirit of God speaks strongly, clearly
To my soul, and I feel I am being called.
I shall confess and follow a new path.
I need to see you. You took me away
From God, you'll give me back to him. What peace1
I go to God, as once to you in Basel.

CHORUS. In St Petersburg, six concerts.
In Lübeck, in Paris,
In Bonn and Köln and Koblenz, more concerts,

NARRATOR. In Koblenz he meets Charlotte von Hagn again.

FRANZ. My visit to Koblenz? Nothing serious.
Such things, when they are over, I forget.
I've barely sufficient presence of mind
To think of them while they are happening.
The best way, the sole way, I always think,
To end such *liaisons* is not to give
Room to them, let them end as they began.
You know how I hate harsh words, noisy scenes.

CHORUS. In Weimar, in Jena, in Erfurt, three concerts,
In Frankfurt, another.

FRANZ. Is it a *quarrel* you want or even
Complete, immediate and final break-up?
Then if you want it sudden and stressful,
Send me some proof of infidelity.
Or if you prefer to be reasonable—
I can't demand that after such folly—
Within the next year I will make the break,
Decently, naturally and quite simply.

MARIE. My sad spirit is wild and wandering,
My anxious soul journeys through stormy clouds
Seeking its country, its lost home once more:
A new Odyssey in which your loved soul

Is the island of Ithaca, far off
But remembered, shifting and out of reach.

CHORUS. In The Hague, three concerts,
In Leyden, in Rotterdam, in Utrecht, three concerts,
In Amsterdam, another.

FRANZ. It seems that I've forgotten how to live.
My dreams are all confused, the passing years
Dig me a pit of misery. I'd drop
All this business, this virtuosity,
Useless, unnatural, as one drops an old coat,
If I thought you'd be happy with me again.
But from some blindness of spirit or heart
I did not feel that I gave you enough,
And so I preferred this vagabond life,
This deadly stagnation poisoning me
And giving no life to you. No pretence!
My life for three years has been nothing else
But fevered excitement, disgust, remorse.
I have had to *spend*—life, energy, time—
Without present joy or a future hope.
Like a gambler I am, without his drive,
His perpetual, insatiable thirst for luck,
Like a man crossing fields, picking as he goes
And throwing away flowers, fruits, leaves and seeds,
Without sowing or digging or grafting.
Is our Ideal still possible? I don't know,
Perhaps you do. It's for you to decide.

MARIE. Your life, poor Franz, is a noble mistake,
And it seems now that mine has been also.
I'm happy enough to be your mistress,
But never just *one* of your mistresses.

FRANZ. Our mistake, I know, was ever to part.
I never think of Florence without pain,
That hour that tolled the death of our best years.
I swear that underneath all the applause,
All the intoxication of success,
And every kind of surfeit and excess,

Yes, even in the banal embraces,
Deceitful too, of many mistresses,
In Prague or Pest, Berlin, Trieste, Vienna,
Anywhere I went, I thought of Florence
And that hour still tolled its pitiless knell.

MARIE. I never loved you more or better, Franz.
Only, I see the sun go down on life
And want before it does to *have had my day*!
Still desperately I hope, and spring and sky
And memory and my imperious heart
Cry out incessantly: his love, his love!

CHORUS. A concert in Münster and six in Berlin,
Concerts in Posen, in Glogau, in Liegnitz,
Three in Cracow, four in Warsaw,
Six in Petersburg and six in Moscow.

NARRATOR. Franz and Marie spend August together, with their children
and friends, on the island of Nonnenwerth. Then Marie returns to
Paris.

CHORUS. Concerts in Solingen, Bonn and Dortmund,
In Köln and Iserlohn, Frankfurt, Würtzburg, Nuremberg,
Four concerts in Munich.
In Augsburg, Stuttgart, Tübingen,
In Heilbronn, Ludwigsburg, Hechingen,
In Donaueschingen, Karlsruhe,
In Heidelberg and Mannheim, concerts, concerts, concerts.

NARRATOR. Franz accepts the post of Honorary Kapellmeister in
Weimar and publishes his *Reminiscences of Norma* with a dedication
to the pianist Marie Camille Pleyel, his 'dear and ravishing
colleague'.

MARIE. Young Icarus, who flew too near the sun,
Compared to you, was sensible and prudent.
This constant moral surfeiting poisons
All natural affections, makes the soul sick.
It's time you were wiser, time you *had taste*.
I don't expect it. You've aged, not matured.
All I gain from speaking truly from my heart
Is anger, insincerity, deceit.

I hope with all my strength that your new post
In Weimar and your work will fill your years.
My courage now comes back. No more laughter,
No more tears, no joy, no pain, no feeling.
I walk more lightly as I brush aside
Those clinging hopes that follow me about,
Like beggars wanting pieces of my soul.

NARRATOR. Franz meets the dancer Lola Montez and travels with her
to Dresden, where they attend Wagner's opera *Rienzi* and stay in the
same hotel.

FRANZ. It's clear we are opposed at every point.
I have thought long and sadly and decide
There's no reply. Receive, therefore, the ring,
The broken sphinx you gave me once in Rome.

CHORUS. In Dresden, three concerts,
In Dessau and Köthen, more concerts,
In Bautzen, Bernburg and Stettin, more,
And more in Berlin, Magdeburg, Brunswick and Hanover.

MARIE. If I was not convinced by now, dear Franz,
That I can only be a pain to you,
I would not do what now I have to do.
You have the power of youth and genius,
They'll drive you on beyond, over the tomb
Where all our sometime love and friendship lie.
Do not be angry! I have some requests
To make. Choose some third party whom you trust!

FRANZ. I count up all the sorrows that I've sown
In your dear heart. Nothing and no one now
Can save me from myself. No wish to see you,
No, nor speak nor write again. An actor
Didn't you call me? Yes, indeed, I play
The dying athlete who has drunk hemlock.
No more. Silence shall seal my tortured heart.

CHORUS. In Paris, four concerts, in Lyon, six.
Concerts in France, concerts in Spain, concerts in Portugal,
In Weimar and Vienna, Prague and Hungary,
Pest and Bucharest, concerts, concerts,

> Concerts in Kiev and Constantinople,
> In Odessa, ten.
> And in Elisabetgrad, one last concert.

NARRATOR. And here, like Mazeppa, in Ukraine, his headlong career as virtuoso ends and his new life as composer/conductor begins. His life with the Countess Marie is already over, his life with the Princess Carolyne has already begun.

IX. Make-believe and Lies

Lola Montez! What a woman! She makes one proud to be British. You've heard of her, of course: the Spanish dancer who rocked the throne of Bavaria and brought down the besotted King Ludwig I, grandfather of Wagner's patron Ludwig II. Imagine the consequence if the Bavarians had abolished the monarchy and declared a republic, as they nearly did in that year of revolutions, 1848, when Ludwig I was forced to abdicate! No generous patron-king for Wagner, no Ring Cycle, no Parsifal, no Bayreuth. What Wagner owed to the weird grandson in the 1860s, he nearly lost years earlier to Lola Montez and the weird grandfather.

To begin with, you'll recall, she was not Spanish, but British, or at least Anglo-Irish, born and bred. Or should I begin with the most salient point? She was stunning to look at and as bold into the breech as Lord Nelson or the Duke of Wellington, with the difference that she did not fight for her country but herself, and her battlefields were not ships of the line or the plain of Waterloo but beds, or the promise of them. Yet she wasn't primarily a prostitute, you couldn't call her that. She was an *artiste*, a stage performer. She made her living partly from rich admirers, partly from audiences who had to see for themselves if she really was such a bad dancer and such a ravishing looker as they'd been told. And they were not disappointed either way. Her dancing was amateur, but what Casanova or Byron or Liszt did to women, she did to men. And yes, she and Liszt got together.

We can observe them first in a railway carriage, in fact, on that same stretch of line between Leipzig and Dresden where a couple of years later we encountered Liszt and Professor List and discussed the Interpretation of Railways.

Lola had performed three dances in Berlin the previous year, with considerable success, her personality and appearance making up for the deficiencies of her technique. Her debut was in the Cachuca 'El Oleano', an early version of her famous 'Spider Dance', in which, accompanied by a repetitive tune, she depicted a girl pursued by a tarantula, which she finally kills. For this dance she wore a tight black velvet top over a skirt of red, white and blue satin squares, with red and white camellias in her hair and a black hat on the back of her head. Her second offering was 'La Sevilliana' and her third and most spectacular 'Los Boleros de Cadix', performed in the interval between the two acts of Beethoven's *Fidelio* and for which she was dressed in silver and white. She was even invited to dance at the Prussian Court for a State Visit by Czar Nicholas I of Russia and she followed this up with a tour of the outlying parts of Prussia. On her way back to Berlin through Tilsit she happened to spot an advertisement for Liszt's concerts in Dessau and Köthen, both by now connected to Berlin by rail, and determined to see and hear the great star for herself.

She was overwhelmed, of course, and having caught his eye as he played—Liszt had a trick of leaving his hands to dart over the keys while he 'swept the auditorium with the glance of a smiling master'— she sent him a note asking him to call on her at her hotel. He replied politely that he wished he could, but unfortunately had to catch the train in Leipzig so as to be back in Dresden for another concert in two days' time. Lola replied that she would go with him. As the Duke of Wellington said, 'I never miss an opportunity to relieve myself or to bring the enemy to battle'.

What a magnificent pair they make, as we take our seat opposite them in their first-class compartment! Next to the window, the tall, spare, thirty-three-year-old megastar in his grey three-piece Parisian suit, with his shoulder-length brown hair and flashing green eyes, and close beside him the twenty-six-year-old black-haired beauty in black velvet with her generous curves, large dark blue eyes and perfectly oval face, sometimes pale, sometimes flushed as she puts questions to him or answers his. She does indeed look Spanish. Her mother, Elizabeth Oliver, illegitimate daughter of a High Sheriff of Cork, had some Spanish blood through *her* mother. Lola's father, however, was impeccably English, Ensign Edward Gilbert of the 25th Foot Regiment, stationed at the time of his marriage and her birth, which almost coincided, with the British garrison in Ireland. Lola was baptized Elizabeth Rosanna Gilbert.

The second salient point about Eliza Gilbert—as her parents knew her—is that she was middle-class. Her charming drawing-room manners—much appreciated at the Prussian Court—were formed at a young ladies' establishment in Bath. After the death of her father in India—his next posting—Eliza had been sent home by her mother's second husband, another Indian Army officer, Captain Patrick Craigie, to live with his Scottish relations. She had already become a wild and wilful child and was passed on by them to the family of General Sir Jasper Nicolls, who had distinguished himself in the Peninsular War (another Spanish connection) and was only too glad to pass her on in his turn to the boarding-school in Bath. I remind you of these details now, because she is certainly not going to reveal them to Liszt. No, she's already telling him that she was born in Seville, five years later than her actual birth in Cork, that her father was a Spanish general and that although she's always known as Lola, her real name is Maria—a little pang there for Liszt perhaps, since he still hasn't made his final break with the Countess Marie.

How on earth did this well-brought up, well-educated young lady from a British military background turn into a Spanish dancer? It was at least partly the doing of her mother, who, having lost her second husband, returned from India, escorted by a Lieutenant Thomas James, and arranged for her eighteen-year-old daughter to marry a man of sixty. Eliza refused and eloped with her mother's escort. They married in Dublin and she lived in an Irish village with his relatives until he was promoted to Captain and posted back to India. There they quarrelled violently, Eliza walked out on him and returned to England alone. Not long alone, however, for on the ship she met a Captain Lennox and when they reached England she moved into a hotel in Covent Garden with him.

Captain Lennox was taken to court by Captain James, her husband, but Eliza peeled off to join Fanny Kemble's drama-school, only to be told that she had no talent for acting and might do better as a dancer. That was the start of her career as Lola Montez, which began with a one-off performance of her Cachuca, 'El Oleano', as the entr'acte to Rossini's *Barber of Seville* at the Haymarket Theatre. There was a distinguished audience, including the Duke of Wellington, and although she found it hard to keep time to the music, she was clever with her castanets and her lissom figure and got applause and good notices. Unfortunately, word soon spread around town that she was really the disgraced Mrs James. Dauntless, impulsive and tempestuous, Spanish in temperament if not origin, she left England and set out to conquer the Continent.

Her conversation with Liszt is necessarily limited, since her French is as minimal as his English. She must be grateful that he has no Spanish, her own being strictly for non-Spanish-speakers. But she has been picking up a little German recently and he has been refining his Austrian patois. It is rather wonderful to overhear these two choice spirits of the age communicating like people in the beginners' class of a triple language course—'Wo hast Du been all ma vie?'—that sort of thing. But the advantage is that if I address her in English and him in French, I can be fairly certain that my discourse with each will be incomprehensible to the other. I wait until they are both silent, both perhaps wrestling inwardly with thoughts too deep for their vocabulary.

'Señora Montez, forgive my ignorance of your own language,' I say in English, with the faintest hint of irony, 'but tell me if you will, what plans you have for performing in Dresden.'

'Not at all. I go just to hear more of Monsieur Liszt. His music carries me away. I am enchanted.'

She lays her lovely hand with its delicate pink nails on his knee. He covers her hand with his mighty fingers.

'Monsieur Liszt,' I say in French, 'I wonder if you have any plans to join forces with Señora Montez?'

'Join forces? What exactly do you mean by that?'

'The famous pianist and the famous dancer on stage together?'

'No.'

'It would be a tremendous attraction to the public.'

'No doubt. And they'd like it still better if she strummed the piano and I jigged about with the castanets.'

'Señora Montez,' I say, 'there's a story going about that you were arrested in Berlin for hitting a policeman with your riding-crop. Is there any truth in that?'

'Which story have you heard?'She has already forgotten to lay on her pseudo-Spanish accent and is speaking pure Bath Ladies' College, with a touch of Indian Army drawl.

'Only what I read in the newspapers.'

'Every newspaper has a different story.'

'That's why I wanted to get the truth from the horse's mouth.'

'Oh, the horse would tell you the truth all right. The policeman hit him with the flat of his sword. That was not nice. I am very fond of horses and the more high-spirited the better I like them.'

'I can imagine. So why did the policeman do that dastardly thing to your horse?'

'Because my horse was showing his high spirits . . . prancing about . . . he was disturbed by a burst of gunfire.'

'This was a grand parade in front of the King of Prussia and the Czar of Russia.'

'That sort of thing.'

'And the artillery fired a salute and your horse was stampeded into the royal enclosure?'

'Not at all. I had him fully under control. I was looking for a friend in the royal enclosure. It was the stupid policeman who nearly made me lose control.'

'So you gave him a crack of your whip?'

'Not the horse, no.'

'The policeman?'

'One has to be firm with flunkeys.'

'And after the parade was over they came to arrest you.'

'They brought me some piece of paper which I immediately tore up and threw in their faces.'

'And then?'

'Then nothing.'

'The authorities didn't pursue the matter?'

'Why should they? It was only some low types in the police who wanted to make an issue of it.'

'But I read that you were taken to court and convicted, with a sentence of several months in prison.'

'What nonsense!'

'The same report said that you were pardoned by the King himself.'

'All right.'

'Is that what happened?'

'If it makes a better story.'

'You don't mind if it's not true?'

'Listen, I'm an artist, not a philosopher. The most important thing for me is the publicity.'

'Even bad publicity?'

'This was good publicity. People like to hear of stupid officials being whipped. They would like to do it themselves.'

Liszt had not been following this very well and was growing impatient.

'*Was sagen Sie, gnädige Fraülein?*' [What are you saying, dear lady?]

'Make-believe and lies,' she said in English.

Liszt didn't quite understand this.

'*Poses et mensonges,*' I translated helpfully, borrowing a phrase Liszt himself used nearly twenty years later to dismiss the Countess Marie's dodgy account of their relationship in her Memoirs.

'A fine phrase,' he said. 'I must remember it.'

'Monsieur Liszt,' I said, relishing the wonderful whiff of inverse déjà vu in this response, 'you've told me that you have no plans for performing with Señora Montez, but I do feel that this meeting of two such celebrities must lead to something. It seems fateful. What do you think?'

'What sort of thing are you thinking of?'

'I hesitate to say.'

'Just as well. So do I.'

He could not know, of course, that I was not referring, as he suspected, to nights in hotels together, but to the complex labyrinth of future events and relationships which would bifurcate and trifurcate and go round in circles from this apparently simple joining of two paths. I have described how Lola would go on to seduce King Ludwig I and alienate him from his people, with the fatal effect that might have had on Wagner's career and greatest works. But there is also the fact that when they reach Dresden, Lola will introduce Liszt to the fourteen-year-old Hans von Bülow who, with his father, the writer Edward von Bülow, has been very kind and helpful to her in Berlin. Young Hans, at Lola's insistence, will play for Liszt in Dresden, greatly impress him and be inspired to devote himself to music. In time he will become Liszt's most brilliant pupil as both pianist and conductor—not only that, he will marry Liszt's second daughter Cosima. Not only that, he will conduct the first performance of Wagner's tragic opera of adultery, *Tristan und Isolde*, under the beneficent patronage of King Ludwig I's grandson, King Ludwig II. Not only that, Hans von Bülow's wife Cosima Liszt will deceive him with Wagner, bear Wagner a daughter called Isolde on the very night that husband Hans conducts the first rehearsal of *Tristan und Isolde,* and eventually leave him to marry Wagner. Their children, of course, Liszt's grandchildren, will inherit Bayreuth. Meanwhile, in Dresden, where Liszt and Lola are about to arrive, they will attend together a performance of Wagner's early opera *Rienzi* and meet the composer.

I was greatly tempted to reveal all this wonderful tangle of circumstances to Liszt and Lola themselves, but I realized they would think I was simply a madman and would not believe a word of it. I could also have told them that their brief relationship, reported everywhere, would soon reach the ears of the Countess d'Agoult and cause her finally to give up on her faithless Franz. Didn't he care or was he so entranced by Lola Montez that he forgot about everything else during those few nights in Dresden? A bit of both, no doubt. Lost in the contemplation of all this foreknowledge, I lay back in my seat and left them to their own halting conversation. I should have noted it down, I suppose, but what was the point? It was lame. They were only filling in time until they could get to Dresden and the Hotel de Saxe, where Liszt's suite awaited him, but she had made no booking.

I caught up with them again some nights later at the performance of Wagner's *Rienzi*, a five-act saga of the people versus the nobles in fourteenth-century Rome. The hero, Rienzi, sung by the famous tenor

Joseph Tichatschek, is the Tribune of the People—ironic in view of Wagner's later obligation to the King of Bavaria, but prophetic of the year 1849, when Wagner joined an abortive people's revolution in Dresden and had to flee for his life and live in exile for a long time afterwards. At this time, however, in 1844, the thirty-one-year-old Wagner, still not widely known, was Director of the Dresden Court Opera, under the patronage of the King of Saxony, another culturally enlightened monarch. Wagner had arranged this unscheduled performance of *Rienzi* specially so that the great star Liszt could hear it before leaving the city, after his own series of sell-out concerts. The five-hour performance went well and Liszt admired it, but since it was written and sung in German his companion Lola could hardly understand a word and was almost beside herself with boredom. Her only consolation, clinging close to Liszt, was soaking up the audience's admiring and envious stares during the intervals.

When the thing finally ended, with the burning of the Roman Capitol and the death of most of the characters, Liszt took her backstage to congratulate Tichatschek and they had scarcely got into his dressing-room when they were joined by the composer. I was already pressed up against the wall—a Daniel in a den of lions—and if my account of the following incident sounds a little different from those you have read elsewhere, well, that is often the way with Montez stories, including her own Memoirs.

(*Editor's Note: All other accounts have Liszt, Lola and Wagner visiting Tichatschek's dressing-room during one of the intervals, not at the end of the opera.*)

It was a small, hot, foetid place. Tichatschek, naked to the waist, was seated in front of the mirror removing his make-up, Lola was given the only other chair, partly draped with the hero Rienzi's cloak, while Liszt and Wagner, who had met before but didn't know each other well, stood on either side of the door. They were like a pair of comically contrasting commissionaires, the one tall, thin and fair, the other thickset and dark, with a huge head and craggy face—Siegfried and Hagen, as it were, though those Wagnerian antagonists were still to be created. Other friends and admirers of the singer continually knocked and tried to open the door, but Wagner barred their entrance.

'*Noch nicht*!' he said fiercely and shut the door again in their faces.

Now since they were all speaking German, Lola was once more being left out of the action and she'd had enough of that. She tugged Liszt by the sleeve and said in a stage whisper:

'*Cheri*, let's get out of here!'

Liszt was in earnest conversation with Wagner on the subject— what else?—of Wagner's music and future plans and merely nodded without even looking at her. Lola got out of her chair and seizing a lipstick from beside Tichatschek wrote on the mirror:

¡*VAMOS*!

Liszt smiled, but remained preoccupied with Wagner, who was now embarked on a virtually seamless monologue. Lola took up the lipstick again and wrote in even larger capitals:

LET'S FUCKING GO!

Still getting no reaction from Liszt, who perhaps did not understand the f-word, she put her lovely hands on Tichatschek's naked shoulders, slid them down to his chest so as to cover his nipples and kissed the top of his head.

'*Auf Wiedersehen*, darling! *Wunderbar*!' she said enthusiastically and Tichatschek leered at her in the mirror. Then she returned to her chair, took up the hero Rienzi's cloak and threw it over Wagner's head as if he were a parrot in a cage.

'You talk too much,' she said in English, as Wagner clawed the cloak off his head and emerged red in the face and hopping mad.

By that time she had pulled open the door.

'What an egoist!' she said. 'You don't make people sit through five-hour operas in German if you have any thought for others.'

Then she pushed past the people waiting in the corridor outside and headed for the stage-door. Liszt made a hasty apology to Wagner and hurried after her.

It was hardly surprising that Wagner later called her a 'demonic creature without a heart' and complained for some years afterwards that Liszt might be a great musician, but kept bad company.

Lola accompanied Liszt to various other German towns, but they soon parted. One story had it that he locked her in his room to prevent her following him, and bribed the hotel porter to keep her there for at least twelve hours. A variant version has him paying the hotel manager in advance, for the damage she would do to the room. Neither sounds like Liszt, though either might have been another *pose et mensonge* of Lola's for publicity purposes. A month later, Liszt missed her debut in Paris, which was a disaster ('Mlle Montez is probably more at home on a horse than a stage,' wrote Théophile Gautier), but by then she had attached herself to a Parisian journalist, who died not long afterwards in a duel.

However, she clearly bore no ill-will towards Liszt. On the contrary, she continued to remember him fondly and proudly, since the following year she attended the unveiling of the Beethoven monument in Bonn, at which Liszt was the leading celebrant. He had stepped in to galvanize a lack-lustre local committee and to contribute his own funds—nearly a quarter of the total costs—in honour of the musician he admired above all others. Due to the incompetence of the committee, the whole week-long festival was chaotic and even the unveiling, in front of King Friedrich Wilhelm IV of Prussia, Queen Victoria and Prince Albert, was a bad joke. It turned out that the cover had been put on the statue the wrong way round, and as it came off, the distinguished guests found themselves facing Beethoven's back instead of his front.

But fortunately the royals did not stay for the closing banquet in the Golden Star Hotel, which became a riot as guests and interlopers fought for seats. Lola, claiming she was Liszt's guest (she may well have been), secured one of them. But when the banquet had got under way and Liszt, speaking in halting German, welcomed the Dutch, the English and the Viennese but forgot to mention the French, there were angry protests from one of the French guests. Liszt tried to explain that he had not meant to insult his adopted country, but another Frenchman wanted to know why toasts had been drunk to the King of Prussia and the Queen of England but not to the King of France. An Englishman shouted back:

'Why not the Emperor of China and the Shah of Persia? They didn't attend the unveiling either and have as much right as your Citizen King to be left out.'

Liszt was still trying to make himself heard, when Dr. Bernhard Wolff, author of the words of the Liszt cantata sung at the unveiling—a homage to Beethoven recycling a theme from the Master's Archduke Trio—got up on a table and tried to restore calm. He was howled down. Now it was Lola's turn. She too got up on a table and shattering glasses and knocking over champagne bottles began a bolero. That silenced the guests for a moment, when waving a champagne bottle as if she meant to bring it down on the head of anyone who dissented, she screamed:

'*Sprechen Sie, Herr Wolff, bitte sprechen Sie*! These French *clochards* have no manners.'

Infuriated Frenchmen rose to pull her down, Englishmen, Dutchmen and Germans rose to defend her. The violence breaking out around her table began to spread to the rest of the banqueting hall. The hotel's proprietor ordered his brass band to play its loudest, gradually driving most of the guests out into the night, and at that moment a spectacular thunderstorm broke over the city, dispersing and drenching them.

Lola's greatest days were still to come, of course, her dominance over King Ludwig I and transformation into the Countess von Landsberg. Perhaps from Liszt's point of view she might have been better titled the Countess von Landmine, for although he had no further effect on her and she had no further direct contact with him, the effects of their very brief liaison would continue to erupt like buried explosives in his life. She put an end to his long almost-marriage with the Countess d' Agoult, mother of his three children. She started his lifelong friendship with Hans von Bülow, his most faithful acolyte and for a while his son-in-law. She introduced discord almost from the outset into his long and complicated relationship with Wagner, and *via* Bülow, indirectly maintained it. Above all, perhaps—though this was a more intangible, more nebulous effect—she vulgarized his reputation as a sexual predator, because she was so much more publicly a sexual predator herself than any of his many other mistresses.

It was certainly fitting, given the variety, complexity and controversy of Liszt's life and music, that his crucial intervention in the Beethoven Festival in Bonn, seen by many as a shining example of his legendary generosity, but by others as a calculated assumption of

Beethoven's mantle—following on from the famous kiss when Liszt was eleven-years-old—should have ended in drunken chaos, Lola's bolero among the broken champagne glasses and, from the Heavens, whether in sympathy or rebuke, thunder and lightning over the Master's birthplace.

X. *Fairy Tales*

In 1852 Hans Christian Andersen visited Weimar and got to know Franz Liszt and Princess Carolyne von Sayn-Wittgenstein. During a visit to their house he read them a story, 'The Nightingale', from his best-selling Fairy Tales, *published three years earlier. He said his hosts were 'like spirits of fire, burning and flaming wildly. They can warm you for a moment, but one cannot get near them without being scorched'.*

1. THE SNOW PRINCESS

There was once a princess who loved her father very much. She was not born a princess, but her father owned fourteen estates and thirty thousand serfs in Ukraine and was very rich. In those days Ukraine was part of Russia. The princess, who was called Carolyne, and her father, were not themselves Russian or Ukrainian, but Polish. In those days, after any number of wars and rebellions, Poland had been swallowed up by its neighbours and most of it was inside Russia.

Carolyne's father, Peter von Iwanowsky, had married a beautiful woman with a lovely singing voice, but after Carolyne's birth they had disagreed and separated. Carolyne's mother liked the busy social life of cities and spas, but Carolyne's father preferred the country, so he and the child continued to live on one of his estates.

Peter Iwanowsky's wealth came from growing and selling grain and he was good at it, but what he liked best was reading books, so he would often spend much of the night in his library. His daughter had an equally inquiring mind and great intelligence and from quite an early age would join him in the library, where they would read and talk and smoke cigars together. By day she and her father would ride out on horseback to visit one or other of his fourteen estates with their thirty thousand serfs and every year they travelled a hundred miles to the city of Kiev to arrange for the sale of their grain. In this way she learned how to manage the business that made them so rich, for it was clear to her father that he would have no more children and that when he died she would be his sole heir.

But although Carolyne was quite as clever and energetic as any son could be, there was one thing that worried Peter Iwanowsky. In those long ago days, before the emancipation of women, it was necessary even for a woman with Carolyne's advantages to be married, and there were few suitable suitors in that remote part of the country. Not one of them could begin to match her intellect and learning or carry on the lengthy discussions of philosophy, religion, literature or science which she was accustomed to have with her father. Furthermore—this pained him very much, but he could not ignore it—she had inherited her father's brains and intellectual interests, but not her mother's beauty.

Nevertheless, when she was barely seventeen, a suitor did appear and a particularly eligible one. He was Prince Nicholas von Sayn-Wittgenstein, the youngest son of a famous general who had been raised to the nobility after defending St Petersburg against Napoleon Bonaparte. This family's estates were quite near the Iwanowskys' and the young prince was himself now a cavalry captain and aide-de-camp to the Russian Governor of Kiev. As a youngest son, he could only expect to inherit one of his father's smaller estates, so it was no doubt her prospective wealth more than her person or accomplishments that attracted him to Carolyne. Like most young military men of his class he enjoyed dancing, gambling, eating, drinking and flirting with women and his tastes were expensive. He was twenty-four years old when he was told by his father that it was time he began to settle down and think of the future, and accordingly, with *her* father's cordial permission, he proposed to Carolyne.

If she had been an ordinary girl she would surely have been flattered and delighted. Princes do not grow on trees, nor are many plain girls of seventeen offered the chance to become princesses. All the same, she turned him down. Very much surprised, Prince Nicholas consulted her father, who advised him to try again. He did and was again rejected, not once but twice. At this point her father, who loved her as much as she loved him, had to make a hard decision. Should he allow Carolyne to do as she wanted, when he was quite sure she would never find anyone better? Or should he compel her to marry Prince Nicholas against her will but ultimately for her own good? He decided on the middle course of persuasion, and spent many days and nights of argument and cigars with her in the library. And because she loved him so much and understood that he was only considering her welfare, even at his own expense, for he no more wanted to lose her constant companionship than she wanted to lose his, she did at last consent.

The marriage duly took place and Carolyne became a princess. Both families were Catholics, so it was a Catholic ceremony. But since his daughter was such a reluctant bride, Peter Iwanowsky made use of an old Polish custom. He slapped her face before handing her over to the bridegroom, signifying to all those present that she was only marrying Prince Nicholas because her father ordered her to.

The prince was at first very attentive to his new princess, and even gave up his pleasurable life in Kiev and resigned from the army in order to live with her on the estate at Woronince, which her father had given them as a wedding-present. They had a daughter, Marie, and tolerated each other for three or four years, until Prince Nicholas' boredom with their isolated life and Carolyne's intellectual interests, matched with her contempt for his impoverished mind and shallow thoughts, drove them to separate.

Then one day in church, her beloved father suddenly died of heart failure. This was a dreadful blow to her and she did not think she could ever smile again. She was sure he had died of distress over her unhappy marriage, blaming himself for it. She put seals on all the doors of her father's house just as he had left it, and returning to her own house at Woronince, where she continued to live with her little daughter, mournfully applied herself to the business of managing fourteen estates and thirty thousand serfs. Prince Nicholas, however, though he had liked and respected Peter Iwanowsky, could not feel great regret at his passing, since his own life of leisure and pleasure was much enhanced by his share of the princess' new wealth.

Things might have continued like this indefinitely, except that one January, a few years after her father's death, she travelled to Kiev, as she did regularly every year, to market her grain. And it was in Kiev that she met a man she could love and admire as much as, or even more than her father.

* * *

There was once a musician who was very unhappy, although he was the most famous and successful pianist the world had ever seen. He had played in virtually every city and self-respecting town throughout Europe. He was the first musician to be treated on equal terms by noblemen and monarchs, and was admired and envied by music-lovers and professional musicians alike, for his almost supernatural gifts. News of his prowess had even reached the Sultan of Turkey, who invited him to play in Constantinople. And since it was so far to go in those long ago days when railways were only just being laid and people still mostly travelled in horse-drawn coaches, he went there by stages, playing in some of the more remote parts of eastern Europe that had so far never heard him. One of these was the Ukrainian city of Kiev.

But behind his charming smiles, his sophisticated manners, his tall, elegant figure and extraordinarily handsome face, Franz was exhausted and dispirited. His long love-affair with a French countess, the mother of his three children, had recently ended in acrimony after he had indulged in brief affairs with some of the innumerable women who adored him. He was tired of playing the piano, tired of travelling, tired of hotels, tired of weekend love in hotel rooms, tired of being always on show, tired of the endless applause and adulation which had once excited him. He had begun to see himself as the wretched hero of Lord Byron's poem *Mazeppa*, bound naked to the back of a wild horse, galloping on and on until it dropped dead of exhaustion. Perhaps he even hoped that by coming to the Ukraine, where Mazeppa had at last been released from his torment, he too would find release.

But none of this was evident to the citizens of Kiev and the surrounding countryside who flocked to hear his first concert. To them, as to all those other audiences who had already heard him, his playing was a revelation, his genius seemed like a meteor flashing across the dark sky of their humdrum existence, his presence in their midst was like the brief appearance of a shining prince or even an angel. After his first concert, of course, there were still more people eager to attend his second and third and among these was the wealthy Princess Carolyne, visiting Kiev in order to market the grain from her fourteen estates. She attended both the second and third concerts, and enraptured by the experience, gave a large sum of money to one of the charities Franz supported.

The donation was anonymous, but in that small world of Kiev and its environs, Franz easily discovered the identity of the benefactress and wrote to thank her. His letter led to a meeting and the meeting led to an invitation from the princess to visit her home at Woronince and attend the tenth birthday-party of her daughter Marie. Franz, who had other concerts arranged for some of the small towns around Woronince and was intrigued by this unusually intelligent princess from the back of beyond, accepted. A short rest from his galloping schedule would be more than welcome.

The visit was a success. Franz liked the princess even more in her own setting than he had during their brief meeting in Kiev. The house was very large, built in the classical style with a grand two-storey portico of Ionian columns, standing in the midst of a park with fine trees and a lake, but the interior was not at all luxurious. The furniture was plain but comfortable, the wallpaper was faded and mainly grey, except in the dining room, which was decorated with large red and blue parrots. There was a music-room, a library, a billiard-room and a chapel. The princess was a devout Catholic, and since there was no resident priest, she and her daughter would often themselves read the Latin mass to their servants. These servants were everywhere. They had their own ramshackle huts round the back of the house, but many of them seemed to live mostly in the house itself, sleeping in the corridors.

Prince Nicholas was also staying in the house. He had come to celebrate his daughter's birthday and perhaps also to make the acquaintance of his wife's distinguished guest and lend respectability to a visit which might otherwise have aroused unpleasant gossip among the princess' neighbours. Franz was soon on friendly terms with the prince, but his relationship with the princess was more than friendly. During the whole ten days he was there, they did almost nothing but talk. She had had no one to talk to like this since the death of her father and he had had no such close intellectual attention from a woman since the best days of his liaison with the Countess Marie d'Agoult. Each was astonished by the other's range of learning and depth of feeling. They were two disillusioned idealists who suddenly saw their disillusionment evaporating like morning mist in the rays of the sun and their old ideals reappearing fresh and bright.

When they parted there was no doubt at all that they would see each other again.

* * *

Many months passed. Franz went to Constantinople and played for the Sultan of Turkey. Princess Carolyne made a long and difficult journey through the spring floods to St Petersburg, the capital of Russia, to settle various business affairs, and then went to her mother's house in Odessa to meet Franz on his return across the Black Sea.

Franz was surprised to find that Prince Nicholas had also come to Odessa and was staying with the princess at her mother's house. Franz took rooms in a hotel for himself and his secretary Gaëtano Belloni, who had accompanied him to Constantinople and arranged for him to give concerts in Odessa. The prince and princess attended these concerts and took Franz with them when they went out into fashionable society. But much of the time he and the princess sat on her mother's sofa together, and talked and talked.

What did they talk about? Chiefly themselves, of course. To begin with, their tastes and opinions, but then their own experiences. He had lived longer than her, thirty-five years to her twenty-eight, and her life had been uneventful compared to his, but to him it was strange, even exotic. The Countess d'Agoult owned a large house in the country, but she did not grow or sell grain or have thirty-thousand serfs, let alone live right in the midst of them like Carolyne. The countess' château was just outside Paris, a rural fantasy, while the princess' was in the middle of nowhere, a rustic reality. Yet the princess, because of her unusual childhood with her father in his library, was even more learned and intellectual than the countess. Furthermore, she was extremely religious and to Franz, who had once wanted to become a priest but had more or less lost interest in religion during his years as a travelling virtuoso, this was deeply stimulating. Above all, although she was a princess, she did not live in the world of fashionable salons and courts like most of the noblewomen he had met. The muddy peasant world she lived in reminded him of his early childhood in Hungary, when his father managed a sheep-station for Prince Esterházy. Except that the princess with her fourteen estates was more like an Esterházy than a peasant. It was all a little like a fairy tale in which the hero, after many adventures, at last comes home to his humble cottage, but with a princess on his arm. And when she invited him jokingly in those very words to spend the winter in 'my little cottage at Woronince', how could he refuse?

As for her, she had enjoyed music before she met Franz, but she had never heard music of the kind he made or even imagined its power over her emotions, and besides there was hardly a woman in Europe who did not find Franz irresistibly handsome and charming, even before he played a note. Perhaps Carolyne might have been the exception if it had not been that in addition to his looks and his music he was so widely-read, so devoted to intellectual argument and inquiry, so keen to return to the Church he had temporarily set aside, so dismissive of what he had achieved, so determined now to give up his travelling circus, make a home for himself and concentrate on composing. On top of all that he liked smoking cigars. For her the fairy tale was a different one. With the loss of her father, first by her marriage and then by his death, she had closed down her emotions, fallen asleep, as it were, to the world beyond her estates, with only her love for her daughter and her Church to sustain her, behind an impenetrable hedge of briars. Now a true prince in all but name had broken through the briars. He had not yet kissed her fully awake, perhaps he would if she invited him again to Woronince.

But what of Prince Nicholas, who although he was separated from the princess and did not even like her, was still legally married to her and still the father of their daughter? He could hardly ignore the growing intimacy between Carolyne and Franz, and many men might have considered themselves insulted and dishonoured. Not he. Unlike Carolyne and Franz, he was a realist not a romantic. He could no longer live with her, had no wish to, and so long as she made him a generous allowance, he had no objection to someone else living with her. If there was insult and dishonour in that, he thought it adhered more to her than to him. Besides, he liked Franz, could see that he and the princess were very well suited to one another and would have plenty still to talk about through a winter at Woronince. He judged that after that Franz would be off on his travels and his amorous interludes again and that he himself would still be married to Carolyne and still guaranteed his generous allowance.

So as their summer holiday in Odessa ended, Franz set out for the little town of Elisabetgrad to give another concert, Prince Nicholas hurried off to the bright lights of Berlin, and the princess went to Woronince to prepare her 'little cottage' for a winter with Franz.

* * *

It was still autumn when Franz and Gaëtano, his secretary, reached Woronince and were given a suite of rooms, in one of which was a piano for Franz. His own piano would arrive later from Odessa. Soon after their arrival, the princess gave a party for Franz's thirty-sixth birthday. She already knew him well enough to know that he always liked to celebrate his birthday. The party was out-of-doors and the guests included hundreds of the princess' tenants and serfs, all of whom were to be let off their usual taxes for a year to mark the occasion. But the special treat for Franz was the arrival of a band of gypsies. Carolyne knew that Franz particularly loved their music, which he had first heard on the other side of the Carpathian Mountains, in his native country, Hungary. Gypsy music, he had told her, was like opium to him, something he needed from time to time as a restorative. Its contrasts of fast and slow, its improvised ornaments, its unwritten variations, discovered and explored by a whole group of players only while they played together seemed to him the essence of music, the heart of its power over the emotions, owing nothing to civilization or academic training. The gypsies proved, he said, that music was as natural to man as breathing.

So the gypsies played, the peasants danced, the sun shone and everyone was happy. But the happiest of all were Carolyne and Franz. Although they did not say so openly, they both knew by now that this was not just a birthday party, but also a secret engagement party. Carolyne's ten-year-old daughter had noticed, of course, how much her mother admired this glamorous man but she thought he was meant to be a husband for her, Marie. She was taken aback when someone—it was no doubt her governess from England, 'Scotchy' Anderson—hinted that her mother might be going to marry Franz. 'But she has a husband already!' said Marie indignantly.

Franz and Carolyne did not consider this to be an insuperable problem as they laid their plans for the future. She would apply to the Czar of Russia, who was the head of the Russian Orthodox Church, for an annulment of her marriage to Prince Nicholas, citing the incident at her wedding when her father had slapped her face to show it was a forced marriage. Franz, meanwhile, would go to Weimar where he had been appointed Kapellmeister-in-Extraordinary to the Grand Duke, whose music-loving wife Maria Pawlowna had enthusiastically encouraged the appointment. A generation earlier, when Goethe and Schiller lived there and directed the theatre, Weimar had been the cultural capital of all Germany, but had since become a backwater again, and it was the ambition of the Grand Duchess Maria Pawlowna and her son Carl Alexander to restore its prestige. This was why they had invited Franz to be their Extraordinary Kapellmeister, although they already had an ordinary one called Hyppolyte Chélard. The Grand Duchess Maria Pawlowna, as luck would have it, was the Czar of Russia's sister. She would surely persuade her brother to grant the annulment of Carolyne's marriage.

Then Carolyne would join Franz in Weimar, where they would be married and set up home together. Franz would conduct and compose, she would support him with her love and if necessary her wealth, and together they would make Weimar one of the great musical centres of the world. All these plans they discussed and embroidered in detail as the snow began to fall and winter set in at Woronince. But Gaëtano, Franz's secretary, who had managed his concert tours and was also spending the winter there, had to be told that he had lost his job. Franz had finished for ever with being a travelling virtuoso and there would be no more concert tours. Gaëtano did not seem to mind, or perhaps, because he was a polite and reasonable man, did not choose to show it.

'I have seen the world,' he said, 'as much of it as I want to. I am tired of travelling and I shall go back to Paris and enjoy the comforts of civilization.'

Those comforts were largely absent at Woronince under snow. The winds from the north and the east blew pitilessly across the open steppes. Carolyne's hordes of servants kept the Russian stoves burning fiercely, but the corridors were icy and the big rooms with their high ceilings full of draughts. During his six years as Franz's manager and secretary, Gaëtano had got used to bad conditions and difficult situations, but here he had nothing to occupy him except trying to keep warm. No wonder he thought longingly of Paris.

The princess, however, was used to the cold, while Franz hardly even noticed it. He was very busy at his piano, improving and completing compositions which he had begun long before, and trying out ideas for new pieces, including a tune he had heard sung by a blind girl in Kiev, and others he had heard at Carolyne's party. He was warmed also by the love of Carolyne's little daughter, princess Marie, who soon became as dear to him as his own two daughters living far away with his mother in Paris. But most of all he felt the constant heat of Carolyne's adoration, and the excitement of knowing that they were starting on a new life together and were secure in each other's love. She gave him a gold ring in the form of a Gordian knot and he wrote to the Countess d'Agoult in Paris to tell her, though not too directly, that he had entered a new relationship with a person of 'great character united with a great spirit'. His former mistress wrote back sarcastically to warn him that such a person would not want to *share* his life with others or be '*one of your mistresses*'. When Franz showed this letter to the princess she was not at all offended.

'I'd be happy for her to know that, on the contrary, there are devotions without limits. One really wants to be *one of the mistresses*.'

She and Franz did not take the countess' taunt too seriously. They were going to be married. In the New Year, as soon as it was possible to travel, Franz left Woronince for Weimar to take up his post there and find a suitable house for them to live in, while the princess went to Kiev to sell some of her estates for ready money, and from there to St Petersburg to submit her petition for the annulment of her marriage. Gaëtano Belloni hastened back to Paris, only to find that the city was on the brink of another revolution. He tried to look on the bright side:

'As between ice and fire,' he said, 'I prefer fire.'

* * *

It was not easy for the princess to part with her estates. The buyers in Kiev began by making derisory offers, thinking they could take advantage of a mere woman, but found she was too sharp for them and too conscious of what she was losing. On her way to Kiev she had visited her father's old house, removed the seals and looked for the last time at the rooms and especially the library where she had grown up. All was exactly as he had left it when he went to church and never returned. Her bitter sorrow was only sweetened by the thought of the man she was going to marry and that her father, if she had sat and talked all night to him in the library, where his box of cigars still lay open on the desk, would surely have agreed that between a conventional prince with no particular talent and a prince of musicians whose work would live forever, there was really no competition. Her eyes full of tears for both the dismal past and the bright future, she mounted her coach and continued her journey to Kiev.

Returning from St Petersburg to Woronince she gathered up her daughter Marie, with her governess, Scotchy Anderson, and a personal maid called Alexandra, hid her jewels and the large sums of money she had taken out of the bank in her luggage and on her person and under the seats of her coach and, without telling any of her neighbours, least of all the Wittgenstein family, set off towards the Russian frontier. It was the beginning of April, very cold still, but as she knew from experience, it was easier to travel before the ice melted and the rivers flooded.

There was a different problem when her coach at last reached the frontier. News had come of a revolution in Paris. Louis-Philippe, the 'Citizen King', had lost his throne and fled to England. And another revolution was breaking out in Hungary. The Hungarians were demanding their independence from the Austrian Empire. There was also unrest in Germany. The people seemed to be turning against their traditional rulers everywhere. The Czar and his ministers were uneasy and were already thinking of closing the borders of Russia to keep out this revolutionary contagion. Meanwhile the border-guards had been told to be particularly vigilant. Instead of accepting a few roubles and waving the princess' coach through their barriers, they carefully inspected all the passports and discovered that Scotchy Anderson's was out-of-date. The whole party, they said, should return to Kiev to get the document renewed.

The princess was sure that if they did, the Wittgenstein family would hear of it and intervene, demanding that her daughter should be left behind in their keeping. And even if they did not, she was afraid that when the party got back to the frontier they would find it completely barred. So she sat down privately with the captain of the border guards and promised him a large sum of money, if he would send one of his own men on horseback at great speed to renew the passport in Kiev. The captain was doubtful, so the princess bowed her head and removed a magnificent pearl necklace from around her neck.

'Have you no wife, Captain?' she asked.

No, he had no wife, but he did have a girl in mind whom he hoped to marry.

'For your future wife, then,' she said, giving him the necklace.

The captain sent his man to Kiev and the princess' party waited several days at the frontier, increasingly nervous as more news came in of the insurrection in the Hungarian city of Pest. But at last the man returned from Kiev, all the passports were stamped and the coach rolled on across the Russian border into the Austrian province of Galicia, edged to the south by the Carpathian mountains.

* * *

One of Franz's closest friends at this time was a young Polish nobleman, heir to large estates in Prussia. Prince Felix Lichnowsky was not on good terms with his parents, who disliked his liberal opinions about politics and had cut off his allowance. Franz had lent him a substantial sum of money earned from his concert tours, and the grateful Felix often urged him to make use of his castle in Silesia, close to Prussia's border with Austria. This was where Franz decided to meet the princess' coach. Prince Felix himself could not be there to receive him since, as a prominent liberal politician, he had to attend a meeting of the parliament in Berlin, but he gave orders to his servants to prepare the rooms and urged Franz to stay in the castle for as long as he wished.

Krzyzanowicz Castle, with thick walls, battlements and towers, standing on a rock above the River Oder, surrounded with wooded hills, might have come straight from a fairy tale. Franz kept lonely state there, surrounded by servants, with his own manservant to look after him personally and his own coachman to drive him about the countryside. But he was too worried that he might be out when the princess arrived to make many excursions and he became more and more worried as she did not appear. He paced the battlements, went up into the towers and stared southwards, started book after book and got no further than the first few chapters before throwing them down. He drank and smoked too much and did not sleep well. He had written to give the princess precise directions from the Russian frontier through Galicia, but perhaps she had not received his letter or had lost it. Worst of all he was afraid that the Wittgenstein family or the Russian authorities or both might have stopped her from leaving and he tried not even to think about the dangers three women and a girl of eleven in a coach full of jewels and cash might run from soldiers or robbers or revolutionaries.

Days passed and Franz began to think that he could not wait any longer, he had to set out across the frontier with Austria to meet her or discover whether anyone had seen her. And then one evening as the sun was setting, he wearily climbed the steps to the battlements for a last look at the road far below, beside the river. Yes, there was a coach coming from the south, but he had so often seen others travelling that way towards Ratibor that he only stifled his hopes, sighed, lit a cigar and turned to look westwards at the gathering clouds streaked with red. 'And suppose she never comes?' he asked himself aloud. 'Suppose she has been prevented from coming or has changed her mind or her coach is lying on its side in a ditch? Then I would rather throw myself down from here than return to Weimar without her.' And he threw his cigar-stub down on the rocks below. But at that very moment he heard horses' hooves and the rattle of carriage wheels over cobbles. Leaping down the steps, he reached the outer courtyard as the coach passed through into the inner one, and running under the archway, saw the coach pull up. He pushed aside the servant who was about to open the coach-door and opened it himself. There she was, his princess, smiling, just as he was, her eyes brimming with tears, just as his were, utterly astonished, just as he was, that they really were together again, as from now on they always would be.

* * *

Or would they? Do not ask, as Franz pulls down the coach's step, as she descends from the coach and they fall into one another's arms, as talking both at once, his arm round her shoulders, hers round his waist, they go inside the fairy-tale castle, followed by Princess Marie hand-in-hand with her governess and the maid Alexandra behind them. This tale ends here in the castle of Krzyzanovicz, where the snow princess and the prince of pianists lived happily for the next ten days.

2. THE NIGHTINGALE

There was once a Grand Duke of Weimar, Carl Alexander, whose city had been famous in his grandfather's time. It was a small city and neither rich nor populous compared to other German cities such as Frankfurt or Munich or Berlin or Hamburg or Leipzig or Dresden, but it was home to the poets Goethe, Schiller and Wieland, the philosopher Herder and the musician Hummel. After the death of the Grand Duke's grandfather, Carl August, and of these five famous men, the Grand Duke's father, Carl Friedrich, was content to rule his duchy wisely and well in the sunset of its glory, but his wife, the Grand Duchess Maria Pawlowna, and their heir, Carl Alexander, wanted the sun to rise again on Weimar.

When they heard the magical playing of the great Hungarian pianist Franz Liszt and learned that he intended one day to cease travelling and settle down to composing and conducting, they asked him to make Weimar his home.

'We are proud of our city's past,' said the young Carl Alexander, but the past is like the Chinese Emperor's mechanical nightingale in the fairy tale. It sings beautifully, but always the same tune. What we want is a real, living nightingale singing new tunes for new days.'

'You are quite right,' said the pianist. 'The law of nature is transformation, the never-ending flow of the past into the present and the present into the future. And this is also what poetry and music are. Nothing would give me greater pleasure than to be your real, living nightingale in Weimar.'

So the Grand Duchess and her son persuaded the Grand Duke, Carl Friedrich, to create a special post for Liszt at the court of Weimar and eagerly awaited his coming. But nothing is ever quite what we expect it to be and when, after a year or two, he did at last arrive, he brought with him a wife. That would have been acceptable enough, since even nightingales need wives when they make a nest for themselves, but unfortunately, although he was a real nightingale, she was not a real wife. Or rather she was a real wife, but not his. Princess Carolyne had every intention of becoming Liszt's wife, but because of her wealth, her real husband, Prince Nicholas, did not wish to give up being married to her, although he no longer wished to live with her. He signified as much to his sovereign and namesake, Czar Nicholas of Russia, who in spite of the intercession of his own sister, the Grand Duchess of Weimar, refused to annul the marriage of Prince Nicholas to Princess Carolyne.

This refusal created a very unpleasant situation in Weimar. To begin with, in order not to offend the court and people of Weimar, where adultery was a crime punishable by a prison sentence, the nightingale and his princess lived apart, he in the Hotel Erbprinz in the middle of the city, she in a large house called the Altenburg on a hill overlooking the city from the far side of the River Ilm. But when word came that the Czar had refused to grant an annulment, Liszt lost his temper:

'Enough of this!' he said to Princess Carolyne. 'We have done our best to spare their sensitivities, but we are not children to be cabined and confined by mechanical rules. If they want me to sing Weimar into glory again, they must allow me the happiness of living with you. I shall move into the Altenburg and we shall be man and wife in spite of this pair of ill-willed Nickol-asses. If they threaten us with prison, we shall simply go elsewhere and there will be no more real, living nightingale and no more glory for Weimar.'

Of course there was no threat of prison, although people in the city complained that there was one law for the well-connected and another for the rest. It had been just the same in the time of the great Goethe, who had lived for many years with a woman who was not his wife. But Goethe's companion had been a peasant and there was never any question of receiving her at court or in Weimar society, whereas Liszt's was a wealthy princess and should have been welcome in the highest circles. As it was, she was entirely excluded, treated as if she didn't or shouldn't exist. No respectable lady could even appear in the same room as her or acknowledge her presence in the theatre, let alone speak to her. For a woman of Carolyne's proud temperament, this was a punishment almost worse than prison. She soon became ill, afflicted with boils, abscesses, nervous pains and rheumatism, and began to spend long periods away from Weimar, seeking cures from the healing waters of Carlsbad, Bad Eilsen and other spas. Whether or not the waters made much difference, the absence from the unforgiving people of Weimar was no doubt a relief in itself.

Liszt, meanwhile, deeply distressed by her afflictions, was further irritated by his own treatment in Weimar. True, the Grand Ducal family continued to value and encourage him in spite of his embarrassing 'wife'. But in creating a special post for Liszt, the Grand Duke Carl Friedrich had neglected to consider that he already had a kapellmeister called Hyppolyte Chélard, whose taste in theatre and music was as dismal and old-fashioned as Liszt's was discriminating and advanced and whose ability to interpret music and conduct an orchestra was lamentable even by the standards of an ordinary kapellmeister. This might not have mattered if the two kapellmeisters could have operated entirely separately, offering the people of Weimar a choice of entertainments in two different buildings. But there was only one theatre in Weimar and this was where all plays and operas, as well as orchestral concerts, had to be performed. One can imagine how unpleasant a task it must have been for the theatre's intendant, Baron von Ziegesar, to arbitrate between these two irreconcilable kapellmeisters and the artistic director of the theatre.

There was only so much that Carl Alexander could do to make things easier for his nightingale. After the death of Czar Nicholas, Princess Carolyne renewed her plea for her marriage to be annulled. The new Czar's response was to summon her to St Petersburg to put her case in person. Afraid that if she obeyed she would not be allowed to leave Russia again, she ignored his summons and he retaliated by sentencing her to exile and sequestering all her property in Russia. Fortunately, on Liszt's advice, she had already given half her estates to her young daughter, Princess Marie, and it was the income from these which for the time being supported Marie, her mother, Liszt and their staff, including Marie's governess, Carolyne's personal maid, Liszt's valet, the housekeeper and two manservants. Since the small state of

Weimar was always in debt, the Grand Duke could not afford to pay Liszt a salary nor even think of building him a concert-hall or   another theatre, but he did at least pension off the incompetent Hyppolyte Chélard. The Grand Duchess, who had an income of her own, gave Liszt some money from time to time, which more or less paid, as he said, for his cigars. But she also bought the Altenburg, the house on the hill, from its previous owner and let Liszt and Carolyne live in it rent-free.

* * *

The young Carl Alexander, meanwhile, treated Liszt as his friend rather than his servant and tried to make up in kindness and affection for all the many ways in which a mere Grand Duke could not emulate an Emperor of China, when it came to keeping a real, living nightingale as a regular part of his court. Soon after the death of Carl Alexander's father, Liszt, who had been away at the time, called on the new Grand Duke at one of his castles outside Weimar—he had several. Ettersburg Castle was surrounded with woods, where Carl Alexander, who was a shy, romantic young man, liked to walk alone. That was where Liszt found him and they walked on together, Liszt condoling with him for the death of his father.

'It was very sudden,' said Carl Alexander, 'no one expected it, least of all me. Quite apart from the shock of losing my dear father, I thought I had many more years to prepare myself for taking on all his duties and responsibilities. But there is one good thing to come out of this. Now that I am Grand Duke I shall be able to make everything easier for my nightingale. The *word* must now become the *deed*.'

Liszt did not like to ask if this meant making more money available, perhaps even building a concert-hall or a second theatre, so he temporized:

'In many ways, sire, it already has. But we need more musicians for the orchestra and they need to be the best.'

It was a fine summer day and Liszt who had hurried to catch up with Carl Alexander and was never much of a walker, wiped the sweat off his face with his handkerchief.

'It's very warm, isn't it?' said Carl Alexander. 'Shall we sit down under that oak tree in the shade and talk about your plans for the future?'

So they sat side by side, with their backs against the trunk and their legs stretched out on the dry earth.

'When you first invited me to be your nightingale,' said Liszt, 'you said that you wanted new tunes for new days. That is exactly what I mean to give you. Not just my own, but those of the greatest composers of our time, whose music is still little known or appreciated. I mean particularly Hector Berlioz and Richard Wagner . . .'

'Wagner!' said Carl Alexander, with a frown. 'That dangerous revolutionary from Dresden?'

'Not at all dangerous,' said Liszt. 'Or only to old-fashioned musicians and audiences. The people of Weimar—your people, sire—will almost certainly be suspicious of and perhaps dislike our new music to begin with. They will criticize me and even perhaps you for encouraging me, but I do believe that in time they will change their minds and be proud to see their city recognized all over Europe as the cradle of new music. It will not be easy, but I promise you that we will change the history of Weimar as well as the history of music for ever afterwards.'

Carl Alexander picked up an acorn from the ground beside him and tossed it from hand to hand.

'Large streams from little fountains flow,' he said in English.

'Sire?'

'"Tall oaks from little acorns grow." We learnt that verse at school,' and he translated it into French, since they were speaking French and Liszt's English was patchy to say the least. 'I will do all I can to support you, but must you include Wagner in your plans? I know that he's a friend of yours and that when he was fleeing from Dresden after the failure of the revolution there, you sheltered him here in Weimar and helped him escape to Switzerland. But he's still wanted by the police in Dresden. Am I to offend my good friend the King of Saxony by encouraging this wanted man's music? In any case, he will certainly not be able to come here to conduct it himself or even hear it, since we have a treaty of extradition with Saxony.'

'I understand that,' said Liszt. 'But we cannot do without Wagner's music. As a man he has many faults, as a musician none but soaring ambition, which is only a fault in those who cannot match it in their work. He can and will. Without Wagner, our new music will be a carriage with only three wheels. But perhaps by performing his operas here, we shall persuade the Germans, even the authorities in Dresden, that it's time to forget and forgive his brief folly in joining that revolution.'

'What I can never understand,' said the Grand Duke, throwing his acorn at an inquisitive squirrel, 'is why artistic people so often support revolutions. It's not at all in their own interests to overthrow the kings and princes who employ them. Revolutionaries and republicans have little interest in art—they're too busy with their own politics.'

'Artists are seldom very rational people,' said Liszt. 'Their emotions smother their reason and they confuse the world they create for themselves with the real world. And perhaps that's understandable when you consider how difficult it is to go from one to the other, from dreams to reality, from reality to dreams. Even more so when you are trying to make your dreams stick—I mean to create something which will not dissolve in the light of day, something which real people out in the real world will recognize and value as a real thing. And such a real thing that it will even outlast the real world of its time and all the real people in it and still be there, and still valuable in a hundred years in another world and to other people. The artists who make such things are revolutionaries of the spirit—as Beethoven was—and if they sometimes behave foolishly and go out on the streets to join actual revolutions—as I once did myself, when I was very young, in Paris— they should no doubt be punished, but only mildly, like children. Otherwise the real world might lose things of incalculable value. Imagine if Wagner had been caught, imprisoned for life or even executed like some of his associates, what riches of the spirit would have been extinguished!'

'When the people of Weimar came out on the streets during that time of revolutions,' said Carl Alexander, 'my father went to meet them and listened patiently to their grievances, which were chiefly with particular officials in his government. Then he agreed to all their demands and immediately dismissed most of his ministers. The people went home quietly and we had no violence in Weimar. I have often wondered—especially now that I occupy my father's place and the same may happen again one day—was that courage or cowardice?'

'Weimar has no soldiers to speak of,' said Liszt, 'so I suppose your father had little alternative. But he was a wise ruler and his ministers probably deserved to be dismissed.'

'And now I am to support this musical revolution of yours, and even take up the cause of Wagner. Is that so wise?'

'More than wise, sire, farsighted. And certainly courageous.'

* * *

Carl Alexander may have underestimated the courage as well as the cost and difficulty involved in bringing new glory to Weimar, but he was not disappointed by the result. His Extraordinary Kapellmeister indeed began to compose with extraordinary energy. He wrote new pieces for the piano and revised old ones and for the orchestra he wrote two piano concerti, two symphonies and twelve symphonic poems, a new kind of orchestral music which he himself invented. He also wrote many songs for voice and piano.

The new Grand Duke might well have been satisfied if his nightingale had composed only half the music he did. But in addition Liszt attracted and encouraged other musicians, both those of his own generation and those of the next. Young musicians flocked to Weimar to be near him and learn from him. He reorganized his lamentable predecessor's lamentable orchestra, picking the best instrumentalists he could find to lead it, and for the operas of Berlioz and Wagner, which no one else at that time cared or dared to perform, the best singers. And although these artistes could have earned more in larger cities with more famous orchestras, they were glad to come to Weimar to work with Liszt. Then, with the help of his new orchestra, he himself mastered both the art of orchestration—something he had hardly attempted before—and of conducting. In fact, the new generation of musicians learned not only how to make a piano sing from this greatest of all pianists, but also how to make an orchestra sing from this first of modern conductors.

So glory returned to Weimar and for a few years, in spite of the Princess' illnesses and the hatred of the citizens of Weimar, which made it almost impossible for her to walk down a street without being insulted, she and Liszt presided over the Altenburg, with its flock of young pupils from all over Europe and America, and a constant stream of distinguished visitors—writers and artists as well as musicians. The place was like a rival court to the Grand Ducal palace in Weimar, with the difference, as the elderly poet Hoffmann von Fallersleben remarked, that the palace was for those who *had* something, whereas the Altenburg was for those who *were* somebody or had *done* something. Since he was himself a former revolutionary wanted by the police and had been given protection and a salary by the Grand Duke so that he could edit a Weimarian cultural magazine, this remark, if it ever came to the ears of Carl Alexander, could only have borne out his opinion of artists and their ingratitude to princes. However, Hoffmann's support for revolution was perhaps less for republicanism than for the unification of Germany. It was he who wrote the words for what eventually became the German national anthem: *'Deutschland, Deutschland über alles'*.

Soon after Hoffman's arrival in Weimar he and his pretty sixteen-year-old wife Ida attended a grand lunch party at the Altenburg to celebrate Carl Alexander's thirty-sixth birthday. The table was laid with silver and flowers, course followed course, fine wine followed fine wine and they drank the Grand Duke's health in champagne. The other guests were all musicians, including the brilliant young Russian pianist Anton Rubinstein, who liked and admired Liszt, but did not share his enthusiasm for what the Princess had christened 'the music of the future'.

'Music is just music,' he said, when the Princess raised the topic over lunch. 'And everyone composes and plays it according to his own skill and taste. But how can you say one composer's music looks back and another's forward? We all look back to Bach and Mozart and Beethoven, we all live and work in the present. What do we know of the future?'

'The music we are composing and encouraging here,' said the Princess, 'will set the patterns for the future, rather than simply repeat the patterns of the past.'

'But how can you be so sure of that?' asked Rubinstein. 'Future musicians will pick and choose from the composers of the past, just as we do. In my opinion they will prefer almost anyone else at all to that tedious Frenchman Berlioz.'

'If you call him tedious,' said Liszt sharply, trying not to sound as angry as he felt, 'it must be because you don't know his music well enough yet. Berlioz is surprising us all the time with new sounds and colours, and his music will sail gloriously into the future because no future musician will be able to ignore his discoveries.'

'But is music like science—a kind of knowledge that's always progressing? We have railways now instead of stage-coaches—a great improvement, true progress. Is music like that? Is Beethoven better than Bach? I don't think so.'

'It's not a question of progress, no,' said another guest, Franz Brendel, the editor of an influential music magazine in Leipzig, 'but of newness. We have already got Bach and Beethoven, we can play their music whenever we like. But we do not want a generation of sub-Bachs and sub-Beethovens.'

'Well, God forbid there should be a future generation of sub-Berliozes!' said Rubinstein. 'It would be the end of music.'

Hoffmann listened to all this with interest and decided there and then that he would support Liszt and the music of the future. But he was a little nervous. He had promised a surprise for the feast and didn't yet know his hosts well enough to be sure how they would take it. After the toast to Carl Alexander had been drunk and they had all sat down again, Hoffman rose, a little unsteadily after all that fine wine and read three odes he had composed the night before, one to the Princess, one to her daughter Marie and one to Liszt. The Princess had tears in her eyes as she thanked him. And from then on Hoffman became an assiduous court-poet to both courts, the Ducal Palace and the Altenburg.

* * *

The news of Liszt's productions of strange new operas by Berlioz and Wagner, and of Liszt's own ground-breaking compositions, began to spread, and like the passage of more powerful boats on a calm sea, caused waves and swells which severely unsettled the people in older, more traditional craft. Music lovers formed factions. Those, like Rubinstein, who supported the old music denied that this new Liszt was any sort of nightingale and likened him more to a crow, whose 'music of the future' was a coarse and cacophonous affront to the music of the real nightingales of the past, Haydn and Hummel, Mozart and Beethoven. They ignored the fact that Liszt was not attempting to displace these composers, whom he greatly admired, but to travel further into the unexplored regions of music on paths they had first opened up. No one, indeed, had done more than he to make Beethoven's music better known and appreciated. As for Hummel, the former nightingale of Weimar, Liszt had once wished to study with him and in his days as a virtuoso had often played his music, but Hummel's family, who still lived in the city, blackened Liszt's name and would have nothing to do with him.

There was still another thing that separated Liszt and his princess from the people of Weimar: their religion. Weimar, with the other states of northern Germany, had long ago followed the recalcitrant monk Luther in rejecting the authority of the Pope and the Catholic Church, and becoming Protestant. But Liszt and especially Carolyne were fervent Catholics and became all the more so now that they lived among Protestants. It would have suited them much better if they could have changed their allegiance, since the Protestant church would have allowed Carolyne to divorce her husband and marry Liszt. But this they could not even consider and the princess, having failed to move the Czar, began to approach the authorities of the Catholic Church, bishops, archbishops, nuncios and eventually the Pope himself, for the annulment of her marriage. Along with presiding over the musical court at the Altenburg and seeking cures at spas, this became her chief occupation. She and Liszt would sit together in his room, he composing, she writing long voluble letters to anyone and everyone who might further her cause.

After some years Prince Nicholas himself fell in love with another woman, sought and obtained a Protestant divorce from Carolyne and remarried, but in the eyes of the Catholic Church he was still married to Carolyne and since she would not abjure her faith, she still could not abjure her marriage. The situation was quite ridiculous but inexorable: only the Pope, advised by his cardinals, could release her, and meanwhile, in spite of the sixth commandment imposed by the faith she would not give up, she continued to commit the sin of adultery by living with Liszt.

How much more complicated people's lives are than nightingales'! The songs of this human nightingale directly reflected his unsteady circumstances, the free flight of his creative powers, the curbs and checks administered by his detractors and enemies, the sorrows and sicknesses of his princess, the obligations he felt towards those less fortunate than himself, the longing to serve and be worthy of that strange three-person Christian God he believed in, who was at once the force that drove the universe and the perfect model of humility, resignation and passive suffering.

The symphonies and symphonic poems Liszt composed were all based on the poems or plays or paintings he admired, but became, when translated into pure music and infused with his own feelings, less stories than streams of mood, confluences of conflicting emotion. Goethe's *Faust* and *Tasso*, Dante's *Divine Comedy*, Shakespeare's *Hamlet*, Byron's *Mazeppa*, the Greek classical heroes Orpheus the singer and Prometheus the bringer of fire to men, all became extensions of himself, models of strife and struggle, hope and fear, creative inspiration, endurance, error and redemption. In *The Battle of the Huns* he took his theme from a famous painting by Kaulbach and shared victory with a Christian army over pagans. In other musical poems suggested by the poems of Hugo and Lamartine, he conjured up the grandeur and solitude of mountains and the gamut of human experience—love, suffering, despair, triumph. But of all the music he created at Weimar, the most personal and most perfect was his 'Piano Sonata', for here he explored on his own instrument, with all the skill he possessed, his deepest feelings. Here he sang of his love for the princess and his love of God, of his battles to overcome the brutish nature of the material world both in himself and in those who constantly opposed him, of his doubts and resolutions, excitements and hesitations, but finally of his quiet contentment at having found true love and its true musical expression.

No, Carl Alexander could not conceivably have expected that his nightingale would sing like this, nor could he, any more than most other people, appreciate how rare and wonderful this music was, as if a great painter had filled all the rooms of his castle with the colours and forms of human life. Nor surely could he see the true glory of what he had done by bringing this particular nightingale to Weimar when he could not really afford such an exquisite and expensive luxury. For if Liszt's life there had been as smooth and easy as that of the mythical bird in that far-away Chinese Empire, his music might have been as sweet, but never as original or profound as it became when painfully distilled from the infuriating reality of Weimar.

Perhaps, therefore, this fairy tale ends happily, as most fairy tales do. But not for Liszt and his princess. After eleven years of mingled pleasure, triumph and torment, the nightingale resigned his post, and he and his bedraggled mate left Weimar. They never did succeed in being married, even after the death of Prince Nicholas, and though they remained friends, they chose to live apart. Their best days were over, their hopes frustrated, their love muted, their hearts saddened.

XI. A Faust Symphony

1. MEPHISTOPHELES

My principal occupation is to spy on human affairs, and if it seems expedient, to manipulate them. An enviable occupation, you will agree. What could be more intriguing and entertaining than to observe and play on people's quirks and contradictions, their vanities and weaknesses, but also their pride and strength, their principles and ambitions, their judgment and prejudice? It keeps me in a perpetual fever of anticipation, activity and adjustment. It is a constant pleasure to pull one string and then another, to see them dance with delight or slump in dejection.

Yes, the metaphor is just. I do see myself as a puppet-master, though of course the actors in my theatre are not lifeless puppets, nor even professional artistes with learned lines and business, but in their own eyes, free agents. And the more sensitive and intelligent they are, the greater their gifts and potentialities, the better the show. Because the more they demand of me the more I demand of myself, the higher the wire we all walk on, the narrower the gap between success and failure. But I flatter myself that I seldom fail—not solely because I am clever and experienced, but because I nearly always have the advantage. Working as I do in the shadows, invisible to my 'actors', I am already well informed about their habits and characteristics and have made my plans for them even before I bring them into the light of my stage.

Free agents? That is most people's view of themselves, but I wonder if it really is so and I must say that my plans are mostly based on the opposite assumption, that if you know enough about the person you are approaching, it is not all that hard to predict his or her reaction in certain given circumstances. Consider those famous characters Doctor Faustus and Don Juan, both fictional types rather than living people—though they may once have been based on living people—but representing two of the highest aspirations of humanity. Faustus stands for intelligence and knowledge, the pursuit and understanding of science, mathematics, theology, even magic—the mastery of the mind. Don Juan stands for aristocracy, glamour, charisma, the arts of persuasion and seduction—the mastery of the emotions. If he had not been so concentrated on women, he would no doubt have been a consummate politician.

Now are these two really free agents? Can one envisage them exchanging roles: Don Juan grubbing in libraries and laboratories, Faustus fumbling petticoats? Yes, Faustus does fumble a petticoat, but only when magic puts it in his way. As for Don Juan, the very idea of learning, let alone study and research, would be anathema to him, simply despicable. And although living people are seldom either as highly-defined or as gifted as these two, they are certainly at least equally limited by their ideas of themselves as well as their actual shortcomings.

For a long time now, I have had my eye on a person who seems to combine several aspects of both Faustus and Don Juan, the pianist and composer Liszt. His learning is narrower than that of Faustus, but hardly less enthusiastic, and Liszt's preeminent skill as a pianist and power over all who hear him amounts to a kind of magic equivalent to, if less dangerous than Faustus' power over spirits. With Don Juan, Liszt shares social graces, glamour and persuasiveness, even if he lacks aristocratic ancestors and has seduced fewer women. Liszt, however, has other characteristics (apart from his musical talent), entirely absent from either Faustus or Don Juan: he seems to be unusually generous, especially towards other musicians—*most* unusual—compassionate towards the unfortunate, and idealistic. And there are curiously conflicting elements in his makeup—this is, of course, one of the main and most fascinating differences between a fictional character and a living person.

Liszt is a believing Catholic of the reactionary, ultramontane variety—that's to say he fully accepts the Pope's authority and what could

be more reactionary than that?—yet he sympathizes with revolutionaries. Although, apart from visiting Hungarian barricades in Vienna,
wearing their colours in his buttonhole and writing a chorus for the
workers, he has only once—in Paris, when he was very young—taken
an active part in their manifestations. Meanwhile he is at present living with a Polish aristocrat, the Princess von Sayn-Wittgenstein, who is
if possible even more fervently Catholic and more idealistic than he is,
though they both somehow manage to overlook the fact that she is
married to somebody else and that they are therefore breaking the law
of God and the social *mores* of man. But no, they don't overlook this,
because they are continually trying to obtain an annulment of her
marriage and she is shunned, in spite of her rank, by all the
respectable ladies of Weimar, where they are currently living. They
don't overlook it, they *override* it, which does suggest perhaps that they
are truly, proudly, ostentatiously free agents.

I myself employ agents who are decidedly not free. They get their
instructions from me and they report back to me regularly. They have
a certain freedom of manoeuvre, of course, a tactical freedom, but the
strategy is always in my hands. Am I then a free agent myself? Not
absolutely. I too follow instructions, though of a much broader kind
and I have a considerable voice in choosing the field of operations. I
am, if you like, an important member of a general staff—not the most
important, but not the least—and once the field of operations has
been agreed upon, I am absolutely free to draw up the detailed plans,
to organize their implementation, to issue the necessary instructions
to my subordinates and to change or countermand initiatives as the
plan unfolds.

The watch I keep on Liszt is partly out of personal interest—he is
one of the most remarkable individuals of our time—but also partly
for larger political reasons. Since the upheavals of 1848–49—when
Liszt, incidentally, sheltered the fugitive Richard Wagner, who had
taken part in the revolutionary violence in Dresden, and helped him
escape to Switzerland—Germany has become a much more volatile
part of the world. The German Confederation, set up by the Congress
of Vienna after the defeat of Napoleon Bonaparte in order to control
and simplify relations between the multitudinous independent states
of Germany, is showing serious cracks and probably cannot now be
mended. Its two most powerful members are surely on a collision

course. Mighty Austria is on the decline, upstart Prussia on the rise. Which way will all the other states jump?

The sovereign state of Weimar, small as it is, is especially interesting in this context. The Grand Duke has only recently succeeded his father. His mother is the sister of the late Czar of Russia, his wife is the daughter of the King of Holland, his sister is Princess Augusta of Prussia. Under his father, Weimar was allied with Russia, Hanover and Prussia, but will this continue under the new ruler? Liszt's importance on this chessboard is minimal, of course—hardly even that of a pawn—nevertheless it was the new Grand Duke who, wanting to revive Weimar's international reputation as a centre of cultural excellence, which faded with the death of the great poet Goethe, invited Liszt to Weimar and created the post of Honorary Kapellmeister specially for him. They are as close friends as two men of such different stations in life can be, so that scarcely anyone is better placed to know the mind of the new Grand Duke than Liszt. He himself does not seem to be a political animal—except in musical matters—but his mistress the Polish princess undoubtedly is and they receive many odd visitors at their house who would not be *personae gratae* in less liberal states than Weimar or under rulers less indulgent to his tame genius than the new Grand Duke. In addition, both Liszt and his Princess have many friends in the foreign embassies, especially those of France and Russia.

I have an agent, of course, at the court of Weimar, but rulers do not always share their inmost thoughts with courtiers and I therefore placed another agent in what I may call Liszt's court—that's to say among the ambitious young musicians who come to Weimar to learn from him. This particular young man, K219, more talented as a musician than a spy, was frankly not much use to me, so when he informed me that he wished to leave Weimar and move to England to pursue his musical career, I quickly agreed and sent a more reliable substitute, sufficiently talented as a musician, though not quite in the same class. A77's huge advantage was in being a very pretty young woman, and in Liszt's eyes that makes up for a great many wrong notes on the piano. Imagine my vexation when she too had to leave Weimar only a couple of months after her arrival! She was pregnant—not by Liszt, she had not been there long enough, but by one of my other agents during her previous assignment. I reprimanded her severely, her mother took her off to Hamburg to bear the child early this year, and she was pencilled in to return to Weimar and get to know Liszt better—he had already shown a marked interest in her—in late autumn.

But meanwhile, in those important months when the new Grand Duke was feeling his way, and no doubt seeing much of the man he had installed as Weimar's latest Goethe, I had no agent in place. In my occupation one may be irritated and incommoded by checks like this, but one neither wrings one's hands nor washes them, one acts. The rest of my organization was functioning smoothly, so, curious to observe this celebrated man in person rather than simply through my files on him, I decided to bridge the hiatus myself. I adopted the identity and disguise of an English baronet, Sir George Eliot—my English is excellent and the former revolutionary Liszt has almost as much time for a title as he does for a pretty face—and took the train to Weimar.

'The Athens of the North' is a small place—ridiculously small and provincial considering its reputation—and by discovering the inn where Liszt and his pupils are often accustomed to drink together far into the night, I was soon able to brush shoulders with the great man in a particularly happy mood and elicit an invitation to visit him at his large house, on a hill overlooking the town. I presented myself as an ardent student of Goethe, which indeed was a comfortable alibi, since I am reasonably well versed in Goethe's work and besides it explained my fluent German. In fact, Liszt's German was not particularly fluent and he preferred to speak French. That was no problem—my French is excellent—and we were soon on friendly terms. Indeed, I can claim that one afternoon when we were sitting in his library discussing *Faust*, I had a hand in one of his major compositions.

Liszt had been introduced to Goethe's masterpiece a quarter of a century earlier, by his friend Berlioz, who many years later composed his opera *La Damnation de Faust* and dedicated it to Liszt. This was one of the works performed in Weimar under Liszt's regime during his Berlioz Festival a year or so before and he told me that he had had the greatest difficulty in assembling the very large orchestra it required. Three of his own piano pupils had to be drafted into the percussion section. I asked their names and was amused to learn that my initial agent, K219, had played the cymbals. Meanwhile, however, the subject of Faust had been constantly on Liszt's mind and he had thought of writing a Faust opera himself. That didn't surprise me, since as I've suggested, I'd already marked him down as a partly Faustian character. What did surprise me was that he too saw himself as Faust.

'Yourself particularly?' I asked. 'Or do you mean that all intellectuals are potential Fausts?'

'Myself particularly,' he said. 'It is kind of you, Sir George, to call me an intellectual, but I don't think I am. For me, the essence of Faust is his longing for something beyond this material world. Chemistry and mathematics fail him, theology fails him, even dabbling in magic fails him, he wants the infinite. So do I. At the same time he is a sensual person, easily seduced by material pleasures, though equally easily bored and disgusted by them. So am I. And he is a person of wildly fluctuating moods, passing from ecstasy to despair, from doubt to confidence, from scorn to admiration, from contentment to anger, almost at the turn of a phrase or the rattle of a window-frame. So am I.'

He suddenly stood up, closed the offending window against the rising wind outside, fetched a box of cigars from a table, offered me one and, sitting down again, lit one himself.

'I have not noticed such moods in you,' I said. 'In our admittedly short acquaintance you have been nothing but calm and gracious and, if I may say so, princely in your attention to a complete stranger.'

'No longer that, I hope,' he said. 'But if you knew me better, you might be shocked by an inner person whom the world seldom sees, because I choose it should not.'

He waved his cigar in the air, making a circle of smoke around himself.

'Tobacco, coffee, wine, brandy, young men and women at my heels—I need all these calmants and stimulants to keep me steady. And really what is Mephistopheles to Faust but his other self, a mocking self, but also a necessary self, supplying constant short-term distractions, a variety of calmants and stimulants to keep him from plunging into the abyss? Mephistopheles is far from enticing Faust into hell, he is keeping him *out* of hell for the period of his life.'

'An interesting interpretation,' I said. 'But where does the episode with Gretchen fit in—Faust's seduction and abandonment of that innocent girl whom he has made pregnant and ruined?'

Liszt looked at me slyly.

'I'm sure you know my bad reputation, Sir George,' he said. 'Are you inviting me to confess that I have ruined far more women than Faust ever did?'

'Perish the thought!' I said. 'I know that many women have loved you, but I have never heard that any of them at all resembled the naive, lower-class Gretchen or that you *ruined* anyone. I did not mean anything personal by my remark, but only to discover how the third person in what is, for all its many subsidiary characters, really only a three-person drama, fitted in with your singular interpretation.'

He was silent for a while, and when he spoke, seemed to have forgotten the main drift of my question.

'Yes, you are quite right. Three persons.'

Then, muttering to himself, 'Three movements. A symphony in three movements,' he got up, left me to consult a book on his shelves, which was my excuse for calling on him, and went to preside over one of his master-classes.

I had to leave Weimar soon afterwards to attend to some crisis at headquarters. Liszt was away in the early summer conducting at a music festival in Rotterdam. When I returned in August and renewed my acquaintaince with him, he offered to introduce me to his friend and patron, the Grand Duke. Now here was an opportunity! But no, I rejected it, saying that I was afraid my studies in the Goethe archive— I was pretending to be researching a biography—would suffer if I was swept up into court occasions, which with my supposed rank I certainly would have been. My real reason, of course, was that somebody at court, if not the Grand Duke himself, would surely see through my imposture. Noblemen of all countries are jealous of their status and privileges and with their almost encyclopaedic knowledge of everybody's bloodlines, have many subtle and not so subtle ways of sniffing out intruders. I had chosen to be a baronet, rather than something grander such as a viscount or earl, precisely because people with this peculiarly English hereditary title are a little more obscure, often with only relatively brief family histories and limited connections with the real aristocracy, but the risk of being exposed was still not worth running for all I, as a foreign visitor, would be able to learn from meeting the Grand Duke.

Yet all of a sudden—such are the chances of my trade—I was threatened with a far greater likelihood of exposure from a much more unexpected quarter. Invited by my ever obliging host to a 'second breakfast' at his house at eleven in the morning, I arrived in good time and was shown by Heinrich, the manservant, into the garden, where the breakfast was charmingly laid out under trees which arched over and formed a kind of roof to this alfresco dining-room. Several other guests were already there, standing about awaiting their hosts. There was a well-known German poet, a less well-known German artist, a German professor—author of a work, I overheard him boasting, on the eleven-thousand virgins—and Liszt's musical assistant, Raff, who told me that Liszt had begun to compose a *Faust Symphony* in three movements. But the sting in the tail was a pair of authors from England, introducing themselves as Mr and Mrs Lewes. Fearing that these people would soon see through my disguise, I was about to plead a sudden indisposition and depart. But at that moment our hosts appeared, Liszt himself, his Princess and her seventeen-year-old daughter, Princess Marie, a young nephew, Prince Eugène, and the daughter's governess.

Having lived in London at one period myself, and keeping watch on it through agents, as I did on all important European centres of activity, I knew of Mr and 'Mrs' Lewes by repute, though fortunately not personally. She was not, in fact, his wife, but an unmarried woman called Mary Ann Evans, who wrote articles for *The Westminster Gazette* and had translated two German religio-philosophical books, Strauss' *Life of Jesus* and Feuerbach's *Essence of Christianity*. George Henry Lewes was much better known, partly from his multifarious writings—novels, blank-verse tragedies, in one of which he acted himself, and biographies, including the four-volume *Biographical History of Philosophy*, in addition to innumerable articles—partly from his reputation as a man-about-town, and partly from the scandal of his private life. He had married a beautiful woman, daughter of a Member of Parliament. They had produced several children before she fell in love with her husband's friend Thornton Hunt—they were fellow-founders and editors of *The Leader*—and began to have more children by Hunt. This did not end the marriage, since Lewes gallantly treated these cuckoos in the nest as his own and continued to live with his wife, as Hunt did with his. One has to admire the English—they are clearly leading the way into a new world domestically as well as industrially. But now here before my eyes was a fresh twist in the already ravelled Lewes ménage, Miss Evans posing as Mrs Lewes for a kind of honeymoon in Germany.

They were an ill-favoured couple on the verge of being middle-aged. Miss Evans had the large nose and jaw of a man, while Lewes had a receding chin and a little screwed-up face like a monkey. But what they lacked in looks they made up in intelligence. Both of them spoke French and German and knew the literature of both, while Lewes, it transpired to my alarm, had come to Weimar to research a biography of Goethe. Liszt, of course, with his usual generosity of spirit, thought this was the more reason for us to get to know each other and share ideas.

'And both of you called "George",' he said with his winning smile. 'This must be a lucky coincidence.'

I could see that Lewes thought, as I did, quite the reverse and that Miss Evans was almost equally distressed on his behalf. They asked me, of course, where I lived, and this was a fraught moment, because I was afraid one or other of them might have grown up in the very place I had chosen for my 'seat'—as the English call their aristocrats' country-houses.

'Trewenna,' I said, 'in Cornwall'. I had reckoned this was about as far from civilized life in England as one could find—even Liszt had not been there on either of his tours of the country.

All was well. Cornwall was indeed beyond their knowledge. She had been brought up in the Midlands and he had spent his childhood in Brittany and the Channel Islands. But something was worrying Lewes.

'You have quite a noticeable German accent, Sir George,' he said, fixing me with his beady little monkey eyes.

'Really?' I said with genuine pique, having always prided myself on my pukka English.

'Your "w"s,' said Lewes. 'Trevenna . . . Cornvall.'

'I spend much time abroad, especially in Germany,' I said, silently cursing my unlucky choice of location.

But we were now urged to take our places at the table. I began to edge away from Lewes, but Liszt would have none of this.

'You must have a great deal to say to one another,' he pronounced and seated us opposite each other, either side of the Princess.

Miss Evans was at the far end of the table, between Liszt and the Princess Marie's governess, another English person—or perhaps Scottish, since she was known as 'Scotchy'.

I have to say that our hostess looked, if possible, even less attractive than Miss Evans. The Princess' dumpy appearance—she was dressed in black with a black bonnet—astonished me. Was this the woman with whom the ladykiller Liszt intended to share the rest of his life? What did he see in her? The only answer I could find was: a mother. Her intelligence and her breadth of knowledge, especially on theological topics, were another possible answer or perhaps further aspects of the first answer. Liszt was self-educated, always aspiring to learn more, and by now, as if to make up for his years of Byronic excess, distinctly pious. This was a woman, I soon realized, who would have cramped even Don Juan's style and that must have been in part what Liszt wanted. I recalled what he had said about Faust—that it was Mephistopheles, his mocking, other self, who kept him *out* of hell. With the Princess at his side, perhaps he felt less danger of falling into the abyss.

Lewes and I, meanwhile, had tacitly and absolutely agreed, with but a single glance between us, that one topic we had no wish to discuss was Goethe, but the Princess immediately broached it, with such an imperious tone that the whole table had to listen. She spoke at inordinate length, so I will only summarize the gist of it.

'You will correct me if I'm wrong, gentlemen,' she said, speaking French, with a nod to the rival Goetheans on either side of her and no intention whatever of being corrected, 'but it has always seemed to me that Goethe was not the great man he thought he was or as many people still think he was. A great egotist, certainly, and he would have done better if he had not tried to be so many things at once—poet, dramatist, novelist, botanist, biologist, entrepreneur, administrator. He never quite amounted to the sum of his parts.'

'But that is just what makes him so great,' said Lewes, himself a man of many parts, 'that he would not rest on any single achievement, but needed to explore every corner of human knowledge and experience'.

'Exploring is all very well for young men,' said the Princess, 'but achievement is what one looks for from middle age, and from old age, mastery. For that, concentration is necessary, rather than a diffusion of creative energies.' She was looking at Liszt as she spoke, evidently reading him a lesson, and evoked one of his wonderful smiles. I saw that Miss Evans, next to him, was already smitten, but—given Liszt's weakness for pretty faces—Lewes was not, I thought, in much danger of losing his latest 'wife'.

'Do you not think, Madam, that Goethe created at least one masterpiece in his old age—the full version of *Faust*?' I said.

'Masterpiece it may be—that is a rather vague term,' said the Princess, 'but, if so, a very unsatisfactory one, both dramatically and theologically. The saving of Faust' soul at the end seems to be entirely arbitrary, with no basis whatever in what has gone before and certainly none in Christian doctrine.'

'How right you are!' I said. 'And surely he recognized that and found it unsatisfactory himself, since it was not published until after his death.'

'I cannot agree with you there,' said Lewes. 'The doctrine may not be narrowly Christian but it is a doctrine of redemption. Faust is on the side of human progress and finds happiness at last in the knowledge of having bettered mankind.'

'He imagines he has,' I said, 'but his great scheme for rolling back the sea and creating new land for development is all devil's magic and will swiftly be negated when the sea rolls back again to drown the population.'

'Not at all,' said Lewes. 'You are seeing it from the point of view of Mephistopheles, for whom everything is negation. The population may or may not perish, but Faust's intention was good. From Faust's point of view his soul is saved by angels. And that is also Goethe's point of view. Mephistopheles' negation is negated in its turn by the power of love, both human and divine.'

The argument rolled on for a while without any dramatic or theological resolution. The Princess took grave exception to Lewes' 'merely humanist' interpretation of Christianity, which, she said, negated its essence almost as effectively as Mephistopheles' ephemeral magic.

The other people round the table were mostly silent, except for a few whispered exchanges—I wondered, in fact, how many of the Germans present could follow their voluble French. After a while, Liszt managed to change the subject by handing round cigars and asking the poet to read some of his verses. But then it began to rain and we hurried indoors, where Liszt was persuaded to play one of his own compositions, a gently rapturous piece called *Bénédiction de Dieu dans la solitude*. Its choice was no doubt a graceful way of demonstrating whose side he took in the theological dispute between Lewes and the Princess.

I had seen and heard him play in public during his *Glanzzeit* and was prepared for his brilliance, but not for the irresistible insinuation of his playing on this occasion. It was still a 'performance', but perfectly adjusted to capture the hearts and souls of a dozen people instead of thousands. His smile came and went during the quiet, contemplative passages, his head went further back and his nostrils dilated when the music became more intense, and his fingers lingered on the notes or leapt up and down the keyboard as if quite independent of their owner, whose eyes occasionally rested on individual members of his audience, most of all, I thought, on Miss Evans. Perhaps he meant to draw her away from the modern rationalist version of Christianity favoured by Lewes—and which, to judge by the books she had translated, she favoured too—towards a more traditional, devotional one. What a seducer the man must be when he wants the woman's body as well as her mind!

I hastened to leave Weimar after this episode. Liszt was preoccupied with the composition of his symphony and I did not intend to knock heads with Lewes over the manuscripts in the Goethe archive. He and Miss Evans were going to be in Weimar until the end of October. By then I hoped to have A77 back in station and if there was any useful information to be got out of Liszt on the subject of the Grand Duke's policies, she would surely elicit it.

I should mention perhaps that Lewes' biography of Goethe was published at the end of the following year and was very well received— as a machine for writing the man was certainly a phenomenon. Miss Evans, however, became eventually the more famous and successful author of the two, under the masculine pen name, George Eliot. Did she borrow my false identity unconsciously or did she have more of a sense of humour than I detected? She and Lewes must surely have made inquiries about me when they returned to England and quickly discovered that I did not exist. So I like to think that although my visits to Weimar gave me no political leverage, they had at least some influence on both English literature and German music.

As for that *Faust Symphony*—one of Liszt's finest works—he finished it in two months and it was indeed constructed in three movements, entitled 'Faust', 'Gretchen' and 'Mephistopheles'. Each movement bore the character suggested, but all were built out of the same musical material, so that the whole was, as it were, seen subjectively from Faust's point of view, with the last movement transforming his dreams and aspirations into mockery and negation. Although this seemed to reflect my own remarks at the breakfast-party, I did not think it could be very pleasing to the Princess and sure enough a few years later Liszt tacked on a new ending, a setting of the last chorus from Goethe's drama: 'All that passes is but appearance . . . Eternal Womanhood draws us upwards'. Yes, indeed! Or possibly downwards, depending on what sort of womanhood you are drawn by. So much, anyway, for the idea that anyone, even Liszt, is really a free agent.

2. GRETCHEN

Report 111154/FL/001/A77. I think this is going to work. The Princess likes me and so does Liszt. Only *he* likes me a lot and she is just friendly. It's rather an ordeal playing for him, of course. It's not that he scolds me for my mistakes—he is very gentle—but I have to perform in front of all those young lions and the odd lioness around him and some of them are really good. Still, cousin Karl was a young lion himself, so they treat me with some respect for his sake.

Marginal note: 'no names! Agent K219 in future.'

Mr and Mrs Lewes left just over a week ago. They couldn't go to Dresden as they intended, because they ran out of money. She got some out of Liszt by translating an article of his, for her husband's journal in London. The subject was 'The Romantic School of Music'— Wagner and Meyerbeer. I think the Princess helps him with his writings, but she's very long-winded and this one had to be cut down a lot.

I've found a nice little apartment in the old town and a woman to look after George, who is crawling now and I'm sure will soon be walking. I called him after you, not his father, since I really don't like the name Ernest, though I do still have a soft spot for the person and we worked really well together in Leipzig until that sharp-eyed Anton Rubinstein recognized me in spite of being dressed as a man. I was, I mean, not Rubinstein!

Marginal note: '*no names*!'

Report 25/11/54/FL/002/A77. L. has been to my apartment! Not on his own, but with two other pupils. They came to see George—I'm allowed to write his name, aren't I?—it will be quite a long time, after all, until he's ready to be an agent. He didn't behave particularly well—he's teething, of course—but they all agreed he is a very handsome boy. So he ought to be, with me for mother and E26 for father.

Very bad blood between L. and the people who run the theatre. Last year L. didn't conduct anything here for six months, he was so angry at being kept out of the theatre by a play called *The Maiden from the World of the Fairies*. But this is artistic politics and you want the real thing. I'll try to oblige.

Report 3/12/54/FL/003/A77. L. has been to my apartment on his own, after dark. I did not let him go too far, don't want him to think I'm an easy catch. But it's hard to resist him, not because he's a pouncer, far less a rapist, but because he is so very eloquent, so very handsome, so very kind and straightforward, so very lovable. And that's before he begins to play his music. I wouldn't let him play on the piano in my apartment, (a) because it was late, (b) because anyone hearing it from the street would immediately know who was playing, (c) because I really would be helpless under such enchantment. We did not discuss politics at all, I'm afraid, but I'm sure we will one of these days—or nights.

Report 18/12/54/FL/004/A77. L. came again to my apartment. I had almost decided the moment had come to fall into his arms, when George began crying and I had to go to him. I'm sorry about this. Agents shouldn't, of course, have children around them, but whose fault is this? Well, partly mine, I know, but also partly yours. You expect me to use my charms for the sake of information, but information obtained in that way sometimes has to be paid for later. Never mind! L. is coming back the day after tomorrow in the afternoon and I have arranged for my woman to look after George all day.

Report 21/12/54/FL/005/A77. Yes, we are lovers! I know it's supposed to be all in the day's work, but work is sometimes a pleasure and you know I wouldn't have done this if it meant getting into bed with just anyone. I'm sure you have other agents who are more professional. L. is a practised lover, of course, not at all tentative, but as passionate and also as tender as you can imagine—like his music. He told me that music is really only an inferior substitute for the real thing—for love— the love of a man and woman or the love of God.

Report 2/1/55/FL/006/A77. Bad news, I'm afraid. Oh, not about L. We have a wonderful relationship. At night when I'm at home and George is well tucked in, I light a candle in my window and if L. is free for what he tells the Princess is one of his night-walks, he taps very gently on the window-pane. The candlestick in which I place this special candle he calls our oboe—not just the crude reference which would spring to most people's minds, but also meaning the '*dolce semplice*', sweetly simple first theme of his new *Faust Symphony*'s second movement, which is played by the oboe. And he often calls me his 'Gretchen', pretending that, like Faust in Goethe's drama, he has wickedly seduced an innocent young girl. He knows perfectly well, of course, that since I already have a child by an unknown father, I am not that innocent. But he does not know that I came here to seduce him. What does it matter? We seduced each other, we love each other very much. But I have not yet told him the bad news. I am pregnant again. It is not his child. We have not been lovers long enough. It must be E26's again, conceived in Leipzig, and I really think this time E26 ought to acknowledge our marriage and that this is his child. As for the G.D., L. is convinced that he will never take Weimar out of Prussia's orbit. It would not be rational, he says, because little Weimar is so near Berlin and anyway there are family connections.

Report 22/1/55/FL/007/A77. Glad you agree about E26 making an honest woman of me—well, an openly honest woman. Brussels will be fine and I should think I'll need to leave here early April. L. will be very upset—so shall I—but what can one do? Quite honestly I think it was a crazy idea of yours to put an agent on to L.—all right, he used to mix with revolutionaries, and he once gave shelter to R.W., and still corresponds with him and of course puts on his operas. But these musicians are complete innocents when it comes to politics—they live in another world. It's almost as ridiculous for you to spy on L. because he might give you useful information about German politics or revolutionary movements, as for L. to spy on you because you might hear that someone was planning to write another *Faust Symphony* or conduct a rival music festival. I almost wish I could tell Franz the truth, because he'd find it so funny. Especially that you roped in cousin Karl and then came here yourself and took everybody in with your disguise.

Not that I'm sorry you did have this crazy idea of sending me here—it's been bliss, the music-making and the love-making—and George has been sweet too since the teething let up for a bit. Unfortunately he's caught a cold now.

Marginal note: *Names*! *Names*!

Report 25/3/55/FL/007/A77. Sorry I haven't been in touch. There was nothing to say, unless you wanted intimate details. I told Franz about the new child—well, it became fairly obvious—and he is devastated that I've got to leave in about ten days now. I also had to tell him why I came here in the first place—he found your last message on my bedside table and it was so cryptic that he thought I must have another secret lover. I couldn't let him think that and spoil our last few days together, so since you've taken my advice not to send any more agents to watch him, I thought it could do no harm if he knew. Of course he's sworn to say nothing about it to anyone and he took it very well. He looked at me with a very severe face for a few moments and I thought he was going to be angry, but then he smiled and kissed me and said that he knew the Austrian secret service used to spy on him in his travelling days as a virtuoso—they thought he might be in touch with dissidents in Italy and Hungary—but so far as he knew he'd never fallen in love with a spy before. And then we had a good laugh about the whole thing. I didn't tell him you'd been here in disguise, but I did tell him that I was your daughter, otherwise he might have thought I was just some brazen whore hired by some faceless department of state, instead of part of a family business. And you didn't intend me necessarily to go to bed with him, I said, but just to send reports on him. Going to bed with him, I said, was entirely my idea and, of course, his. I'll see you soon in Brussels. The baby's due in July.

3. FAUST

My dearest Gretchen/Agnès, light of my life, beautiful spy,

How sad I am now, how I miss you! I pass your window and try to imagine I see the candle lit in the darkness, and the oboe plays the *dolce semplice* in my gloomy thoughts. My only consolation is composition. Thinking always of you, I am revising my symphonic poem *Héroïde funèbre* which was based on an old piece of mine, my *Revolutionary Symphony*, begun long ago in Paris, when I *was* a revolutionary or thought I was. It is immeasurably sad, as I am. Everything in our life changes and passes, except sadness and loss. Those never change, never leave us for long.

I am even sad—though it would have been devilish awkward—that your new child is not mine. You have given a new meaning to that old Faust story. Not only does innocent Gretchen turn out to be a spy, but she is working for Mephistopheles, who is her father! That should give a jolt to selfish and self-conceited old Faustus, who thinks he controls his own life and the lives of others! And perhaps a jolt to Mephistopheles, who also thinks he controls the lives of others, but finds that his daughter Gretchen spoils the plot—why? Out of love, sheer love! It's wonderful! All that elaborate dance Mephistopheles leads Faust in Goethe's drama becomes in this revised drama of ours a little hop, skip and jump of Gretchen's because she and Faust really do fall in love and she is a modern woman, not afraid of scandal, not afraid of her father, least of all afraid of her foolish old Faust.

But this must not be the end of our love. I shall be conducting at the Lower Rhine Music Festival in Düsseldorf at the end of May. Surely that is not too near your time? We can meet there or, better still—out of the way of spies and gossips—in Köln?

'Out of the way of spies'! No, there's one spy I cannot do without. One spy has stolen my secret—my love—and made off with it to Brussels!

Your sad, disconsolate, oboeless, lightless, lost and loving F.

Extracted from the private files of Georg Klindworth, spymaster to the Austrian Government of Prince Metternich and later to the kingdom of Württemberg, arms-supplier to Russia during the Crimean War, father of Agnès Street-Klindworth. After the birth of her second child Agnès divorced her husband, Captain Ernest Denis-Street, and became the mistress of Ferdinand Lassalle, friend of Karl Marx and founder of the Revolutionary Workers' Party of Germany, and bore him two children. It is not clear to whom the first section of these papers was addressed, but perhaps Klindworth wrote it for his own amusement and attached the other papers to it as a kind of inverse Faust Symphony *of his own.*

XII. A Dog's-eye View

Liszt arrived at Triebschen on Wednesday, 9 October [1867] at three
o'clock in the afternoon. He and Wagner had not seen one another
since the summer of 1864, and neither of them could have relished the
circumstances under which they were now obliged to confront one
another. For six hours they were closeted together, but nothing is
known of their conversation.
—Alan Walker (*Franz Liszt*, VOL. III, p. 125)

It was like visiting Napoleon on St Helena.
—Liszt

. . . dreaded but pleasant.
—Wagner

*Richard Wagner, 54, is accompanied by his large Newfoundland dog Russ,
nearly half his own height, as he emerges from the front door of his isolated
house beside Lake Lucerne. At the same time his carriage, despatched to
Lucerne to collect his visitor from the railway station, pulls up in the drive. The
coachman climbs down from his box, opens the carriage-door and the tall
figure of Franz Liszt, 55, wearing a black cassock, gets out. Wagner, followed
by the dog, goes forward to greet him, As they meet the contrast between their
relative heights is very marked: Liszt stands more than six feet tall (1.85m),
Wagner less than five and a half feet (1.66m).*

LISZT. What a peaceful place!

WAGNER. Triebschen! How we love it! We fell for it the moment we saw
it.

LISZT. We?

WAGNER. Cosima and I.

LISZT. Well, we have to speak about that.

WAGNER. Shall we walk? Beside the lake? That's the Rigi over there across the water. Or towards Mount Pilatus? There behind you. Lovely walks in all directions.

LISZT. I'm not a walker.

WAGNER. Come inside, then!

They go inside and enter the salon, whose large windows overlook the lake. Wagner sits down, with the dog at his feet, but Liszt declines a chair and stands looking out of the window.

LISZT. It can't go on, Richard. It's a huge scandal, ruining your career and Hans' and tearing Cosima in two.

WAGNER. Fate brought us together. We cannot be parted. Even Hans understands that.

LISZT. This is childish talk. Operatic talk. The cartoonists enjoyed themselves depicting you as Tristan, Cosima as Isolde and Hans as King Mark, but the stories don't quite fit, do they? Life is less straightforward than myth. It was not Fate or even a magic love-potion that brought you together, but principally Hans himself. It's true that he saw you as a god and in the myths gods steal pretty ladies from their husbands, but in reality . . .

WAGNER. When they came to see me in Zürich on their honeymoon, there was already something in the air. I had just completed the text of *Tristan* and read it to them. When she went up to bed, she took the manuscript with her and spent several nights re-reading it. Hans told me that. But I made nothing much of it at the time—it was Hans who was in love with me, in love with my work, at anyrate. He sat down at the piano and gave wonderful performances of Karl Klindworth's arrangements of *Rheingold* and *Die Walküre* and he sight-read my sketches for the first two acts of *Siegfried*. He was beside himself with excitement. She was shy, she barely looked at me all through the visit.

LISZT. She was nineteen years old and she'd only just fallen in love with Hans.

WAGNER. Had she? What do we mean by love? She was more like his mother or his nurse than his lover. When they arrived in Zurich he'd managed to lose his luggage and all their money was inside it. Then he was crippled with rheumatism. She saw him as someone who needed her, and of course he did, and no doubt she needed to be needed. Their marriage was the direct result of that concert in Berlin when Hans conducted bits from *Tannhäuser*. The audience booed and hissed. And poor Hans fainted.

LISZT. It *was* horrible. I was there and took him back to his mother's house, in the early hours. Cosima answered the door and I went back to my hotel.

WAGNER. And of course the poor fellow was still in a very sorry state— as he so often is—and needed a lot of comforting. That's how he came to ask her to marry him. But love? It was *Tannhäuser* and their mutual hurt feelings over its rude reception that brought them together.

LISZT. You know how much I admire your work, Richard. But can't you see the difference between the greatness of your work and the smallness—meanness—of your behaviour as a man?

WAGNER. If that's your opinion . . .

He begins to rise from his chair and the dog, sensing his anger, growls.

LISZT. It *is* my opinion. Throw me out, if you will! But this is what I came to say and you knew very well that I would say it, even though you kept out of my way in Munich, and I had to make this journey to Switzerland for no other purpose than to say it.

Wagner sits back in his chair and waves his hand as if to permit Liszt to continue.

For God's sake, Richard, try to see yourself for once as others see you! As *I* see you, for a start, I who have been your friend and admirer for a quarter of a century, and for just as long the friend and teacher and father-in-law and indeed father-in-music to Hans von Bülow . . . and also I have to say, the loving father of Cosima, my only surviving child after the deaths, so young, of both the others. Didn't I rejoice, wasn't I almost as delighted as you yourself when King Ludwig took you under his wing, paid your debts, set you up in luxury only to be free to create and perform your work?

Wasn't I equally delighted when you persuaded the King that the only person capable of conducting your work was Hans von Bülow? And again when you persuaded Hans that for this great task he should even give up his bright prospects in Berlin and come to Munich? And then what? He comes, he does everything and more to glorify your genius . . . and you steal his wife. This is not *Tristan und Isolde*. No, even though it was on the very day that Hans took the first rehearsal for that great work that his wife Cosima bore a child, my grandchild, whom they called Isolde and who was not, I believe, Hans' child, but yours. No, this is not that noble opera, not by any stretch of the imagination, this is mere mean, squalid betrayal and adultery. How could you bear to do such a thing to the man who admired you above all others in the world?

WAGNER. Adultery, yes, I don't deny that. Betrayal of Hans, I suppose so. But not of Cosima. No, I rescued her from a degenerating relationship with a man incapable of loving her. Did *she* send you on this mission to separate us? I don't think so. Let me tell you, if she has not already told you, how we knew that we must live the rest of our lives together! It was in a carriage, in Berlin. We were being driven about the city to occupy the time while Hans took his classes somewhere. Both of us deeply unhappy—you know, I'm sure, how Hans and his mother neglected her, how the mother froze her with disapproval and how Hans flew into tempers and tantrums, how he was constantly subject to nervous crises and hypochondria. Perhaps you don't know—it's something she only told me after *our* first child was born—that she bore *their* second child, Blandine, alone in her room. Neither Hans nor her mother-in-law took any care of her pregnancy at all. As for my own unhappiness, that was perennial— my unloving wife, my huge debts, my lack of income, my lack of success or any prospect of it, homeless, unable to compose—I need stability, self-confidence for that . . .

LISZT. Don't we all?

WAGNER. So we sat opposite one another in that carriage trotting through the streets of Berlin and we said very little, but our eyes met and we knew in that instant what we had missed in all our previous encounters—that behind her shyness, and my awkwardness and self-absorption, inside those two bodies that were so inexpressive, our souls, our selves knew better. And having seen that, that our souls recognized each other at last, we said nothing. No, nothing at all. We both began to cry, we took each others' hands across the carriage, could not speak, broke down completely in tears and sobs . . . until the carriage put us down again at the door of Hans' home. And did not meet again until eight months later, after I'd received my summons from the King of Bavaria, and persuaded him to employ Hans to conduct my work, and persuaded Hans that I couldn't do without him . . .

LISZT. And was it really Hans you wanted or was it his wife?

WAGNER (*after a pause, in which he seems about to jump out of his chair again, but instead grinds his teeth and pats the dog at his feet*). I was thinking only of my work. In the excitement of that fairy-tale invitation from King Ludwig to rely on him henceforward, to finish the works I had started and create new ones at his expense, I thought of nothing but *Tristan* and the Nibelungs. No, perhaps I had not altogether forgotten that scene in the carriage, but it was so far at the back of my mind that I actually wrote to another woman asking her to come and look after my new house and me. Fortunately—my lucky star still shining—she turned me down. And so there I was, settling into the house Ludwig had provided for me beside Lake Starnberg, when she came—Cosima, with her two small daughters—a week ahead of Hans, to help me prepare for his arrival. And then, then there was no alternative. Our fate was sealed.

LISZT. Your fate! You mean, of course, that a girl who was clearly dazzled by you—a girl, I grant you, not very happy in her marriage, but nevertheless feeling deep loyalty to Hans, as she still does—a girl who is my daughter and whom you should, both from your age and your friendship for me, let alone your friendship for Hans, have treated as *your* daughter . . . that you seized your chance of her, put up no resistance to her admiration for you, behaved as your lowest instincts dictated. Your fate was sealed, no help for it! I can hardly believe that this is you, Richard Wagner, the man who wrote *Tannhäuser, Lohengrin, Tristan and Isolde*, whose *artistic* integrity pulses in every bar, who tell me this.

WAGNER (*getting up abruptly from his chair and confronting Liszt beside the window*). And I can hardly believe that this is you, Franz Liszt, also a model of artistic integrity but at the same time notorious the world over for playing fast and loose with women, old and young, who lectures me about 'lowest instincts'.

LISZT. I have never made love to any woman who had not already broken with her husband.

WAGNER. Oh, is that the criterion, the ethical border-line? Yet most, if not all of them, *had* husbands, who were perhaps not so happy as their wives to be broken with.

LISZT. To none of them did the wives owe loyalty, as Cosima did to Hans. And above all to none of the husbands did *I* owe loyalty, as you did to Hans, in return for his loyalty to you and your work. This is not a case of God's law—I know you are an atheist, so I leave all arguments from religion aside. Nor is it even a case of man's law. It is a case of personal loyalty, personal integrity—nothing more and nothing less than that.

Wagner turns away since he is so much shorter than Liszt and does not like being looked down on. He walks to the fireplace, though there is no fire in it, and stands there legs apart, hands behind his back. Russ, the Newfoundland dog, who lifted his head and observed the confrontation warily, but did not get up from his place in front of the chair, now lays his head back on his front paws.

WAGNER. You've already spoken, I suppose, to Cosima and Hans, together or separately. What do they say, what do they want?

LISZT. I have not spoken separately on this subject to Hans, but what he wants is clear enough: to pursue his career as conductor, pianist and teacher in Munich with all the authority and respect that is due to such a brilliant musician. Can you even begin to imagine what he has suffered in the way of ridicule and humiliation, since it became public knowledge that the composer he worships and does honour to with his talent, was meanwhile sleeping with his wife and having children by her?

WAGNER. Does he want his wife, then, to live with him as before, and now with all four daughters—mine as well as his?

LISZT. Of course, he must want that. And for you to stay away from him and his family—with some reservation, I suppose, for you to receive visits from your daughters. But I don't think he recognizes Isolde as yours.

WAGNER. Then he is a fool. She was the fruit of our first coming together at Lake Starnberg. I don't think there was any coming together of Hans and Cosima at that time or since. Indeed, soon after he arrived at Lake Starnberg he found the door of my room locked, with Cosima and me inside. He left the house in a fury and moved into a hotel in Munich.

LISZT. You talk as if he was the person at fault.

WAGNER. I tell you the facts. We are long past the question of faults.

LISZT. Cosima is not. She blames herself continually.

WAGNER. But does she wish it had never happened? Does she want what you say Hans does, to live with him as if it had never happened and never see me again?

LISZT. She loves you both, of course.

WAGNER. But not in the same way. Tell me, if you can, that she never wants to see me again and I will take her at her word!

LISZT. She does not want to break with Hans. She cannot. She was brought up a Catholic Christian and she is faithful to the Church's teaching.

WAGNER. As faithful as you have been.

LISZT. I have committed many sins and sought forgiveness for them. She too, I'm sure.

WAGNER. But you cannot say that this sin of loving me—if it is a sin, which I utterly deny—is one she can or ever will ask forgiveness for. How could she, when she and I will love each other for ever, in this world and the next?

LISZT. I didn't think you believed in a next world. And that, by the way, was a boast I once dared to make myself—with Cosima's mother—and could not sustain.

WAGNER. No, but we shall. And that's why this idea of yours that she can live with Hans and leave me out of her life is sheer fantasy. We have tried the middle way—all three of us in Munich, where the newspapers and the gossip made it impossible, and then here, remote from the gaping, unforgiving world. It was not a success and the first person to recognize that was Hans. He moved out to Zürich. There is only one solution to this conundrum, Franz, other than the '*Liebestod*' of Tristan and Isolde, and that is for the lovers to become man and wife.

LISZT. Never!

WAGNER. Why not? My poor wife died last year. I am free to marry Cosima.

LISZT. She is not free to marry you. She and Hans were married by the Catholic Church.

WAGNER. Hans is a Protestant and can get a civil divorce. Cosima has only to become a Protestant too.

LISZT. I trust she will never do that.

WAGNER. Then we must live in sin, like you and her mother, the Countess d'Agoult. And our children must remain illegitimate, as yours were, as Cosima herself is. How I hate your Church and all its piddling hypocrisies!

Liszt is silent.

Forgive me, Franz! But you have said hard things to me and I must tell you that I hate to see you in that black cassock—you the Byronic lover, the man who has only to finger a piano to reduce men as well as women to tears of pure emotion, the composer of the 'Sonata in B minor' and the *Faust* and *Dante Symphony*. Yes, I understand your fascination with religion—our souls, whatever they are, are infinitely more important than our bodies—do you think I don't believe that as fervently as you? How could one write true music if one did not? But to submit yourself to the dead hand of that life-denying Church, with its self-indulgent grandees and arbitrary man-made dogmas, that I can't begin to understand. And now you've become one of its priests!

LISZT. Not a priest, no. Only minor orders. I believe there is a next world, you see, and that the Church knows the way to it, since, whatever its failings, it is the only true successor to Jesus Christ and the guardian of a teaching. There is forgiveness for our sins, but not escape from them, not denial of them, however we may pride ourselves on our own freedom and integrity. And so I put on this cassock, and read my breviary and make my prayers every day, so as to correct myself, to remind myself and train myself to be humble and attentive to the teachings of Christ.

Wagner is silent.

But I did not come here, as I said, with any intention of asking you to obey God's law. I know you don't accept it and it would be fruitless to try to change your mind on that point. Nor do I ask you to consider your own prospects, the effect this scandal has already had on your relationship with King Ludwig, his advisers and the citizens of Bavaria, and what further effect it may still have. Long ago your involvement with the rebellion in Saxony drove you out of Dresden and forced you into exile in Switzerland. Now here you are again, driven out of Munich, and what will become of your great works if the King should withdraw your income? I'm sure his advisers, who are by no means your friends or admirers, would dearly like to bring that about.

WAGNER. There are other reasons for my having to leave Bavaria.

LISZT. Yes, of course, your extravagance and your patronizing remark about the boy King, unfortunately reported back to him.

WAGNER. Maliciously. I was surrounded by spies and enemies because of the favour the King showed me.

LISZT. But your extravagance and lack of discretion are mere foibles of your character which your admirers have learnt to accept for the sake of your genius, and the King, I'm sure, as long as he remains under the spell of your music—long may he do so!—can easily discount them. What he cannot ignore is the moral smear of your relationship with Cosima. The Catholic party is strong in Bavaria, and the King must fear that although he is not personally involved, he might go the same way as his grandfather Ludwig I if his people transferred their dislike of you and your behaviour to him, your admirer and patron. Haven't they already called you 'Lolotte', as if you were another Lola Montez? Might not Ludwig II lose his throne for his attachment to Lolotte, as Ludwig I did for his to Lola?

WAGNER. You should not pay so much attention to the gibes of the gutter Press. Ludwig's attachment to my music is not at all the same as his grandfather's to that heartless whore.

LISZT. All the same, the fact is that he made you leave his kingdom in spite of his attachment to your music. And although he may continue to pay you what he promised, it is never quite safe to rely on the word of kings.

WAGNER. I do rely on his word and I think you are wrong to suspect him of either insincerity or weakness. The boy is besotted with my work, he lives for it.

LISZT. Just as Hans did, and still does. But you yourself seem to be quite incapable of keeping faith with the friends your music wins for you. And this characteristic of yours is apt to affect your prospects. As your friend I am naturally concerned about your prospects. I always have been, because you are your own worst enemy. But now that your prospects threaten to become Cosima's prospects, I am more than concerned, I am deeply disturbed. If she were to leave Hans and attach herself to you, what would *her* prospects be?

WAGNER. The same as mine, of course. I would care for her and share my life with her.

LISZT. Exactly! But you are growing old, Richard, as I am. You are almost half-way into your fifties , much more than halfway through your life. Your record so far, you must admit, is not encouraging. I don't mean as a musician, but for steadiness of life, for personal relationships. Your debts and quarrels have followed you like faithful dogs from city to city, country to country. Your personal intimacies have been less faithful. When did you ever care for or share your life with anyone? Your wife? The several women who from time to time took her place in your life?

WAGNER. The pot calls the kettle black!

LISZT. Why trade insults? In this case, it is not your life or mine that matters, but Cosima's. Hers, yes, as a woman who abandons her husband, as a mother of four children, a young woman still, not yet thirty, depending on you, an old man—or nearly so—whose life so far has been that of a musical genius and a vagabond.

WAGNER. 'Why trade insults,' did you say?

LISZT. I did not mean it as an insult. On the contrary. You had every right to live like a vagabond for the sake of your art. Future generations, I firmly believe, will applaud you for it, will understand that, like Beethoven himself, the difficult, unconventional life you led was necessary in order to concentrate all your powers on creation. I hope they may understand the same of me. But do you have a right to impose that sort of life on Cosima, even if she thinks now, in her idealistic, worshipping way, that she could bear it for your sake? Put it like this: if she were *your* daughter and I her lover, what chance would you see of her happiness in dependence on me?

WAGNER (*after a pause*). That capacity for worship came from her dependence on you. She was brought up, as she often says, 'fatherless and motherless,' her mother forbidden to see her, her father far away in Germany, Russia, Italy, England, Hungary throughout her early childhood. But such a very famous father! Such a paragon of genius and success! Such a magician of the keyboard as never walked the earth before! How could she fail to understand love as worship and worship as love? I don't mistake the nature of her love for me, Franz. It is certainly composed partly of worship—and probably her first attraction to Hans, your prize pupil—was an immature version of the same. Her mother too once worshipped you, deny it if you can! But what you taught Cosima in her most impressionable years from your lofty distance, she cannot now unlearn. And how grateful I am for that! For that is our fate, hers and mine, to love and worship mutually, in her maturity and my old age, she the child of the great Liszt and I the composer even Liszt admires—you said so yourself—more than any other since Beethoven. We cannot escape such a love and its fulfilment. Nor can you, nor can Hans. And of the four people who created and formed this love, only one—only you—still tries to frustrate it. No, I will not give her up, not for you, not for all the world. And she, I know, will not give me up, however much it hurts Hans, however much hurting him hurts her. That is our fate, to be true to each other now that we have found each other . . . just as much our fate as the love of Tristan and Isolde, though we mean to do better than they did. No 'Liebestod' for us, but *Liebesleben*. We shall love and live.

Da capo, *as musicians put it. The preceding conversation is repeated more or less from the beginning and then again six or seven times in different combinations of the same themes and arguments, while the two musicians sit or stand, move about the room, look out of the window or at the floor or each other, while the dog lies mostly in the same place with one eye usually open, confident by now that however heatedly he speaks, the stranger is not going to harm his master physically. Finally Liszt sits down exhausted and defeated in a chair and the dog stands up and ambles across to him to be stroked, as if to condole with him. Liszt absently rubs its head and pulls its ears. A long silence, during which Wagner, unsure whether Liszt is going to resume his attack, glances at him from time to time, but otherwise stands with his chin held high and stares through the window at the mountain in the distance.*

LISZT. I've made a paraphrase of the 'Liebestod'. It wasn't easy, but I'm pleased with it. Would you like to hear it?

WAGNER. Hugely. But you know I've been working on my new opera—with a happy ending. That's the good influence of Cosima. I'd love you to play me some of that, if you can read the score. And I'll sing the parts, of course.

LISZT. Where is it?

WAGNER. On the piano.

Liszt gets up, walks round the dog at his feet and goes to the piano, where he finds the score.

LISZT. *Die Meistersinger von Nürnberg*! Good, very good!

He sits down at the piano and turns several pages.

WAGNER. Can you read it?

LISZT. Oh, yes! Wonderful, Richard, wonderful! Send your carriage for our friend Pohl! He's waiting for me at the hotel in Lucerne. He'll not want to miss this.

He turns back to the beginning of the score, throws back the sleeves of his cassock and starts to play the Overture. Wagner goes out to instruct his coachman. The dog follows him.

* * *

Just over a year later, in November 1968, Cosima left Hans and their two daughters in Munich and, taking Wagner's two daughters and her own dog with her, moved into Tribschen with Wagner. Seven months later, after Hans' daughters had joined them there, she bore Wagner's son, Siegfried. In August 1870, by which time Hans had divorced Cosima for desertion, and she had converted to Protestantism, she and Wagner were married. Liszt never visited Tribschen again and was only reconciled with his daughter and Wagner, who had meanwhile moved to Bayreuth, five years later.

XIII. My Third Countess

She claimed to be a Countess and a Cossack. She was neither. She added the title to her name on her Austrian passport, but her name was partly false too. Olga Janina was born Zielinska, the daughter of a Polish manufacturer—boot-polish, I think—and married, very briefly, a man called Piasecki, with whom she had a child and from whom she borrowed his second name, Janina, when she embarked on the career of a concert pianist. She had some talent as a musician, had been to good teachers and played in public even before she attached herself to my band of pupils.

She was small, slim and plain, cut her hair short to look like a boy, and swaggered about in jacket and trousers, with a Circassian belt and dagger and sometimes a pistol in her pocket, smoking cigars. She always had an array of pills and potions, including opium and laudanum, and what she said was poison. Presumably she wanted to think of herself as a boy, though she was woman enough to pursue or be pursued by several different men in the short time I had to do with her. But it was not Liszt the man she pursued—he was an elderly man in a cassock by then—it was Liszt the celebrity.

The type is common enough unfortunately. Lonely, narcissistic people with no strong identity of their own become obsessed with celebrities for quite the wrong reason—the celebrity itself. They want it for themselves, that shiny carapace of fame and success. They perceive only its outside and chase it as greedily as men after gold or gamblers after luck, caring little for who or what is inside. They want to touch it and possess it and be instantly transformed by it into somebody significant, unaware that fame itself has no significance, fame is created *by* significance, not *vice versa*. It's a child's fairy-tale view of the world they have, that one can leap out of one's own small dreary reality into the glitter of stardom without any intervening effort. They are belated Cinderellas, expecting to be magically transported from the kitchen cinders to the fairy coach to the Prince's palace.

Such people may be pitiable, but can also be dangerous. Making no distinction between reality and their dreams, they are brought up very short when, as they always must be in the end, they are forced to recognise the distinction. They can 'explode' into violence at that point, either against themselves or the person whose celebrity obsesses them. This was my case with Olga Janina, and I must blame myself for letting it happen, in spite of my long experience of the effect my celebrity has on such people.

At the time she became my pupil, I was in my late fifties and living my '*vie trifurquée*', commuting between Rome, Pest and Weimar; and I was in Rome when I received her first letter, which I thought was from a young man since she signed it 'O. Janina', and agreed to hear him play.

She could play well, no doubt of that, with fire and spirit, and I took her on, I suppose almost *because* my other pupils disliked her, not wishing that they should dictate whom I would teach. She made out later, of course, in her dreadful, vindictive novels, that I was her lover, but no, that was one of her many falsehoods, even though she did her best to entice me, to the point of stripping naked in front of me in the garden of the Villa d'Este and plunging into one of the fountains. Luckily my friend and host, Cardinal Von Hohenlohe, the Villa's tenant, was absent at the time.

But, yes, I was fond of her in a fatherly way, especially since at that time Cosima, my only surviving child, had turned her back on me. She had abandoned her husband, my friend and former pupil Hans von Bülow and gone to live with Wagner to whom she had already borne two children and was shortly to bear another. I could not approve of Cosima's actions, and did my best to end her relationship with Wagner, and persuade her back to her husband, and I'm afraid she had really begun to hate me. Only those who have themselves experienced such a break with a beloved daughter, will be able properly to understand what this did to me, how it seemed to dry up my deepest feelings and bring a deadly drought to my life. So although I had no desire to sleep with Olga, I did relish having her around me at that time, and she, no doubt, felt something like adoration for me—or rather for my shell, my celebrity.

Her swaggering manner included also a great deal of foul language and opinionating of a provocative kind—free love, atheism, anarchism and so forth—the usual topics appealing to young attention-seekers—but when we were alone together, she was quite ready to moderate both her language and opinions. Indeed, on those occasions when we dined together alone on the terrace of the Villa d'Este, she seemed to become almost a different person, gentler, more intelligent, more impressionable. At the time I thought that this was the real Olga, the woman behind the nervously raucous persona she projected in public, and flattered myself that I was having a stabilizing effect on her. Now I am not so sure. It was probably only another of her roles and adopted purely because she saw it pleased me. How foolish I make myself sound, but then I *am* foolish where women are concerned, their clever fingers play up and down my keyboard and my strings cannot help but respond. Olga's fingers, though, I have to say, were not a pretty sight. She constantly bit her nails until they bled and after a session at the piano—the real one—she often left bloody traces on the keys.

Her body, however, when she revealed it to me in the fountain, was the best part of her—lithe and compact like a gymnast's, worthy of the water sprite she was pretending to be. Nervous as I was that some gardener or other servant would come upon this strange and compromising scene, the naked nymph sporting in the basin under the fountain, while the elderly abbé in his black soutane sat contemplating her from his seat under a tree, I could not help wanting the scene to continue. Nor could I feel that however much the Church and society in general might disapprove, there was anything morally wrong with the action per se. Her motive might have been to lead me into temptation, but since she did not, what harm? What difference, indeed, from looking at a master's beautiful statue, except that this one lived and splashed and was made by the Master of all Creation.

When, many years later, I composed the centrepiece of my 'Third Year of Pilgrimage,' a joyful evocation of the Villa d'Este's fountains to counter-balance the two sad cypress pieces that precede it, I was inspired as much by the memory of La Janina's escapade as by the rising and tumbling water in which it took place. The piece is a celebration of Creation, of course—of the water that gives us life—and of Redemption—the metaphorical 'water of life' offered by Christ to all believers—but our gift of life can only be experienced through our bodies and that was never so strongly brought home to me as in those few moments of anxious delight. It *was* only a few moments, though it seemed much longer, for soon after she entered the water, I heard a clock striking midday in the distance and as she emerged again and stood dripping in front of me, the clock had barely stopped striking. I hastened to give her her shirt and trousers.

She came perhaps more often than any of my other pupils to the Villa d' Este, where the kind Cardinal had put a couple of rooms at my disposal so that I could retreat from the noise and bustle of Rome. It was a tiresome journey—up to four hours in a horse and cart over a rough road—but if they wanted to play to me and get my advice and instruction, my pupils had to put up with that. Olga, of course, had the additional incentive of her adoration of my unworthy self and I was usually glad of her company. She was also an excellent copyist and I made much use of her calligraphic skill in preparing my scores for publishers.

After the episode of the fountain, of course, I was warier and even tried to explain to her, when we had eaten a frugal meal on the terrace and were both smoking cigars, that I could not go on seeing her alone unless our relationship was to be strictly that of teacher and pupil. I cannot, of course, recall exactly what we said, but it was more or less as follows:

'I can't help loving you,' she said, quite simply and directly, 'and I can't help wanting you to love me in return.'

'Then love me as a teacher, as a musician,' I said, 'and I will love you as a pupil of great promise, whom I hope to send out into the world to make a name for yourself.'

'It was your music I first loved you for, when I heard you play in Vienna, but when I came to Rome and got to know you, that was something else, that was personal.'

'I don't think so. I don't think that if you set aside my music and my reputation, you would find anything very lovable about this old person with many ailments and sorrows. And even if you did, I could not return such love.'

'You've loved many women, I know. You're famous for it.'

'Infamous, yes. But I'm no longer the same person.'

'Because you're a priest now?'

'No. I am not a priest. I have taken the tonsure and been admitted to the minor orders. I am not bound by any rule of celibacy. That is not the point. The point is that I have lived a sinful life and that before I die—which may be soon enough at my age and after so much stress and self-indulgence—I want to do better.'

'But is loving someone a sin?'

'Not if it hurts no one else.'

'How can this hurt anyone? You could only hurt me by not loving me.'

'I am old and you are very young. The last thing you need is to waste your energy and idealism on loving somebody who cannot love you in return—or only love you as a sort of daughter.'

'What about your daughter and Richard Wagner? Isn't he much the same age as you?'

'That's not a subject I wish to talk about—not with you, not with anybody.'

'Sorry.'

She was silent for a while, but then returned to the attack.

'You said you *couldn't* love me. Is that because you don't find me attractive enough?'

'There are many kinds of love. What I mean is that I do not wish to be *in* love with you, Olga. That is all there is to it.'

'That's much better. That's not a death penalty.'

So for the moment, I had staved off some attempt at suicide or the threat of it. But the problem with people like Olga is that once you have admitted them into your life, they are virtually impossible either to satisfy or shake off. They are adept at insinuation, and even blackmail and they always have the strategic advantage that, whereas you do not at first take them very seriously, and have many other things on your mind, they are single-mindedly concentrated on what they want from you.

In the spring, Olga and several other pupils accompanied me to Weimar for our Beethoven Festival, and I was much relieved when she began an affair with one of the Russians from their Weimar embassy and disappeared to Heligoland with him. It looked as if she had finally grown out of her childish attachment to me. But my relief was premature. Her affair with the Russian diplomat was over by the autumn and she followed me to Hungary.

In the interim I had almost forgotten her. All my thoughts, and most of Europe's, were centred on the terrible events in France—the invasion of a German army led by Prussia and the swift defeat of the French army at Sedan, with the surrender of the Emperor Napoleon III. Because of my youthful years spent in Paris, my friendship with so many distinguished French men and women, including the Emperor himself and his Prime Minister at the time, Emile Ollivier, who had been married to my dear dead daughter Blandine, and whose son Daniel was my grandson, I was bound to sympathise with France. But I also had innumerable German friends, including, of course, the Grand Duke of Weimar, and had been honoured by the King of Prussia, while my daughter Cosima and her new husband Richard Wagner were rabid supporters of the German cause. The whole conflict, then, was a torment to me, and the thought of so many lives lost or damaged in such an unnecessary struggle over national pride and ascendancy—the original cause was a dispute over who should become the next King of Spain—clouded my days and kept me awake at night. But what did my torment matter, compared with that of the imprisoned French Emperor and his soldiers, the widows and the wounded?

There was little I could do except to give concerts to raise money for them, so that when my bad penny, Olga Janina, turned up again in Hungary I enlisted her, with other pupils, to perform. But about this time her well-to-do father died, leaving her, it appeared, more or less destitute, so that it became necessary to try to launch her career seriously, which we did with a series of recitals in the private salons of several leading Hungarian patrons. Most went well enough, but then there was an unmitigated disaster. Olga was playing Chopin's 'Grand Ballade in G minor' at another charity concert in Pest, before a glittering audience. She had performed this work recently with great success and we were all looking forward to hearing her play it again with perhaps still more elan. She was not, of course, wearing her jacket and trousers, but stepped forward to eager applause in a tightly-buttoned dress of violet-velvet, suggesting, though with perfect modesty, what lay beneath it: the youthful figure I had seen in the Villa d'Este's fountain. She began as brilliantly as we had all hoped and then on the sixth page suddenly stopped. She started again from the beginning and stopped again at the same place. This time, white-faced, she stood up and was going to abandon the attempt. I did not behave well. I was beside myself at this ruination of all her hopes and mine.

'Stay where you are!' I said.

The wretched girl sat down again, began again, and again lost her memory at the same place. Banging out a series of discords, she left the piano and rushed towards the exit. I hurried to intercept her and take her arm, but I was still in no mood to forgive her.

'It's your damnable drugs!' I said.

'What do you expect? I needed something to help me through.'

'And you took something that helped you to complete humiliation.'

'Well, I have something to make me die too.'

'Have you no shame at all? Bad enough to spoil your chance of being an artist, but suicide would be the ultimate failure.'

For the moment, that ghastly occasion and my intemperate anger were enough to relieve me of her company for several months. She did make several attempts at suicide, but they were only attempts, or rather demonstrations. Madame Janina valued herself too much to end her life voluntarily. She went to Rome for a while and stayed with a friend and then in the spring of the next year joined her brother at Baden-Baden, where they both tried to make up for their father's lost allowances with gambling. Who but a person lacking any normal sense of reality could imagine that would be a solution? She sent me a letter from Poland—she had sought refuge, I think, with her relations—virtually demanding money from me, 'the alms of anger and hatred' as she charmingly phrased it, and I, foolishly regretting now that I had not been more charitable towards her childishness, replied with a kind letter for her birthday, assuring her that she still had the ability to be a fine musician if only she would give up her moods, her tendency to show off, and above all her pistol, her dagger and her drugs. I did not send her money, not so much because I had little to spare, as because I knew that if I did, her demands would never cease.

When she announced a few months later that she was returning to my side, I had time to devise a little strategy of my own. Why should she not try her fortunes as a pianist in the United States of America? I would pay her fare and give her introductions to some of my contacts there. In return she was to finish copying a three-volume set of my piano studies which she had begun in Rome and take them with her to the music publisher, Julius Schuberth in New York. He had agreed to pay one thousand dollars in advance for the manuscripts, and she should collect this and bring it back to me whenever she returned to Europe. It seemed to me that this scheme, which laid much responsibility on her to fend for herself but which also gave her the advantage of being received as my pupil and protégé, had a good chance of launching her successfully and weaning her away from her bad habits and childish dependence. She accepted the idea enthusiastically and left for America in mid-summer, taking the two finished volumes of my manuscript and promising to finish copying the third while she was away.

The next I heard of her, some months later, was a letter from Schuberth the publisher. She had delivered the two completed manuscripts, but not the third, and she had received the thousand dollars owed me, but she had found no engagements in America and was now returning to Europe and threatening to kill me. I did not take this last too seriously, but was sufficiently annoyed that once again she had contrived to spoil her chances, and on this occasion mine also, so far as the publication of the studies went. Nor did I look forward to having her evidently insoluble problems thrust back in my face.

She arrived in Pest in November and took a room at the Hotel Europa. Then she came to see me in my apartment. I knew she was coming, and my old friend Baron Antal Augusz and my pupil Ödön Mihalovich, who knew of her threats, were also in the building, so that I was not taken entirely by surprise when my door was flung open and she appeared. I was certainly disconcerted, however, by the pistol she was pointing at my heart.

'This is for you, you, you!' she shouted, 'and in case I miss, I've brought this too.'

In her left hand she was holding a small blue bottle, which she began to shake to and fro in the way one does with medicines.

'The poison will kill you if the bullet doesn't, because I've finally finished with your treachery, you ************'. A string of filthy words at the top of her voice.

At this point my friends rushed in and she turned to point the pistol at them.

'Please!' I said to them, as calmly as I could. 'Leave us alone together, so that Madame Janina can explain what she wants of me.'

'But she wants to kill you,' said Ödön.

'Yes, I'm going to kill him,' said Olga, 'I'm going to, I'm going to send him to his f****** next world, and it ought to be hell not heaven for a b****** like him!'

'Why don't you, then?' I was tempted to say, but didn't, for I already felt reasonably sure that she was not going to shoot, provided I did not provoke her.

'I'll get the police,' said Antal.

'No, there's no need for that,' I said. 'Madame Janina is quite capable of shooting someone if you try to use force. Just leave us alone and I'm sure we can sort it out.'

All this time she was still shouting 'I'll kill you, I'll kill you' and brandishing her two weapons. It was somehow the empty threat of the bottle of poison that reassured me. Would she try to force it past my lips, pour it over my head? No, this was a scene from a melodrama she was improvising, not reality.

'Please do leave us,' I said again to my friends, 'and shut the door behind you!'

I was afraid that one of them would try to overpower her and that then she would pull the trigger. Very reluctantly they did as I asked and I sat down at the desk, where I had been writing a letter to Princess Carolyne in Rome, and pointed to the armchair by the window.

'Now, Olga,' I said. 'You can kill me, if you wish, or you can sit down and tell me what has made you so angry with me.'

She would not sit down, but stood over me at the desk, still pointing her pistol at me when she remembered, but mainly waving it about wildly, likewise the little blue bottle, as she gesticulated and ranted.

'You sent me to America to get rid of me. There was no work, nothing, not one concert. It was the middle of the summer. Everybody was away. There are no concerts in the summer. You knew that. You wanted me to finish up totally destitute in that f****** horrible country and die on the streets or sell my body and never be heard of again.'

'None of that is true, Olga. Of course it was summer. My idea was that you would get in touch with the people I recommended, make engagements for the autumn and have time to practise thoroughly so as to make the best possible impression.'

'And what was I supposed to live on in the meanwhile?'

'Didn't Schuberth give you the thousand dollars he promised me?'

'Yes, he did, but you never said I could use that.'

'I thought that if you needed money you could use it and then pay me back from your concert-earnings whenever you returned to Europe.'

'You should have said so.'

'So what *did* you live on?'

'I lived on that. I took it. I thought you owed me that at least.'

'Well, then . . .'

'And I made your f****** copy of those f******* studies.'

'The third volume?'

'Yes. What else did I have to occupy me in that f****** dreadful place?'

'But I don't think it's reached Schuberth.'

'No, it f****** hasn't, because I f****** sold it. What else did I have to live on?'

The scene went on for some hours, but that was the gist of it, endlessly repeated, and I must admit, that although many people afterwards praised me for my courage, I felt more like laughing than shivering in my shoes. The real root of her fury with me was not that she had failed in her dreams of success, but that she had humiliated herself in my eyes, and her own, by stealing my money and my man-uscript. And I was her celebrity, her ideal. She could no longer live with herself because the fairy tale had turned so sordid, and since I *was* in her eyes, in her fantasy, part of herself, she had somehow to elimi-nate me.

But how could the scene end? I was more and more convinced, from the way she waved it about, that the pistol was empty. So would we come to the little blue bottle and if so, how could it be adminis-tered? Really, it was more farcical than alarming, I thought, as we went over and over the same ground. But then her tone changed. From fury and abuse she shifted to tears and self-pity.

'Love, love!' she said. 'All I ever wanted from you, you cruel, heart-less man, was your love, not success, not money, not fame, just love! And you did love me, you do, you can, I know. You liked my body when I showed it you. Take it, take it, for God's sake! Why must you torture me? Is it because of your f****** princess, that ugly old bluestocking who never stops talking and writing, who lives like a spider in her hor-rible room in Rome and hardly ever goes out? Do you really love her and not me? I am *young*—look at me! I can look after you, I can copy your music, and play for you, and keep you company, and go to bed with you, and give you medicines and even wipe your a*** for you, if that's what you want.'

There was little I could say or do to counter this new barrage. Even to say I loved her, let alone to make love to her, would only have postponed the inevitable reckoning and left me forever at the mercy of her emotional blackmail.

'Olga', I said finally in desperation, 'I cannot love you in the way you want. You must try to accept that I've given you such love, such *father*'s love and loving help as I could, and that because of your own follies and weaknesses you've thrown it all away. I am old and very tired now. Shoot me if you must, or just go away and forget about me!'

And at that, she threw the pistol on the floor, took the cork out of her little bottle and swallowed the contents.

'I am going,' she said, 'you f****** b******, and will never trou-ble you again in this world.'

And then she began to writhe and retch, sank down on the floor in convulsions, closed her eyes and went into a coma.

By now it was the early hours of the morning. With the help of my manservant and Ödön, who had remained within call, I got her through the empty streets to her hotel, where the night porter summoned a doctor. The 'poison', he said, was a harmless sleeping draught and she would soon recover. The pistol, however, when we examined it back at my apartment, was loaded and Ödön took the precaution of removing the bullet before returning it to her next day. She left soon afterwards for Paris, where she had friends, and remained there for some years. I heard that she gave public concerts of my music and even lectured on it and rejoiced that her exhausting scene with me seemed finally to have broken the spell of her fantasy.

It was not so, of course. She only left me alone and took control of her own life the better to 'kill' me more effectively than she had with her pistol and dagger. The world has since enjoyed in many editions her extravagant account of our 'love', *Souvenirs d'une cosaque* published as a particularly wounding slash of her dagger, under the name of my dear friend, the composer Robert Franz. And twisting the dagger in the wound, she followed it with a second novel under the same pseudonym, *Souvenirs d'un pianiste*, purporting to put my side of the case. I am never mentioned by name in either fiction, it's true, but no one can be in any doubt who the heroine's passionate and sinfully tormented musical abbé can be.

At least, I tell myself, I am free of her person, and like that other fictional revenge, my second countess' *Nélida*, these novels are mere rubbish which must be swept away by time. But they *do* hurt me, of course, however much I proclaim publicly that they have nothing to do with me and that I wouldn't dream of reading them. I have written this account not to defend myself publicly, since I have no intention of publishing it, but only to cauterize my wound, to dispose of my gangrenous thoughts on to paper, and then perhaps burn them and be altogether rid of them and of her, that miserable child whose ignoble adoration did so much harm to us both.

XIV. Spiridon Speaks

In short, he was a perfect cavaliero,
And to his very valet seem'd a hero.
—Lord Byron (*Beppo* XXXIII)

'Dr Liszt? No, he's not as complicated as most people think. He just wants to be liked, that's all, wants to please people. What makes him really happy is to have everybody happy around him. Doesn't matter whether it's a few people—his friends or his pupils—or hundreds or thousands in a concert-hall or out in the street. If the few people are talking and laughing and getting on with each other, or if the hundreds or thousands are clapping or yelling with excitement at hearing him play or just setting eyes on him, he's a happy man.

But when he's alone, he's not. No, not at all. Then he's a very sad man. Because, you see, he doesn't make *himself* happy, he doesn't admire or appreciate himself. He just remembers all the mistakes he's made in his life, all the failures, as he sees it. He doesn't think of the successes. Those are water under the bridge, as they say. The failures, though, don't seem to get through the bridge, they swirl about like the dirty water with the bits of rubbish in the corners. The failures are always with him.

What sort of failures? Well, in the first place, his music. There's a bunch of people, music critics mostly, who make sure every time his music is played to tell him it's a waste of time and effort—shallow, uninventive, superficial, that kind of thing. And although he pretends to the world that he pays no attention to these people, he really pays them far more attention than the ones who praise him. Because when he *is* praised he puts it down to favouritism, friends or admirers being nice to him to keep him happy, while the nasty ones he secretly believes are telling the truth. So he can't win, can he?

He used to tell his pupils and admirers not to play his work at all, since they'd only get lambasted by his enemies, and he sometimes goes on as if nobody *does* play his music. It's not true, especially not now in his seventieth year—there are no end of concerts and celebrations planned for him. But again, you see, that vicious circle starts in his mind—this is a tribute from his friends, not from the world at large, so it doesn't count—and you can be sure the hostile critics will confirm his fears by telling him all over again that he shouldn't have bothered.

So why does he bother? Because composing is the only thing that consoles him for his sadness, when he's alone. That's another bind he's in. He thinks he needs more solitude so as to get on with his compositions—and that's what his awful old woman in Rome, the Princess von Sayn-Wittgenstein, is always telling him in the long letters she's always sending him and when he visits her apartment in Rome. She never goes anywhere else—not even to his concerts in Rome—hardly even goes out at all, but just sits or lies in her room smoking cigars and writing letters and books. Anyone that visits her, including Dr Liszt, has to wait half-an-hour in an anteroom before entering her room, so as not to bring in any fresh air or infection. She's a sack of irritations, and illnesses and dislikes and in my opinion she can be held responsible for a lot of his unhappiness, both on her own account and his. His feeling of not being good enough, I mean. She nags at him all the time, tries to run his life for him by post, doesn't want him coming here to Budapest, though it's a big part of his life now, doesn't want him going back to Weimar where they used to live together and where he goes for a month or two in the spring and summer, wants him only to stay near her in Rome and concentrate on composing. Well, it's true most of his composing is done in Rome—or rather at the Villa d'Este in Tivoli. He goes into solitary there, gets melancholy thinking about himself and his 'failures' and then starts composing to keep the melancholy at bay. But then what he composes doesn't please people—nothing could please some of them—and so it doesn't please him and he's into the melancholy again.

And, of course, his past life makes him sad too. His long-ago love for that French countess, who died at just about the time I joined him.

He didn't take that too badly. What takes him badly is the thought of how she began to hate him and wrote a nasty book about him. And their children . . . two of them died when they were barely grown up, and the only one that was left cut his heart out when she ditched his favourite pupil, Herr von Bülow, and went off with his friend, Herr Wagner. She and her father have made it up again since, after a fashion, but he believes the Wagners don't like his music and that makes him sad.

And recently he's lost a lot of his best friends. That's bound to happen when you're as old as he is, but it doesn't add to one's joy in life, I should imagine, to think that you've reached an age when you might expect your friends to die and might equally expect to be the next to go. Wouldn't cheer me up, that, would it you?

He comes to Budapest every winter and leaves at the beginning of April. Then he visits Vienna, and maybe Munich and the Wagners in Bayreuth, before settling in Weimar for the spring and summer. Not really settling, though, because he's off to various places for concerts or operas or music festivals, which he feels obliged to attend because they're playing his music or his pupils or friends are involved. Then he's back to Rome in August and either stays in an apartment near the Princess or goes out to the Villa d'Este to get some peace and quiet. People do visit him there, but not too many, it's still quite a journey, though they've built a railway now. He has rooms there and a nice terrace, courtesy of his friend, Cardinal Hohenlohe, and that's where he mostly composes, as I said. And that's where he's at his saddest, because of the solitude and because although it's very beautiful, that place is sad in itself—all those cypress trees, as if it was a cemetery, and even the fountains can get on your nerves day in, day out—all that water going nowhere but up or down. I have to fight off the melancholy there myself, sometimes.

But then it's back to Hungary and that's quite a relief. The people do love him here, because you see they haven't often, if ever, had a Hungarian before, who was world-famous. So they all get very excited when he comes, grand people meet him at the station, people cheer him and take their hats off to him in the streets, pianists come from as far away as Russia or America to learn from him. Oh, yes, he wears a crown in Hungary, he's more like their king than Franz Josef is, to be honest. They've made him president of the new Academy of Music and given him his own apartment on the first floor of the new building, with a good-sized bedroom/study, a dining-room and a salon in peacock blue, with beautiful embroideries made by Hungarian ladies for the chairs, and there's a small room for me. Of course he's got enemies even in Hungary, but he's nearly always surrounded with friends and well-wishers here and that gladdens his heart. He can't speak Hungarian as I can—yes, I speak good Italian too, as well as German—but he was born here, after all, and he'll do anything to prove his patriotism and they really love him for it. He'll go to any number of insignificant events, concerts given by ladies' groups or children or charities, and even play for them, and he'll turn down prestigious offers from Vienna or Berlin.

And, of course, he never takes a penny for anything. He lives on his small salary from the government. I know how small it is because my wages come out of it and they're nothing to speak of. Not enough even to pay for the hairdressing lessons I'm having, so he's paying for those. No, not just so that I can make his hair look nice. I'm hoping to get married, you see, and open a hairdressing salon. Dr Liszt says he'll write an opera called *The Barber of Budapest*. No, it's a joke, he doesn't do opera, leaves that to his son-in-law. Yes, I shall have to give up this job if I get married, he told me he can't afford to keep more than one person besides himself.

No, really, he's poor. He gets a little extra when they publish his music, which they don't always these days, but that's all. He'd make a fortune if he'd ever give concerts for money, which I urge him to do, if only so as to up my wages, but he won't—he'll play for friends in private or for charities in public and that's it. We always travel second-class in the train, believe it or not—I hate that—cramped seats, humping the luggage in and out whenever we change trains, which on the long journeys we do, mostly by night, is far too often. But when we stay at hotels, it's two cheap rooms for him and one better room for me, to make up for my discomfort in the train, he says. It's not just the cheapness, of course, there's a side of him that *wants* to be humble and uncomfortable. He belongs to a Franciscan order, you know, and poverty is a big thing with them. Yes, it is odd. On the one hand he's the uncrowned king of Hungary who, when he goes to any little town out in the sticks, in Transylvania or some such godforsaken place, the whole district turns up with torchlight processions, bands and public banquets, and on the other hand he dresses in that awful black cassock, spends hours on his knees in cold churches and travels second-class. But then when he's being entertained at some grand banquet, I have to pin all the medals and orders from all the sovereigns of Europe on his black cassock. Did you know he's a knight of the Austrian Empire? No, I don't think it's vanity—or only partly. He wears the things to show his gratitude to the people that gave them to him, wanting to please them again, you see.

And all that travelling! What's that for? To please people. To please the Grand Duke of Weimar, for instance—a nice, friendly man, he even talks to me like a friend—who's lent him a pretty little house there in a park, because he wants him to keep organizing concerts and teaching pupils there, to keep coming there so that people will still associate Weimar with the great Franz Liszt. He goes to Rome to please the Princess, he goes to Bayreuth to please the Wagners, he goes all the way to the Netherlands to stay in the royal summer palace at Loo so as to please the King of Holland, he comes to Budapest to please the Hungarians. And to please himself? Well, he gets a hero's welcome in all those places and more or less wherever he goes, which does please him, but I think it's the solitude and relaxation of the Villa d'Este he really looks forward to, except he gets so sad there.

No, I'm wrong. He doesn't *get* sad there, because underneath he's sad all the time and being on his own just uncovers it. In fact, if you ask my opinion, all that excitement, that admiration, that adoration make it worse. It's not only extremely tiring for a man of his age, it's like drink—the more it raises the spirits while it lasts, the more it drops them down again when it stops. Highs alternate with lows, don't they? Mountains with valleys, waves with troughs—that's the law of nature—and the bigger the waves the deeper the troughs. And he's been cresting huge waves of adulation ever since he was nine years old and gave his first public concert—and just think what sixty years of that would do to your system! Quite honestly, it's a wonder he's still such a sane and kindly man, though he's capable, I can tell you, occasionally, of frightening bursts of anger.

And this please keep to yourself: he's a heavy drinker and smoker. Yes, any number of cigars and a bottle of cognac a day, plus plenty of wine when he's with friends or at parties. And he likes absinthe too. No, you don't see him drunk, but that amount of extra stimulation on top of all the demands on him, and the nervous energy he has to put out to respond to people's enthusiasm—more than that, their real greed to be near him and get a piece of him—imagine what it's like in between, when he's alone, completely exhausted! He doesn't sleep well either. And he won't ever refer to it or even admit it, but he has a lot of aches and pains. I hear him groan when he doesn't think I'm near. His teeth are absolutely terrible, he's had gout, he's very subject to chest infections and he spends the coldest part of the year in this perishing climate to please the Hungarians. No, I'm not Hungarian myself, I come from Montenegro, which can be cold but doesn't have these winds sweeping across or nearly so much rain.

'What does that sound like to you?' he asked me the other day when he was trying something out on one of his Bösendorfers in the salon and I came to call him for his lunch.

'Gloomy,' I said. 'It sounds like the way the sky looks.'

'Grey clouds again?' he said. 'Yes, spot on, Spiridion!'

He calls me that, though my real name is Spiridon. Why? It's a book by his old friend George Sand which I haven't read because French isn't one of my languages.

The other day he fell as he was getting out of a carriage and was quite badly bruised. I think he's still in pain from that. And then we had this accident just after Christmas, when I was shaving him. There was another person present and Dr Liszt was talking away and suddenly stuck his left arm in the air to make some point and his finger collided with the business edge of my razor. Very nasty, it was the index finger. We bound it up quickly and it's healing well, but could he behave like a normal person with a damaged finger? Could he say to the people who'd asked him to play the piano for them at various events, 'No, sorry, pianists use ten fingers, you know, and at present I've only got nine, so count me out for the present'? Oh, no, he didn't want to displease them, so he played anyway with nine. It didn't affect his performance. In fact, I think he rather enjoyed the challenge of changing the fingering as he went along—and when *he* goes along a keyboard, as I'm sure you know, it's not ping, ping, ping, pong, it's zzzrrrooooommmm, bang, trip, twiddle, vvvvrooooooommm, zip, rip, roar, ringa, ringa, over the back and round again and hang in the air a second or two . . . and dong dong dong!

His love life? No, really, you've given me a lot to drink and I don't know exactly what I've already said, but nothing I hope to his discredit, because I really love that man. But I can't talk about his love life. In the first place, it's private, in the second place I've only known him the last five years and in the third place, it's obviously not what it was. And although he'd never say so, because he hates to be thought vain, which so many of his enemies think he is, it must be very depressing to have got so old and rather heavy—yes, he's put on a lot of weight—with warts and lines, and loose flesh on his face, considering he was once—to judge from the portraits and what people say—such a very good-looking young man. People thought he must be more than human, looking like an angel and playing in a way that seemed beyond the power of the human brain or fingers. Well, they say now that his playing has quietened down a lot, but even his enemies—the ones who constantly carp at his compositions—agree that he's still far and away the best. But nobody can say that he still looks like an angel. Of course, he makes up for that with his dignity and poise, in public at least. No, he's no longer an angel from heaven, but more of a battered old saint who's been through a long, hard life. But he's a saint who thinks of himself as a sinner.

The ladies still adore him, of course, because of who he is and his personal magnetism. Ladies care less about a man's looks, I believe, than about his air of authority, his masterfulness. You've got to put on a bit of an act for ladies, I find, but he's never needed to, they come to him like cats to a roast dinner, tails in the air. And even now it's not just the older ones, like his Princess or that Baroness von Meyendorff who keeps a close eye on him when he's in Weimar and often writes to him. The young ones, his pupils especially, are all in love with him still. Oh, yes, they may have boyfriends, even lovers of their own, but I'll guarantee that the man they see in their dreams is him. How does he respond? Like a father, I should say. Daughters are often in love with their fathers, and fathers in love with their daughters, but they mostly restrain themselves physically because it's against nature as well as the law. And after all, he's going to be seventy this year, he's already repenting of his sins of the flesh in the past, and he's very much ashamed of his body for looking and feeling so old and decrepit. So would he really want to strip off his cassock and get into bed with a lovely girl of seventeen?

Yes, of course he would, but then he wouldn't, if you see what I mean, because for him the spiritual part of love and the physical, which once when he was such a handsome and slender young man must have been more or less the same thing, have parted company. Just think what it would be like for him to look into a girl's dark eyes with those flashing emeralds of his and to see her completely in his grip, under his spiritual power, and to feel her excitement—her ecstasy—mounting as he began to take off her clothes and touch her soft, firm flesh—and then to remember that he was no longer Franz Liszt, the angel in human form, but old, fat, warty, Dr Liszt and that in a moment she was going to realize that too, the moment he stopped holding her and started to take off his own clothes. No, it doesn't bear thinking about, it would be obscene and there's no one in the world, I should think, more disgusted by any sort of obscenity than him. So the answer to your question is that his love life is all in his head now, or in his music. You and I will never have women coming for us like cats, will we? So maybe we envy him, but at least when we're old we shan't feel we've lost so much.

Madamoiselle Menter? Do you think so? Sophie Menter? Yes, she's one of the pupils he most admires. Yes, he called her 'the greatest woman pianist of her generation'. Yes, she's very attractive and I'm sure she finds him attractive, at least as a great man and a great teacher. But lovers? Not in my time, I'm sure, though of course he first met her here in Budapest before I ever knew him, when he was still in his late fifties and she was probably not much more than twenty. 'My only legitimate daughter as a pianist'? Is that what he said? Well, that bears out what I said, doesn't it? You don't call your lover your daughter.

No, he wouldn't do so to cover up the real relationship. If you think that, you don't understand him at all. I told him once that he'd do better to be less open with people, even tell some small lies, if necessary.

'A public man like you,' I said, 'is always being badgered and bothered by unscrupulous people who just want something for themselves from your fame. Well, you need to be a bit less scrupulous back.'

'No,' he said, 'I don't agree with you, Spiridion. A public man needs to be *more* scrupulous. Firstly, because being so publicly visible he'll always be found out sooner or later, secondly, because if he has any real value at all, it's not because people know *who* he is but *what* he is, what sort of person they are treating like an icon. And thirdly, I can't help it, I can't disguise my feelings even when I want to. I was never able, you know, to deceive any of the women in my life for long about the other women in my life.'

So, you see, although he's such a sophisticated person in most ways, he's also quite naive. And it comes back to what I said at the start, he wants most of all to please people, to make them happy. And in my opinion that's his chief problem now. He's looking at death these days, he knows death is coming for him—that's what most of his music is about now, where it used to be about love and glory and hope—and he believes in God. So he wants desperately to please God but is quite sure that God isn't pleased with him. That's why he wears his dreadful old cassock and goes to mass every day and kneels for hours on cold stone. I said to him,

'If God isn't pleased with you, after all you've done to please him with your sacred music and your generosity to other people, your help to other musicians old and young, your secret gifts of money and your concerts for innumerable good causes, then God must be very hard to please and probably isn't pleased with any single person in this whole world.'

'That may well be true,' he said.

'Well, then,' I said, 'why did he make us, in the first place, or why didn't he make us different?'

'I can't answer that,' he said, 'but I do know that he came to earth in the person of Jesus Christ to show us how to be different.'

'Maybe so,' I said, 'but *you*'ve shown us how to play the piano to perfection. Does that mean we should all try to do the same? Not much hope. And ditto with Jesus Christ. We can't get near doing the same, so we get discouraged and go back to being our unpleasant selves.'

What did he say to that? He just laughed and said,

'Spiridion, you're my Sancho Panza.'

'That's a character, you know, in that Spanish book about an old madman called Don Quixote.'

—*Spiridon Knezevic* was *Liszt's manservant 1875–81.*

'The replacement for the conceited scoundrel Spiridion has a fine name: Achille. He looks after me much better than his predecessor.'

—*Liszt, in a letter to Olga von Meyendorff, 3 February 1882.*

Achille Colonello died in 1884 and was replaced for the last two years of Liszt's life by the Hungarian Mihály (Miska) Kramer.

XV. *Stations of the Cross*

When an angel is about to die, the flowers of his crown wither, his feather robe is stained with dust, sweat pours from under the arm-pits, the eyelids tremble, he is tired of his place in heaven.

—Footnote listing 'the fivefold signs of sickness' in an angel, from Arthur Waley's translation of the Japanese Noh play 'Hagoromo'.

STATION I: FRANKFURT-AM-MAIN

Old, old man in a railway carriage . . . uncomfortable every way . . . eyes too dim to read my watch . . .

SELF. Isn't it time we started?

STAVENHAGEN. Another minute, Master.

Teeth all gone, dentures don't fit well . . . better without them . . . gums sore, pain in my side, legs and feet swollen . . . too painful to walk without help . . . body swollen too . . . mercifully somewhat concealed by this soutane . . .

STAVENHAGEN. Here we go!

Damn this cough! Feverish? Just a bit. This dear boy, finding it hard to be patient with the hideous old hulk beside him: can he imagine what it's like to be old? Why should he? Better not. When I was his age I never imagined it, never even saw it coming. Symptom by symptom it crept up on me . . . tried to ignore it. With some success. 'If one doesn't enjoy good health, one must create some,' . . . brave words . . . never thought so much could go wrong all at once. Nothing to be done now, not much scope to 'create' good health in a carcase altogether rotten . . .

Dr Volkmann prescribes the water cure . . . great bore, never believed in it . . . Dr Graefe says he can operate on the cataract. And no more alcohol, they say . . . been my main remedy up to now . . . not easy to break the habit, but I've done it—partly . . . given up cognac and absinthe, watered the wine . . . doesn't seem to have done much good so far. And no more cigars. Damn this cough!

SELF. What are you humming, Bernhard?

STAVENHAGEN. The piece you played on Monday, Master, at the end of the concert in Luxembourg. It's been running in my head ever since. That melody from the *Glanes de Woronince*. I don't think I ever heard you play it before.

SELF. A long-ago thing. I don't know why I suddenly chose to play it.

Why I suddenly chose to play at all, at the end of the concert . . . had the eerie feeling it might be the last time . . . might never play to an audience again.

SELF. They were songs I heard the peasants sing on the Princess' estate in Ukraine. And one of them, the *dumka*, I heard in Kiev, where I first met her. There was an old man on the street with an instrument that was new to me, a *bandura*, a kind of bass cittern. And with him was a beautiful young girl with black hair, blind, and she was singing that *dumka*. I had no money in my pocket, so I hurried to the place where I was to give my concert to get some. But when I came back with the money, they had gone.

'The wind is blowing,
The trees are swaying,
How sad I am,
Yet cannot weep.'

The melody ran in my head as I went down the hill and walked beside the river Dnieper, and that night in the concert in Kiev, I improvised on it.

STAVENHAGEN. That was when you first met the Princess?

SELF. Not at my first concert. She heard about it and came to my second.

'How sad I am, yet cannot weep.' Can only cough, damn it! All the other things wrong with me I can forget about if I think of something else, but the cough intrudes . . . noisy, ugly, infuriating visitor that can't be ignored.

STATION II. HANAU

Vanity again, was it, that made me go up on the stage on Monday? To get a last shot of adoration from an audience that wasn't expecting it. Isn't my present condition cure enough—punishment enough—for all those years of preening and posing? One thing to leap up on the stage as a young Apollo, quite another looking like an old monster! Stupid! Stupid! You change outside, but not inside. *They* see the monster, inside *you* haven't changed, you're still Apollo. And to judge by the applause, the acclamation, they still heard Apollo . . . or thought they did.

SELF. What are you doing, Miska?

MISKA. Close window, your Grace. Too much air. Not good for cough.

How they look after me, my manservant, my pupil! And more pupils waiting to meet me at Bayreuth. Why such self-pity? You're old, you're going to pieces, it's natural. How lucky you are to be cared for like this! Damned cough! Lucky to be loved still! Lucky to have been handsome once. What if I'd played like an angel, but looked like a monster? If I'd looked like Paganini, poor fellow? But I saw him only when his diseases had gripped him, thin as a pole, his jaw all eaten away, and he played like an angel still . . . or like the devil, they said . . . he looked like the devil. And I now, fat as an abbot, with warts on my face, what do they say I play like? A hippo? No, they still hear Apollo . . .

Vanity, vanity! Vanity for gifts that God gave me . . . and more vanity for what those gifts brought me . . . fame, success, orders and medals, portraits, busts, biographies . . . the friendship of the famous—writers, artists, musicians—and the noble—counts and countesses, princes, princesses, dukes and duchesses, archbishops, cardinals, kings and queens. How many sovereigns received me as an equal? The Kings of Prussia, Denmark, Holland, the Queens of England, Spain and Portugal, the Sultan of Turkey, the Emperors of France, Brazil, Mexico, Savoy, Austria, the Pope himself. Only the

Czar of Russia treated me like a servant. But Russia is just a vaster version of its capital St Petersburg, a thin crust of borrowed civilisation floating uneasily over a quagmire of barbarism . . .

Vanity, yes! I drank it in greedily, as I drank cognac and wine, and I'm tasting it still with a relish I cannot lose, in spite of my humble abbé's soutane, my monstrous appearance, this second-class compartment and this vile plebeian cold, caught in the streets of Paris. Let every cough drive a nail into my vanity!

STATION III. ASCHAFFENBURG

And what became of the revolutionary? The boy who went out on the Paris streets to bring down the Bourbon king and sat down afterwards to compose his *Revolutionary Symphony*? The Hungarian nationalist who sympathized vehemently with his country's longing for independence . . . knew many of the heroes who led the revolt against Austria's rule . . . composed sad music as their epitaph, when the revolt was crushed with the help of Russia and they were vilely executed . . . and twenty years later composed the Mass for the coronation of the Emperor of Austria as King of Hungary . . . was that a betrayal? No, the so-called Compromise, the Dual-Monarchy, marked a kind of independence, the best that could be found in the circumstances . . .

Rebellion is for youth, compromise for maturity . . . politics for politicians not musicians . . . 'Give unto Caesar that which is Caesar's,' our Lord said. But the fall of the 'Citizen King', Louis Philippe, that was a revolution I welcomed . . . detestable man . . . a former revolutionary favouring the rich bourgeoisie . . . his only principle to have power himself . . . I told him so once to his face in so many words and he paid me out by denying me the *Legion d'Honneur*. But Napoleon III I did like, as he liked me, and his defeat and surrender to the Prussians filled me with grief and horror . . . cough, cough, cough!

SELF. Isn't it too hot with the window shut?

STAVENHAGEN. Miska is right, Master. The draught would be bad for you.

STATION IV. LOHR-AM-MAIN

SELF. Here we join the river Main again and follow it upstream all the way to Bayreuth. Did you post my letters to the Princess and to Olga—the Baroness Von Meyendorff?

STAVENHAGEN. Yes, of course.

Perhaps England has achieved the best, the most mature political compromise. At the dinner the Prince of Wales gave for me in London in April, Olga's sister said to me, 'England is a country of small constraints and great freedoms'. Even Wagner was ready to compromise when it came to accepting help from the King of Bavaria . . . and Wagner was a real revolutionary . . . they would have hanged him or shot him or shut him up in jail for years after the Dresden uprising, if he hadn't had the luck to escape when most of his confederates didn't . . . and the best thing I ever did as a revolutionary sympathizer was to give him asylum in Weimar and when that became dangerous, arrange for him to slip out of Germany into Switzerland with a false passport.

Wagner! Did God make him and his gifts? Wagner didn't think so, but I must think so. And where is he now . . . in heaven or hell? In heaven for his sublime genius? In hell for his unequalled self-love, his profligacy, ingratitude, disloyalty, arrogance, his contempt for mankind as well as God? What would I do with him if I were God? Forgive him, of course. As I did so frequently myself . . . and if I could do it, surely God can?

Especially after he wrote *Parsifal*, the only opera that is not just *about* religion but *is* religion. How could such a man compose such an opera, that's the mystery, the unadulterated Self transmuted into music of pure selflessness?

My son-in-law! My own Cosima, my last surviving child, become so much his slave and keeper of his flame that *my* only function in her life now is to be a publicity agent for Bayreuth . . . to help preserve his monument . . . to carry the ark of his work into the future . . . what can one think about such a man . . . that like Faust he sold his soul to the devil, but unlike Faust was turned by God to his Glory . . . or like the repentant thief on Calvary, was saved at the last moment? I don't believe he was . . . I saw no sign of repentance or belief in him the last time I was with him in Venice . . . no, it remains a mystery to me . . .

Not least that in spite of his faults, I did not just admire the music, I *liked* the man. He was my very good friend, until Cosima betrayed her husband with him and then her Catholic faith and I couldn't continue with either of them . . . but later how glad I was to make it up with both. And now I am on my way to Bayreuth, in spite of my exhaustion, my rotting carcase, my near despair about ever being well again . . . why am I doing this, why am I in this train, coughing, sweating, a pain in my side, dribbling probably, drivelling to myself, tediously stopping at every station . . . my 'stations of the cross' . . . God forgive me the presumptuous comparison . . . Why? Damn this cough! To preserve Wagner's monument . . . his appointment with the future . . . his immortality!

STATION V. GEMÜNDEN

STAVENHAGEN. Would you like me to read to you, Master?

SELF. Not yet. I'm busy with my thoughts . . . enduring my thoughts.

My 'stations of the cross', my *Via Crucis* begun twenty years ago, finished eight years ago at the Villa d' Este, never performed, never even published . . . too unusual and would not sell, said the publisher. Wagner's immortality is already assured, but mine? If he were alive and I were dead, what would he and Cosima be doing to promote my work? A question that needs no answer. They did not even like it latterly . . .

A more difficult question . . . were they right? Wagner deserves immortality—that I don't dispute—but do I? I must be honest with myself . . . I really don't know. Perhaps the early things and the little things—*Années de Pèlerinage*, the *Harmonies poétiques et religieuses*, the *Transcendental Etudes*, the *Liebestraüme*, the *Mephisto Waltzes* and *Consolations*—perhaps the transcriptions and paraphrases of other men's melodies . . . my gifted pupils will play those for another generation . . . and yes, surely, the 'Sonata in B minor', and perhaps the two symphonies and two concertos, but the symphonic poems, the 'Lieder', the 'Masses', the 'St Elizabeth Oratorio', all that 'Music of the Future' which so irritated the conventional music-lovers of Vienna and Dresden . . . who will perform any of that after my death? And as for the *Via Crucis* and all the dark despairing stuff I have laboured over these last twenty years, no one cares for it . . . I'm not even sure I care for it myself . . . and how can anything sail safely into the future which was never even launched in the present?

So shall I after all be remembered only as a virtuoso who turned his back on the public's Lisztomania and abandoned his glitter-years to waste the rest of his life producing music that did not even glimmer? Will they speak with a condescending smile of the *Folies de Liszt*? How long, in any case, can a reputation as a virtuoso last after the hands have ceased to touch the keys? Young men forget . . . what they never experienced for themselves. All things considered, Cosima is quite right . . . better to put her sad old celebrity father on the poop of the good ship Richard Wagner than let him go to waste trying to salvage his own sinking vessel.

STATION VI. KARLSTADT

STAVENHAGEN. Will you be staying with your daughter, Master?

SELF. No. Her house will be full of distinguished guests for the Festival. I believe I shall be lodged in the same street—just opposite Cosima's house—where I stayed for my grandaughter's wedding earlier this month. The wife of a forestry commissioner lets out rooms there.

MISKA. Better you stay with daughter, your Grace. You tell her this.

SELF. I may tell her what I please, Miska, but if her arrangements are already made and her house already full of guests . . .

MISKA. Your Grace is not well. Daughter take in sick father and kick out other guest to forest wife!

SELF. Well, we'll see.

My dearest Cosima . . . of all the children you were the best musician and you look most like me . . . not as I am now, heaven forbid! As I was before I swelled up and lost my teeth . . .

Do I blame you still for your treatment of Bülow? I think so. It was shabby. But I didn't much want you to marry him in the first place . . . knew him better than you . . . in both senses . . . knew him as you did not, and did not really know you . . . Hans was my favourite most talented pupil . . . a musician of the very highest quality . . . but as a boy then—and even as a man—tightly wound . . . all nerves . . . intellectually brilliant, emotionally stunted . . . his awful mother surely to blame for that. And it was he, after all, who put you under the spell of Wagner. On your honeymoon he took you to worship his hero! Oh, the whole story of you and Hans and Wagner is like one of his own operas, a German fairy tale. Damn this cough!

But your widowhood! Nothing in Wagner's work to compare with that, is there? . . . or is it Senta and the Flying Dutchman? You did not cast yourself into the sea like Senta when the Dutchman's pact with the devil carried him away, but you did cast off all friends and comforts, including your father . . . and even the year before last when you reopened Bayreuth and invited me to help publicize it, you never spoke a word to me, but passed me in the theatre corridor with the look of a ghost . . . your mother's motto, I remember, was *in alta solitudine* and your altitude is your widowhood . . . yes, indeed, you were and are Senta, except that you did better than throw yourself off a cliff for love of your Flying Dutchman and stayed alive to save his operahouse. And of course you called your first child Daniela Senta . . .

Is this another wound I'm probing . . . not physical but of the soul? I've tried to ignore it like my physical pains, but yes, it is a deep wound . . . not that she loves and worships her dead husband so much, but that she cannot spare any love for me. I thought once, I boasted to the Princess, that Cosima and I understood each other and were at one. It wasn't true. I wanted to brush away the Princess' constant criticisms of Cosima and perhaps my own unspoken, unacknowledged ones as well. No, we have not been at one for a long time, not since . . . truly speaking, not since . . . cough! cough! cough!

STATION VII. WÜRZBURG

Daniel's death. Must I think of that? My dear boy, so happy in his great academic success in Paris, the national *Prix d'Honneur*, the Emperor's special prize, the ovation by the National Guard . . . true glory for hard work . . . so happy during his long holiday with me in Weimar . . . and then studying law in Vienna, translating Homer, learning Hungarian . . . proud I think, of his father as well as himself . . . only to be struck down . . . in Berlin, on holiday in Cosima and Hans' home . . . coughing blood . . . 'galloping' consumption, well named, horribly well named . . . we three, Cosima, Hans and I taking turns at his bedside . . . how strange to think that then, *then*, at the worst moment of my life and perhaps of hers, Cosima and I were closer than ever before or since. What a fearful journey this life is! What 'stations of the cross' we enter and pass through without recognizing until later—when we reach other stations—their full meaning for us! Your journey was short, dear Daniel, too short for what was promised you . . . and only now I see that after your last station, Cosima and I began to part too.

STAVENHAGEN. Do let me read to you, Master!

SELF. No, no!

MISKA. Your thoughts are not good. You have tears for eyes.

SELF. Tears for eyes! My good Miska, it cannot be helped, *sunt lachrymae rerum*. Tears for things! I beg you not to look at me. Tears sometimes do us good.

Sunt lachrymae rerum. . . my lament for Hungary's failed revolution . . . the title from Virgil, his hero Aeneas remembering the destruction of Troy . . . and I dedicated the piece to Hans, thinking of his tears for Cosima and the way she betrayed him. Not that he was a good husband, far from it . . . violent outbursts and deep depressions, his 'migraine moods'. After the birth of Daniela Senta, Cosima was so ill, so low, I had to take her away from the cold-hearted mother-in-law she hated and the neurotic husband she still thought she loved and put her in a sanatorium to recover. No, I should not blame you for deserting the Bülows, Cosima. They were intolerable.

STATION VIII. SCHWEINFURT

Your first child, Daniela, called after your brother . . . your second, Blandine, after your sister. My beautiful Blandine . . . her child also named Daniel, after her dead brother . . . and then Blandine herself dead soon after the birth. How did we bear these things? How do we? Only in the faith of our Lord Jesus Christ and his promise of the life to come. I do believe . . . do I believe? . . . I *must* believe in the Resurrection and Redemption . . . and if I do, then why should I feel so sad, now that my own life is ending? Shan't I see them again soon, Daniel and Blandine, in a place without sadness, without 'stations of the cross'? But how will Wagner manage in such a place, a place without selfhood? He can only be a Wagner changed almost beyond recognition. And how will I manage, with my vanity and my own selfishness, less blatant than his, less extreme, but scarcely less persistent?

I cry now for my dead children and my living lost child, but what did I give them when they *were* children? Money I gave them—money I saved from my glitter-time and put with Rothschild for their education and dowries . . . a mother I gave them, my own mother, since *their* mother was no use to them and after we parted I feared her vindictiveness too much to let her near them. Money and mother . . . good home in Paris, education and dowries . . . what else? A father? No, I hardly gave them a father, except in prospect and in a distant haze of celebrity. I must have been a sort of Jehovah to them, a Jehovah who sent down stern commandments by letter from his cloudy height far away in Weimar, and, when they grew a little older, a crabbed old maid from Russia to tutor and polish them, she who had been the Princess' own teacher, but was not so much loved or admired by my children. And for eight years I never saw them, nor they me.

Why not? I was too busy with my music, my battles with the reactionaries for the 'music of the future', my ups and downs in the petty politics of Weimar, my conducting, my music-festivals, my pupils, my commissions, my great circle of friends and acquaintances, my deadly piles of correspondence, my railway journeys to distant cities, my promotion of the work of others, my concert performances for charitable causes, my articles to write and scores to proof-read, my Princess and her many illnesses and her long futile struggle to divorce her husband so that she could marry me. No, I could not find time to visit my children in Paris. I loved them dearly, of course, as *my* children, as *concepts* (in both senses) . . . but only when they began to grow up did I meet them and love them as physical beings . . . and even then how briefly! For a visit to the zoo in Brussels! And later still, when they came to stay with me in Weimar, I began to appreciate and love them as themselves, as real and separate people. But how short a time that was before they were fully grown . . . two of them married . . . and then two of them swept away! Oh God, forgive me! You gave me three beautiful, intelligent children and I left them out of my life. Was there ever such a failure of gratitude, of understanding of my own good fortune, of love for those I had most cause to love? Do I wonder, Cosima, that you've left *me* out of *your* life?

SELF. This cough will carry me off.

STAVENHAGEN. Won't you lie down along the seat, Master? That might be more comfortable.

SELF. No thank you, Bernhard. The cough is worse when I lie down. Give me some of that wine!

MISKA. Wine no good for fever. Water better.

SELF. Wine for oblivion, Miska, wine for addiction, wine for relief!

MISKA. With water, then!

SELF. Without water. Not what the doctors say is good for me, but what *does* me good!

STATION IX. HASSFURT

Two people at the door, looking at the empty seat opposite . . . they've decided on it . . . two very young people . . . this is the disadvantage of travelling second-class . . . one's space is invaded . . . they sit down together, very close . . . newly-married, I should think . . . he's not good-looking, nor she . . . country-folk with coarse features . . . but for now they have the attraction of youth . . . strength, freshness, colour, innocence, optimism . . . cough, cough! . . . now they look at me think-ing it might have been better to choose another compartment . . . I smile apologetically and they smile back . . . they don't know who I am . . . they are not the sort of people who go to concerts . . . they don't perceive the world-famous Franz Liszt, who walks and talks with kings, for whom crowds rise to their feet in homage as he takes his seat in a concert-hall . . . just an ugly old abbé with a nasty cough whom they smile at with pity . . .

No, she has a lovely smile and she is so happy that she's almost pretty . . . why do I think of Zerlina in Mozart's *Don Giovanni*? Am I casting myself as Don Juan, eager to draw her away from her bump-kin Masaccio . . . what a grotesque thought! But thoughts are free, why should I not enjoy a last trace of lust, imagine myself the man I was, the man who revelled in that scene in his time of triumph . . . what bewitching mastery of the female heart, what sensual ecstasy I put into my *Reminiscences de Don Juan*, as if Mozart's irresistible lover were my very self! . . . myself at thirty, whose external appearance did not belie the spirit inside but joyously, lustfully reflected it . . . for whom women fell not by any calculated art of seduction on my part, but as if by grav-ity, like ripe plums from a tree . . .

These thoughts are unsavoury, especially for a person in Holy Orders. Shouldn't my 'stations of the cross' include sincere repentance for so many violations of the Ninth Commandment? Not yet, O Lord, not yet! Let me keep that for my death bed! The women in my life were indeed often married, but none still living with her husband. The Ninth Commandment is really about property: it says nothing about coveting another man's wife when he has discarded her. Do I make excuses for inexcusable behaviour? No, the truth is I cannot feel real regret or repentance for love which was felt on both sides, which has been throughout my life its light and warmth, the sun that shone through my clouds of exhaustion and despair, the fire that fuelled my best music. I wanted to be a monk, especially after my first love was cruelly stamped out . . . but suppose they had let me enter the cloister . . . would I, could I have become a person whose capacity for love was all focused on God and his work? I don't think so . . . no doubt, like my father, I would soon have rebelled and returned to the world . . . and now in my dotage I've taken holy orders after all, and the world, I know, laughs and thinks me a play-actor, a *saltimbanque* . . . an acrobat still, who amusingly elects to perform in a cassock. The world is quite wrong about that. I have never ceased to think what I thought as a child, that the service of God outweighs all other things on this earth . . . how could it not when you believe as I do that this life is only the anteroom to another? '*Never* ceased?' I hear them sneer, 'not even in the arms of Lola Montez?' No, not *ceased*. Sometimes in the haste and dazzle of those days I forgot, as I forgot my children . . . an acrobat indeed I was, and it's a risky profession. An acrobat must forget everything, even himself, if his body is to tumble and somersault and snatch the trapeze every time without mistake.

STATION X. BAMBERG

The girl has been glancing at me surreptitiously from time to time . . . . concerned, I think, at my sorry appearance . . . now she is whispering to the boy . . . now he suddenly stands up and opens the window, his potato face breaking into a friendly smile for me as he sits down. Miska is getting to his feet now . . . I wave him down . . .

STAVENHAGEN. Master, don't you think . . . ?

SELF. Let it be! You can see I'm too hot . . .

STAVENHAGEN. For that reason . . .

SELF. Let it be!

Indeed the cool air is refreshing. Cough, cough! She looks at me again, concerned . . . she'll be a good mother, I'm sure . . . I smile and shake my head . . . let it be! How I do love women! Imagine a world without them—a world composed only of men! A world all drive and competition and single-mindedness . . . no mothers to teach them better. How would they be born? Like those seeds sown by the Greek hero, Jason, in the kingdom of Colchis which sprang up as armed men, who immediately began to slaughter each other . . . and the *Battle of the Huns*, Kaulbach's great painting which I translated into a symphonic poem, with the dead warriors' souls rising into the sky and still fighting it out . . . Wagner at least had them carried up by Valkyries—the feminine touch . . . not all that feminine . . . Wagner's female characters seldom are . . . yet Wagner himself was a strangely feminine man with his proclivity for silks and satins and scents all around him as he composed . . . one might have thought he had a preference for men, except that his need for women was almost as great as mine.

Caroline, Adèle, Marie, Charlotte, Marie Duplessis, Princess Carolyne, Agnès, Olga Janina, Olga von Meyendorff . . . .the chapters of my life could be called after them . . . and I didn't sleep with all of them, but did sleep with others too fleeting to remember . . . Lola, yes, I remember her . . . Adèle I treated badly and Olga Janina treated me badly . . . Marie and I were quits . . . but Caroline de Saint-Cricq, that was first-love and not to be compared with the rest . . .

She still loved me when I saw her again, in our thirties, after the break with Marie, at her home in the Pyrenees . . . I loved her too, but not in the way I had . . . her beastly, forced husband had deserted her, she had a child, she was in a remote place, she was desolate and the glowing embers of her love for me could have flamed up if I had blown on them . . . but I was on my way to tour Spain, still bound to the back of my galloping fame, and could only respond to the memory of what we had been . . . How sickening this sounds, the man who has moved on, the girl left behind! No, it was not quite like that . . . we were happy to meet again, sadly happy to revisit the past together . . . only afterwards did I feel sick with myself for not responding with more love and when I made a will, left her my signet-ring as a last vow of love from the grave . . . she never knew . . . died many years ago and the ring is still mine and will go with everything else to my other Carolyne.

STATION XI. ZAPFENDORF

Marie is dead too. She took her revenge with that slushy novel, *Nélida*, depicting herself as the innocent, angelic heroine led astray by a prating artist, whose dreams of greatness collapse in self-deception and ignominy. Was that really how she saw me, how she saw herself? Make-believe and lies I thought and think still. I had the best of the worldly argument since French law gave her no power over children that were illegitimate and on whose birth-certificates I was named as the father, while she had concealed her identity. But some of her venom stuck . . . my enemies were glad to see me wounded . . . and I myself, yes, though I always pretended not to recognize myself, the arrow found its mark . . . she aimed not at my love-affairs but my artistic pretensions, which she knew would hurt more. But what I did not know when Marie and I loved each other was the history of mania and depression in her family and herself. She had threatened her husband with suicide before ever we met, her nephew jumped into the Seine, her sister actually drowned herself . . . in this very river Main we are steaming beside now . . . and in the years after our break, Marie was many times treated by the celebrated Dr Blanche and even on some occasions when she was truly beside herself, straitjacketed. 'Six inches of snow over twenty feet of lava,' she said of herself. If I had known, would I have been more careful of her? Or more careless, aware that her moods were only partly dependent on me? Whatever its faults, ours was an equal relationship. We were both self-willed people, set on our own ways. So long as those ways led into each other's arms, so good, so very good . . . but there was no help for it when I needed to perform and she needed me to hide my light and give all my energy to her.

I was sad enough when we parted, but soon got over it . . . in those last holidays together on the island of Nonnenwerth, it was the past we were trying to recover, not the present or the future . . . so much had changed between us, damaged, soured, lacerated by mutual criticism and abuse . . . and of course her jealousy . . . and of course my promiscuity . . . .We had both grown up and learnt that the other was not as lovely a person inside as each had first thought . . . and that taught us also to be ashamed of ourselves . . . to feel soiled, diminished. If she could have forgiven me, I would have found it hard to forgive myself . . . as it was, I forgave myself quite easily . . . she had already begun to write that poisonous book even before we finally parted. *Basta,* Marie, *ave atque vale*!

STATION XII. LICHTENFELS

SELF. *Ave atque vale*!

STAVENHAGEN. You spoke, Master?

SELF. Did I speak? I have the habit of speaking Latin aloud, I suppose.

STAVENHAGEN. You were saying one of the Offices?

SELF. I'm afraid not. Secular thoughts, Bernhard, entirely secular and not very consoling.

Cough! But no, Marie, it is not quite *vale* and certainly not *ave* when I think of how you behaved to my mother. You quarrelled with her, you wanted to take our children away from her . . . though you were hardly going to look after them yourself, with your salons, your journalism, your procession of lovesick suitors sighing after you in the absence of your Odysseus. The words you wrote about my mother when I was away in England still fester in my memory . . . her 'base language, base feelings', her 'odious bawling', how you would not put up with 'her ass' kick', how she cried and gesticulated and wouldn't lis-ten to a word, but threatened to 'go into service' and was mad . . . was 'one of those people I cannot do with'. And how did I reply? True, I was caught between you, far away in the grip of my exhausting tour, still wanting to retain your love, Marie, knowing that whatever I said or did, I would always retain my mother's, but I am not proud of the way I temporized, promising to sort things out when I returned . . . suggesting you might be making too much of this 'baseness' . . . point-ing out that you had no experience of this way of talking, but that it was the way ninety-nine percent of humanity were used to talking . . . recalling the 'base language and base feelings' of the innkeepers and coachmen which had annoyed me so much in Italy. Shouldn't I have had the courage to say 'yes, Marie, my mother *was* a servant once and I am her son, no better born than those innkeepers and coachmen, though I may have learnt to speak like your friends and conceal my *baseness* with a veneer of *breeding*?' Cough, cough, cough!

STAVENHAGEN. The window . . .

SELF. Leave the window! If I could open every window into myself, I might feel better.

That baker's daughter, orphaned at nine years old, that base Austrian serving-maid who, when my father died suddenly at Boulogne on our way back from our third visit to London, came immediately from Vienna to Paris to take care of me . . . she who, struggling with a language she had never learnt and a city she'd never seen, took me in her arms and made a new home for us . . . she who endured my dark years of arrogance, ignorance, self-love and self-doubt . . . who cooked, cleaned, shopped, made ends meet, and learnt to be a Parisian . . . but when I fell in love with Marie, was left behind without a qualm in that still foreign place. And later, when we returned to Paris with three young children and left them in her care while we pursued our selfish lives, it was she who saw to all their needs and found them good schools . . . and now I feel impotent anger . . . not with Marie so much as myself . . . I should have broken with her then . . . I should not have hovered between her snobbery and my mother's 'baseness', but there and then made the only loyal and honourable choice.

Cough! My musical talent came from father and grandfather, but my sense of destiny, my determination was from her. Dearest Mother, I was far away when you died and was not even at your funeral, but if there is a Heaven you are surely in it and if I ever reach it, I shall see you again . . . and perhaps my thoughts are open to you now . . . I pray you may forgive me . . . I pray you may accept my sorrow for all the pain I gave you . . . you always had my love, but I did not much show it. Cough! Cough!

STATION XIII. KULMBACH

STAVENHAGEN. The last stop, Master. We're making good time.

SELF. *Stabat mater dolorosa, juxta crucem lacrymosa* . . .

STAVENHAGEN. Master?

SELF. Words from the *Via Crucis*, quite apposite . . .

Cough! 'There stood the mourning mother, weeping beside the Cross . . .' And my second mother, I suppose, was Carolyne . . . not at first, not at Woronince, but gradually, as her religion, her intellectual obsessions, her battles with her husband's family, her eccentricity gripped her more and more . . . she retreated to her bolt-hole in Rome . . . and mothered me . . . mostly by letter, long screeds of instruction and correction . . . Suppose we had never met! Would she have stayed as I found her, the lonely queen of her great estates in Ukraine? She abandoned all that for me . . . made that arduous, dangerous journey out of the clutches of the Russians . . . endured the humiliations of Weimar . . . a princess who could not be received at Court or even recognized in street or theatre by respectable ladies . . . a fallen queen, a fallen woman . . . no wonder she was so often ill! . . . and has become, I think, more or less mad. Should I blame myself? Ours was an equal relationship at first, when we were lovers . . . but it changed . . . and she proved the stronger or at least the one who domineered. Wouldn't she, in any case, have become more than a little mad if she had remained alone at Woronince?

Our marriage that never was! It was already too late when she finally broke through all the obstacles and received the Vatican's permission . . . too late at any rate for me . . . but I could not deny what she had suffered for me and therefore allowed myself to deny that my heart no longer endorsed my word. That was a miserable journey to Rome . . . as if I was going to a funeral not a wedding . . . and then her relatives intervened again at the last moment and the church, already decked with flowers and candles, saw neither funeral nor wedding that morning . . . I could hardly admit my inward relief . . . did she feel the same? Surely by then, even for her, this was an act of will, a triumph over her legions of adversaries, not a sealing of love, a true marriage of hearts and minds? Love, I think, which blazed up in that snowbound winter in Woronince, was extinguished over the years by that snowstorm of paper . . . petitions, explanations, appeals, personal interventions, letters, letters, letters . . . And when Prince Nicholas died and there was no further barrier to our union, we were entirely at one—*not* to be united.

When we see each other now it's mostly to disagree . . . about people, politics, music, the church . . . I try to avoid such topics . . . hard to find others . . . When I entrusted her with the proofs of my book on Hungarian Gypsy music, she rewrote it so as to trumpet her own dislike of the Jews . . . under *my* name! Foolish of me not to have checked it before publication . . . but how could I have imagined she would do such a thing without telling me, knowing very well I had no such opinion myself? Whatever damage I have done to her, she more than repaid with that piece of high-handed stupidity which lost me so many friends and supporters, especially in my native country, and which I could not in loyalty to her disown. Stupidity, yes! How she would scold, if she knew I'd used such a word of *her* . . . princess of bluestockings, doyenne of intelligent women, author of innumerable books and pamphlets, including the monumental *Causes intérieures de la faiblesse extérieure de l' Eglise en 1870*, just now, I believe, reaching its twenty-fourth volume . . . but like the circle of colour in which opposites shade into one another, there is a circle in which high intelligence shades into stupidity.

Must all my thoughts about Carolyne be bitter ones? Let me try to think back to those earlier times at Woronince and in the Altenburg at Weimar, when we worked in the same room, drank and smoked and talked together as if we could never come to the end of our discoveries about each other and the world . . . and the world through each other . . . and we had a daughter then too . . . her daughter Marie, who in the absence of my own children became a true daughter to me . . . . We did not think of ourselves as happy then . . . too many anxieties . . . her and her daughter's poor health, our constantly frustrated desire to be married, her outlawry by Weimar society, her struggles to shake off her husband and his family—who only wanted her money—my struggles to bring the best contemporary music to that unenlightened, provincial public . . . but, yes, often and without sufficiently realizing it, we *were* happy. And if that happiness vanished, it was for the same reason as with all my other lovers—not that we changed but rather that we knew each other too little, knew ourselves too little. Paths that meet and inexorably diverge again . . . journeys that reach the same station but never end there . . . harmonies that become discords . . . tones that long for each other and having embraced each other, die away into silence . . . so many of my works end *pianissimo* . . .

STATION XIV. BAYREUTH

STAVENHAGEN. Bayreuth!

The girl is getting out, with her new husband. God be with you both! Be happy if you can! Do not ask too much of each other or yourselves! Have many children and be good to them! Smile, smile . . . cough, cough, cough! I believe your kind thought with the window has finished me . . .

SELF. What are you doing, Miska?

MISKA. Take down luggage, your Grace. We here.

SELF. Here? Where?

MISKA. Terminus. Bayreuth.

SELF. Terminus? I don't want to die in Bayreuth.

MISKA. Die? No, you see opera, see daughter, get better!

STAVENHAGEN. Siloti is here, Master, and Göllerich and Thoman. More of your pupils are expected.

My pupils, yes, I've been a good father to them. They'll not forsake me. Even in the shadow of Wagner's theatre, I shall not be altogether forgotten. Vanity! Vanity still! Cough, cough!

STAVENHAGEN. Can you stand? Put your arm round my shoulder!

O *Traurigkeit, O Herzeleid* . . . O sadness, O heart's pain . . . *Ave crux, spes unica, mundi salus et gloria* . . . Hail Cross, our only hope, salvation and glory of the world . . . *pianissimo* . . .

* * *

Liszt arrived in Bayreuth on 21 July 1886 and attended performances of Parsifal *and* Tristan *on the 23rd and 25th, coughing at the back of his box, but coming forward at each interval to lead the applause and show he was present. He died on 31 July of pneumonia and heart failure. He was 74. His funeral was held in Bayreuth and he was buried there. His* Via Crucis, *the fourteen stations of the cross for mixed choir, soloists and organ or piano, was first performed in 1929 and published in 1936.*

THE END

Chronology

1811	Liszt's birth, 22 October, in Raiding, Hungary
1820	First concerts in Oedenburg and Pressburg
1822	Family moves to Vienna, where Liszt studies composition with Salieri and piano with Czerny. Liszt's first published composition, one of fifty variations by different composers, including Schubert, on a waltz by Diabelli
1823	Liszt plays for Beethoven. Concerts in Vienna, Pest and various German cities. He and his father, Adam, move to Paris, where Liszt studies with Paer and makes his Paris debut
1824	Tour of England, organized by the piano-manufacturer Erard
1825	Second tour of England. Première in Paris of his opera *Don Sanche*, written in collaboration with his teacher Paer
1826	Tours France and Switzerland
1827	Death of Liszt's father in Boulogne on the way back from a third visit to England
1828	Falls in love with his pupil, Caroline de Saint-Cricq, and when her father ends the relationship, Liszt abandons public performances and thinks of becoming a priest
1830	Revolution in Paris, in which Liszt takes part. The Bourbon king Charles X displaced by Louis Philippe, the 'Citizen King'. Liszt meets Berlioz, Lamartine and Hugo
1831	He hears Paganini play
1832	Meets and becomes a friend of Chopin
1833	Meets the Countess Marie d'Agoult
1835	Elopes with Marie d'Agoult to Switzerland. Their first child, Blandine, born in Geneva
1837	Gives concerts in Paris, then travels to Italy with Marie d'Agoult. Their second child, Cosima, born in Como

1838   Goes to Vienna to give a concert for Danube flood victims

1839   Birth of his and Marie's son Daniel in Rome. Start of virtuoso concert tours and his so-called *Glanzzeit* (Glitter-time)

1840   Meets Richard Wagner. Tours of Germany and England

1841   Tours of Britain and the rest of Europe

1842   Visits Russia, accepts post of Extraordinary Kapellmeister in Weimar

1844   Break-up with Marie d'Agoult, after his brief liaison with Lola Montez

1845   Unveiling of Beethoven monument in Bonn, partly organized and paid for by Liszt

1846   Tours of France, Spain, Germany and Eastern Europe. Meets Marie Duplessis, '*la dame aux camélias*'

1847   Meets Princess Carolyne von Sayn-Wittgenstein in Kiev. Plays for the Sultan in Constantinople. Ends his career as virtuoso

1848   Settles in Weimar with Princess Carolyne and embarks on his most sustained period of composition and conducting, which continues for the next ten years

1849   Shelters Wagner, on the run after the Dresden uprising, and helps to arrange his escape to Switzerland

1853   Agnès Street-Klindworth comes to Weimar as one of Liszt's pupils

1858   Resigns his post as kapellmeister in Weimar

1859   His son Daniel dies, aged twenty

1860   Princess Carolyne leaves Weimar for Rome

1861   Liszt's and Princess Carolyne's marriage in Rome stopped by her relations at the last moment

1862   His daughter Blandine, married to the French lawyer and politician Emile Ollivier, later briefly Prime Minister at the time of the Franco-Prussian War, dies soon after the birth of their first child

1864   Stays for the first time in the Villa d'Este

1865   Enters minor orders in the Catholic Church

1866	Death of his mother in Paris
1868	His daughter Cosima leaves her husband Hans von Bülow to live with Richard Wagner
1869	Beginning of Liszt's *vie trifurquée*, commuting between Rome, Budapest and Weimar
1871	Involvement with his pupil Olga Janina
1875	Becomes President of the new Royal Academy of Music in Budapest
1883	Death of Wagner
1886	Triumphal visit to London. Gives last concert, in Luxembourg. Travels to Bayreuth, where he attends performances of *Tristan* and *Parsifal*. Dies in Bayreuth on 31 July and is buried there

A Selection of Liszt's Music

PIANO

Années de pélerinage, Books I, II and III
Consolations
Harmonies poétiques et religieuses
Hungarian Rhapsodies
Etudes d'après Paganini
Etudes d'exécution transcendante
Liebesträume
Mephisto Waltzes
'Rákóczy March'
Rhapsodie espagnole
'Sonata in B minor'
St Francis de Paola Walking on the Waves
St Francis of Assisi: the Sermon to the Birds
Trois études de concert
Schaflos! Frage und Antwort
Unstern! Sinistre, disastro
Valse oubliée
Nuages gris

PIANO TRANSCRIPTIONS, PARAPHRASES, REMINISCENCES

Danse macabre (Saint-Saëns)
Paraphrase of Ernani (Verdi)
Paraphrase of Rigoletto (Verdi)
Reminiscences de Don Juan (Mozart)
Reminiscences de Lucia di Lammermoor (Donizetti)

Reminiscences de Simon Boccanegra (Verdi)
Transcriptions of the Symphonies of Beethoven
Transcription of the Liebestod from Tristan und Isolde (Wagner)
Transcription of the March of the Knights of the Holy Grail from Parsifal (Wagner)

ORCHESTRAL

Dante Symphony
Faust Symphony
'Piano Concerto no.1 in E flat major'
'Piano Concerto no 2 in A minor'
Totentanz for piano and orchestra

Symphonic Poems:
Ce qu'on entend sur la montagne
Festklänge
Hamlet
Héroïde funèbre
Hungaria
Hunnenschlacht
Die Ideale
Mazeppa
Orpheus
Les Préludes
Prometheus
Tasso
Von der Wiege bis zum Grabe (*From the Cradle to the Grave*)

CHORAL

Christus (oratorio)
Legend of St Elisabeth (oratorio)
Missa choralis
Missa solemnis (*Gran Mass*)
Via crucis

and a great many lieder for solo voice and piano

NOTE: *No dates are given, since he often reworked earlier pieces.*